Pennies from Heaven

Danielle Palli

With each book I write, I am reminded of how lucky I am to have the support and friendship of so many wonderful people in my life. These are the people who helped bring Pennies From Heaven to life…

Thank you, Lisa Ramirez, for painstakingly editing for me and loving my characters as much as I do! To Cindy Readnower, for her ongoing advice, beta reading and publishing support. Thank you, Graham Mack, for co-narrating all of my books with me and giving each character a unique voice. And thank you to my partner in love and life, John Palli, supporting this book through beta reading, lending technical and historical knowledge, and always encouraging me to pursue what I love.

I also need to send a special thanks to Mike Costello, tour guide extraordinaire, on my recent trip to Ireland. Mike shared much about the rich history of Ireland, and these wise words, "Never let the truth get in the way of a good story." Thank you, Mike.

Contents

Prologue

The year is 1998 and still at the height of the tech boom. Startups are all the rage, and a select few have access to inventions that won't be readily available to the public for several more years. The Internet is considered a passing fad, and only a small percentage of people carry cell phones.

Emma Post is a force to be reckoned with. Living in a run-down studio apartment in the Lower West Side of Manhattan, and earning a modest living as a figure model, she has a general "punch first and ask questions later" approach to life. She distrusts technology and people, particularly cops. The recent death of her two friends only reinforces her inherent belief that the world is a dangerous place.

She might be right…

Chapter 1
"Because You Just Can't Trust Cops"

"Why are you here, Officer—" Emma Post struggled to remember his name.

"Dennis," he answered awkwardly, police hat in hand as he shuffled nervously from one foot to the other. "But you can just call me Dennis."

"That's right," Emma remembered. "You were one of the cops who interviewed me a few months ago, after my two best friends were murdered."

The last time Officer Dennis had paid a visit to Emma's apartment complex, it was to help investigate the murder of a singer named Clarissa Sauer, and her art model friend and actress, Ursula Gorky.

Not much had changed since he'd last visited… she still occupied the same bland-white studio apartment with noticeably low ceilings, cracked tile, and an efficiency kitchen that melded into the bedroom. Frankly, while Officer Dennis' digs were not that much bigger, he had to admit to himself that his living arrangement was far better.

What had changed, however, was Emma Post's hair. He remembered. The last time, it had been a short brown-haired cut that curled under once it reached her shoulders, coupled with a few blonde streaks through it. He smiled to himself. While she still retained the same athletic look today, she had obviously bleached her hair blonde and had it permed. Officer Dennis decided she looked just as pretty both ways. He even thought that her plain gray hooded sweatshirt and jeans, with no makeup on, suited her.

"Yes." Officer Dennis glanced sheepishly at the floor. "I guess I just wanted to see how you were getting on… er… seeing how you lost two people who were close to you."

"That seems highly uncustomary for a police officer, doesn't it?" Emma answered. She had let him in her apartment, nonetheless, and Officer Dennis' husky frame took up an enormously large amount of space, made evident when he sat on a small metal chair with a tiny plastic seat that was one of Emma's two kitchen seats. They looked as if they once were used in an elementary school classroom… they probably had been.

Officer Dennis thought a moment, as he shifted his weight uncomfortably in the chair. "How would you know that?" he asked curiously. "I mean, what makes you think it's uncustomary?"

"It just seems like a nice thing to do and —"

"Cops aren't nice?" Officer Dennis finished.

"Your words, not mine," Emma answered flatly. While Officer Dennis sat, she began unpacking the groceries she had procured just prior to his arrival. She paused for a moment as she put a carton of milk, eggs, and fresh vegetables into her refrigerator. Emma let out a sigh. "The truth is, I've been better. It's like there's this giant hole in my heart. And sometimes—" she paused at the door and looked over at Officer Dennis. "I forget they're gone, like when I get good news I want to share or feel like catching a movie. I pick up the phone like old times and then it hits me. I've no one to call." She closed the door of the refrigerator. Then, as if remembering, "You want some coffee or juice or anything?"

"Nah, I'm good," Officer Dennis answered. "Thanks, though."

Emma returned to the kitchen counter and reached into a second paper bag, pulling out two pink candles, a round rose quartz stone, and what looked like a small bag of dried rose petals. The name on the bag read, 'Elementals Magickal Gift Shop.'

"You know," Officer Dennis suggested, "I wouldn't be opposed to catching a movie with you sometime." He coughed slightly. "Just so you wouldn't have to go alone and all." He eyed the objects Emma was holding curiously.

Emma blushed. "They're for a money spell," she lied, disappearing behind the large accordion screen that separated the kitchen from the bedroom. Officer Dennis couldn't see much into the room, but it appeared as if she placed them on a little table that sat low to the floor. On it, was what looked like an incense burner, several gemstones and a small gold ring. He couldn't see what else was there.

"Officer Dennis—" Emma called from behind the screen. "Er… Dennis." She peered around it like a curious cat. "Were you just asking me out?"

"Well, that depends" He grinned cautiously. "If you were accepting, then definitely yes. If you weren't, then definitely not."

"Hmm." Emma returned to the kitchen and hoisted herself up onto the counter, sitting with her legs dangling below her as she rested her hands on each side of her hips. "What did you have in mind?" She eyed him suspiciously.

"Well, there's a really great steakhouse near the movie theater on—"

"I'm a vegetarian," she interrupted, pursing her lips distastefully.

"Oh." Dennis recoiled slightly. He wasn't entirely sure what vegetarians actually ate, mind you. He assumed a lot of lettuce. But he was quick on his feet. "Well, there's a nice vegetarian Japanese restaurant in Midtown that we could try… at least, I think it's good. I've never been there."

"And the movie?" Emma asked. "What would we see?"

"Anything you like, really." Dennis sat up optimistically. "A romantic comedy, a foreign flick—"

"What makes you think I want to see either of those?" she challenged. "Because I'm a woman?"

"Fine, an action movie?"

"Too violent."

"A drama?" Dennis tried again.

"Too depressing." Emma bit back a laugh. It was then that Dennis realized that Emma Post was having a little too much fun messing with him.

"You know, Emma," he said, leaning forward, resting his elbows on the table. "Your love spell might work better if you don't shoot down every guy you meet."

Emma's face dropped. "What? How did you?" She glanced toward the altar in the bedroom and back at Dennis.

"My little sister, Rose, got herself kicked out of Catholic school on account of practicing witchcraft." Dennis laughed at the memory. "My folks were fit to be tied, the only one out of the six of us to have to go to public school." For some reason, Dennis thought this was hilarious.

The color drained from Emma's face. "So you're—"

"Roman Catholic, yes," he confirmed.

"And you're one of six—"

"Kids," he nodded, finishing for her.

"Officer Dennis," Emma began, suddenly appearing woozy. Dennis sat upright. Her reverting to addressing him by title set off alarm bells in his head. He had pushed too hard and said too much. "I really don't think you and I would make a good match at all."

"Well, I wasn't asking for your hand in marriage or anything. Just a dinner between friends."

"We're not friends," Emma scowled, sliding off the counter and standing. "It was really nice of you to check in on me, but —" She moved toward the front door and held her hand on the doorknob leading out of her apartment.

Dennis stood. "So, you're going to shoot me down because my family is Roman Catholic?"

"Do you have any idea what the Catholic Church did to Wiccans throughout history?"

"Not really," Dennis confessed. "But I can tell by your expression that it wasn't good."

"No, Dennis," she answered anxiously. "It wasn't good. They were tortured and brutally murdered—"

"But I wasn't there *then*," Dennis pleaded. "And I hardly ever set foot in a church… except for Christmas and Easter."

Emma sighed again, this time more loudly. Dennis was quite a bit taller than she was and a little chunkier around the middle. He obviously didn't exercise regularly and probably visited that steakhouse he mentioned a bit too much. From what she could tell, he was also several years younger than her. Honestly, Emma wouldn't have given him a second glance if she passed him on the street. And yet, after two brief encounters, she sensed there was something really… sweet… about him.

"How old are you, Dennis?" She eyed him curiously.

He knew where this was going. "What does that matter?" he answered defensively. "How old are you?"

"None of your business," she retorted. Then she remembered, she told him her age the last time she met, when he and Detective Ortega, his boss, were investigating the murder of her two friends. "Thirty-six," she finally answered.

"Well, I'm thirty-one. Now that we've gotten that out of the way—"

"Officer Dennis, I have been nothing but difficult since the time you arrived. Why on Earth are you so set on taking me out on a date?"

"Well," he thought about this. "You just seem really put together is all."

Emma's face became flushed. "What do you mean 'put together'? You mean my body?!"

"No, no," he tried again, holding his police hat in his hands and rotating it awkwardly in a circle. "I mean, as an overall person. You seem to know what you're about. You're obviously smart and independent and… will I get tossed out on my ear if I tell you I think you're kinda cute?" Dennis turned his head away, glancing sideways sheepishly.

Emma smiled despite her attempts to be as disagreeable as possible.

"If I'm remembering correctly," Dennis cleared his throat, "the last time I was here, you told Detective Ortega that you, and I quote, 'have terrible taste in men.'"

"Yes," Emma nodded. "That is true."

"Well, have you ever thought of going against the grain — trying someone different?"

"Like you, you mean?"

Dennis nodded. "Yes, I'm an omnivore who comes from a long line of Catholics. I'm a little younger than you and am obviously not as athletic as you are. And… drum roll please… I also happen to be a cop, which you hate. In fact, I'm probably the last person on Earth who would be considered your 'type'." Dennis put the word 'type' in air quotes. "And yet I'm asking you, Emma Post, will you go on a date with me?"

Emma couldn't recall the last time anyone made that much of a fuss over her and couldn't believe he hadn't given up at the start. He was definitely a determined young fella, that was for sure. Finally, she smiled. "Okay, Officer Dennis. I will go out with you. Vegetarian Japanese food, then? With a movie to be determined?"

"Perfect," Dennis smiled back, placing his police cap on his head. Emma cringed a little out of habit, but quickly recovered. He reached into his shirt pocket and procured a small pen and notepad. He scribbled a note, peeled off the slip of paper, and handed it to her. "Here's my number. How does Saturday at 6:30-ish sound? I can meet you here and we can catch a cab together?"

Emma opened the door for him, reaching out to take the paper. She smiled with the tiniest glimmer of hope. "Saturday at 6:30-ish," she agreed. "See you then."

She closed the door behind him and leaned against the door, glancing at the note, wondering if this was a good thing or the biggest mistake of her life.

Chapter 2
The Call

Two Weeks Ago; 1998

"Detective Or—" Detective José Ortega caught himself. "This is José," he said as he answered his cell phone. It was given to him by Cyber Forensic Consultant and Private Investigator Darwin Fennec after the two men became unlikely allies in solving a multiple-homicide case in Manhattan nearly a year ago.

"Detective Ortega," Dennis could be heard on the other line. "It's me, Officer Dennis. It's good to hear your voice, Sir."

Ortega smiled despite his typically sour mood. "It's good to hear from you too, Officer Dennis. But you can call me José now. As you know, I am retired."

"I know," Dennis clucked into the phone. "I know all too well. The detective they assigned to us after you left is a real pain in my ass, if I'm being honest."

"I have it on good authority that you said the same thing about me when you and I first began working together years ago," Ortega laughed. Dennis' awkward silence on the phone let Ortega know his suspicions had been correct, and that Dennis was embarrassed about it now. "Just give the new detective a little more time. I'm sure it will work out."

"Er, maybe… But, Sir?"

"Yes, Dennis?"

"I'm not staying in New York. I'm in Florida."

"Really?" Ortega was surprised. When his wife Nancy insisted he retire early in an effort to 'save their marriage,' she also got it in their head that they should move to a warmer climate and get away from the crime-ridden city. Ortega agreed, and had since spent the last nine months bored out of his skull.

No longer conducting murder investigations, he became one of their HOA's worst nightmares, always reporting to the Home Owner's Association in their sub-division if someone parked on the street during a weekday, watered their lawns on non-approved days, or failed to pick up after their dogs at the poop station at their community dog park. He'd even once wrongly accused his 83-year-old neighbor, Bob, of stealing his *Tampa Bay Times* from his front porch, only to find that Nancy had already retrieved it — leading to a very uncomfortable apology to Bob.

"What business do you have in Florida?" Ortega asked. "Are you on vacation?"

"No, actually, I requested a temporary exchange with another officer to see what it's like down here for a bit. I think I'm near you. We've moved into a small house in St. Pete."

"We?" Ortega was curious.

Dennis paused. Ortega could actually feel him blushing on the other end of the phone. "So, you remember the woman we interviewed during the murder of the singer Clarissa Sauer and the figure model Ursula Gorky?"

"Of course, I remember. It was my last case before retiring. Emma… Emma Post, I believe, was her name."

"That's her."

"What about her?" Ortega was suspicious.

"Well, we've been sort of… seeing each other."

"I'd say it's a bit more than that if you're living together, wouldn't you?"

"It's not like that," Dennis explained. "We're living in the same house but have separate bedrooms. It's temporary... unfortunately."

"Things not working out?" Ortega was sympathetic. There was a lot of that going around lately.

"It's working out just fine... though, a little slower than I'd like, if I'm being honest. I'm never 100% sure how Emma really feels about me. But that's not why I'm calling."

"You want to plan a double date with Nancy and me? We're close. Parrish is only about an hour from you."

"Well, no," Dennis admitted. "I mean, yes. But that's also not why I'm calling."

Ortega gave Nancy a quick peck on the lips as she headed out for her weekly tennis lesson. Nancy gave a playful twirl to show off her new pleated white skirt as she headed out the door, blowing him another kiss. Ortega smiled. *Gotta take in the good moments when you got 'em*, he thought to himself.

He drew himself back into the conversation. "So, why *are* you calling Officer Dennis?"

"Emma has suddenly come into some money... a *lot* of money."

"Oh?" From what Ortega could remember, she was a woman of very little means, living in a tiny hovel on the Lower West Side of Manhattan. He shuddered to even think of it.

"Yeah," Dennis explained. "She had been modeling for this artist and philanthropist Erasmus Vandenberg."

"The tycoon whose family fortune came out of selling vitamins?"

"The same, though I'm told they prefer to refer to them as nutritional supplements or nutraceuticals. Probably some hoity-toity rich thing," Dennis reasoned. "Must have worked for him, though. Seems to have died in his sleep just shy of his 89th birthday... heart failure."

"That's a pretty good run," Ortega admitted. Ortega wasn't sure he wanted to live that long. His joints were already a little achy, and he couldn't imagine thirty or more years with bad knees. "So, am I to assume that he left Emma something in his will?"

"Nearly everything," Dennis answered.

"Everything? As in… his entire fortune? Were they having an affair?" Ortega blurted out before he could stop himself.

"They most certainly were not!" Dennis all but yelled into the phone. "He was like a grandfather to her!"

"But his *entire* fortune?" Ortega was incredulous.

"*Nearly*," Dennis clarified. "He donated much of his wealth to some charity that supports women in crisis, another for at-risk youth, and a third to provide mental health services to men and women who can't afford them."

"Sounds like a pretty upstanding guy," Ortega had to admit. He rarely thought fondly of those with money, Nancy's family being the exception. He had spent too much of his career uncovering the shady dealings of wealthy men doing their best to cover things up.

"That amounted to only 30% of his fortune. The rest… his estate on Treasure Island, his high-rise in Manhattan, and his manor in Leitrim… he divvied up between Emma, his nephew, and one granddaughter. Emma got the house in Florida and the remaining 70% of his financial assets."

"That doesn't make sense," Ortega insisted.

"I agree. So does Em. I think she's a bit overwhelmed by it all."

"I'll bet." Ortega cleared his throat. "Might wanna talk to a good accountant and hire a lawyer."

"She's done that… only, they were Erasmus Vandenberg's accountant and his team of lawyers. I recommended she talk with someone without close ties to the family."

"Smart thinking, Officer Dennis. But what does any of this have to do with me?"

"The thing is," Dennis lowered his voice, "I don't think Erasmus Vandenberg died in his sleep at all. I think it was murder."

"Who would murder a nearly 90-year-old man who probably didn't have that many years left, anyway?"

"I don't know, but the family is acting all fishy if you ask me."

"Wouldn't you act fishy if your family fortune was handed off to an art model that their dearly departed Erasmus couldn't have known very well?"

"That's just it," Dennis answered. "You would think they would contest the will, call her a gold digger and tie the estates up in court."

"Exactly."

"But that's not what they're doing," Dennis explained.

"It isn't?"

"No, they've already been all over the news celebrating her new fortune. They say that dear old Erasmus had a heart of gold, through and through, and who more deserving of his fortune than the one woman who gave his life purpose and was a friend to him in his older years?"

"That's surprisingly... generous of them," Ortega eventually found the words.

"It's bullshit, if you ask me... er, sorry Sir," Dennis apologized.

"Dennis, I'm no longer your boss. You can curse any damn time you want to. I don't care. And please, call me José. Call me Ortega. Call me whatever you want, but don't refer to me as 'sir' or 'detective' anymore. Okay?"

"Okay... Jo." Dennis thought carefully and decided he liked that nickname (even though it likely only made sense to him). Ortega didn't, but since he gave him free range to call him 'whatever,' he'd have to learn to accept it. "As I was saying, it's bullshit if you ask me. I believe Erasmus Vandenberg was murdered, and the family is being agreeable because they're all hiding something."

"Did you report your suspicions to the proper authorities in each district?"

"I did," Dennis sighed. "But no one believes me. And, if they do, they're not willing to disturb the potential hornet's nest that is the Vandenberg family."

"So, I'll ask you again. What does any of this have to do with me?"

"I wanna hire you, Jo," Dennis answered simply. "You can't be happy being retired. Help us figure out what's going on here, else Em won't be able to accept the fortune with a good conscience."

"Did she know you had plans to contact me?" Ortega asked.

"Of course," Dennis answered. "It was Emma's idea."

Chapter 3
Erasmus Vandenberg

Two Months Ago in Manhattan; 1998

"**B**eautiful, my Dear," Erasmus complimented. "But could you lift your chin just a smidge upward… yes, perfect," he praised. "Now the light catches the side of your face, just so.

Emma Post had been the private model of wealthy philanthropist Erasmus Vandenberg for the past six months. While she was hesitant about accepting the position at first, the model coordinator at the Artist Atelier, an art school where Emma had been a figure model for years, vouched for his character. Several models, both male and female, had sat for him over the years in his home studio on the Upper East Side of Manhattan — always draped, never nude.

In fact, Erasmus was typically fond of Rococo-era art, often renting ball dress replicas for Emma to wear during her sessions. While it was a far cry from her everyday jeans and sweatshirt, she found that she rather liked it.

More than the dress, she appreciated that Erasmus treated

her like a lady and never felt the need to call attention to the fact that he was wealthy and had plenty of money, whereas she had almost none. He was respectful and kind and, in Emma's world, that combination was rare.

On this day, Erasmus had his back to the window, where the sun beamed brightly over his shoulder. The light landed directly on the model stand where Emma lounged across a gold-trimmed, light blue sofa with stiff padding and ornate patterns across it. She was wearing a contrasting indigo ball gown with a base so wide that it was literally impossible for Emma's slight frame to fall over, even if she tried. Frankly, she had no idea what she'd do when it was time to take a bathroom break.

Erasmus hunched over his easel, as he had done for over six decades. It was a little harder for him to hold the paintbrush now, the knobs on his arthritic hands becoming more prominent with each passing year, but he learned to be patient, waiting for his hands to stop trembling before he applied the next stroke. His vision was challenged too, and while his earlier work was a precise mix of complex lines, colors and subtle light shifts, he'd learned to adapt his later work to meet the needs of his aging body. For example, there were fewer lines on the canvas, but they were purposeful. Any intricate shading he would work on after the model had gone home, where he could take as much time as he needed waiting for the natural light in the room to shift just so. His brush strokes were larger and his colors bolder.

"Do you have time for a late lunch today?" Erasmus asked, absentmindedly humming for a moment before catching himself.

Emma waited for him to finish his tune before answering. "Sorry, Raz. I promised Dennis I'd meet him for an early dinner since he's working late tonight." *Raz* was Emma's pet name for Erasmus, since it was the only logical one she could come up with for someone with a name like Erasmus. It should be noted that Emma was the only person permitted to give him a nick-name. He hadn't even let his late wife do that.

"Ah." Erasmus nodded, glancing up for a moment, holding his paintbrush at arm's length to measure. "The police officer. How is it going with Officer Dennis?" He fought back a knowing grin.

"Good, so far." Emma resisted the urge to scratch the unfortunate itch under the folds of her gown. She didn't know how she'd reach it, anyway. The muscle behind her left shoulder ached, but she dared not move. Instead, she took a deep breath, as if willing it to soften. It did, slightly.

"Well, that's encouraging," Erasmus smiled. "Though I am a little cross at the young man for interfering with our late lunches."

"Next time," she smiled. "I promise."

"Yes," he nodded. "And one of these days, I'll have you and your par amour to dinner so I can size him up properly. Make sure he's good enough for you."

Emma thought this was sweet. Her own father had skipped out on her mother at a young age, and unfortunately, her mother's love life comprised a revolving door of men, each one worse than the last. That's why Emma was so particular now. In all matters of the heart, she kept her wits about her. Though, if she were being completely honest with herself, Officer Dennis was carving out a neat little spot in the center of her chest that seemed to flutter slightly when he was around. But she'd never tell her boyfriend that, lest he get the wrong idea.

Erasmus began humming again. Emma immediately recognized the tune and began singing along softly. It was 'Pennies from Heaven.'

Erasmus stopped humming, surprised. "You know the tune?"

"Yes," Emma chuckled. "You sing or hum it almost every time I sit for you."

"Do I?" Erasmus mused, taking out a white cloth and wiping a small spot on the corner of the canvas. "I had no idea. Sorry, my dear."

"Don't be," Emma smiled. "I like it."

After a moment's pause, Erasmus hummed and sang quietly under his breath, *"Hmmm… hmmm… each cloud contains…"*

Emma joined in, *"Pennies from Heaven."*

There was a knock at the door. They both stopped singing, their smiles dropping simultaneously at the interruption.

"Ex… ex… excuse m… m… me… gra… grandfather." A mousy young woman peeked a nervous head around the large mahogany door. Her hair was raven black, cropped short and framing her round face, her dark bangs a stark contrast to her pasty complexion.

"Elsbeth." Erasmus was delighted. "How nice to see you. Please come in." The young woman cautiously entered the room and shuffled her feet toward her grandfather. "Shut the door behind you, please. It's drafty."

She turned to obey.

"Emma, have you met my granddaughter Elsbeth before?" Elsbeth looked as if she'd rather fade into the deep blue painted walls, a little challenging as she had on a plain toffee-colored dress. Elsbeth eyed Emma's gown and then glanced at her own, blushing a little.

"I have not," Emma smiled pleasantly. From her estimation, Elsbeth had to have been in her early twenties, probably not much more than a decade younger than Emma. And yet, she carried herself like a small child. "It's nice to meet you, Elsbeth," Emma offered softly.

"Hi." Elsbeth curtsied, tucking her head as she absentmind-edly clung to her dress with both hands, rocking nervously from side-to-side.

"Elsbeth is visiting with her mother, my daughter, Edwina, from the Hamptons."

Apparently, the family liked names that began with the letter "E."

"What is it, Elsbeth?" Erasmus persuaded.

After a pause, she said, "M… M…. Mother… w… wants to

know if y… y… you'll be taking us to a B… Broadway… sh… show this w… w… weekend." She kicked the side of the very expensive couch where Emma was posing.

"Emma." Erasmus turned to his model. "Why don't we break for today? We can continue on Thursday." Emma nodded, standing up with some difficulty. Her joints were stiff, and she attempted to stretch her arms overhead. Unfortunately, the dress was as stiff as her joints, and wouldn't allow her to raise her arms more than about shoulder high. Instead, she twisted her neck from side-to-side and then lowered her arms.

"You're b… b… beautiful," Elsbeth blurted out and then shrank back, clasping her hands over her mouth.

Emma smiled at the young woman's abruptness but was careful with her reply. She realized Elsbeth was a bit… different.

"Well, thank you, Elsbeth," she offered. "But I'm certain it's the dress."

Elsbeth furrowed her brow, confused.

"Elsbeth," Erasmus addressed his granddaughter gently, while putting his paints away. "Are you quite certain it's not you who really wants to go to the theater and not your mother?" Elsbeth turned a beet-red and fought back an embarrassed giggle. She wrapped an arm around her face as if to hide herself. "It's okay, my dear. Tell your grandpa what it was you were hoping to see."

Elsbeth looked at Emma for a moment, her mouth dropping in a frown. She dared not say it aloud. Instead, she ran over to her grandfather and motioned for him to bend over. She cupped her hands around his ear and whispered.

"Really?" Erasmus confessed. "I'm afraid I don't know that one." He shook his head. "But maybe Emma does. Why don't you ask?"

Elsbeth was unsure, looking down at her Mary Jane shoes and simple, ankle-length dress and then over at Emma, whose hair had been pinned up to reveal long, toned shoulders and a gown fit for royalty. Elsbeth seemed to have difficulty understanding fantasy from reality. She lost the concept that Emma was only pretending to be from the Rococo time period and hadn't actually magically appeared from the past so that her grandfather could paint her.

Still, she let Emma in on her secret. But instead of answering aloud, even though there were only the three of them in the room, Elsbeth suddenly darted over to Emma, having taken her into her confidence. She tugged at her arm until the slightly older woman leaned over to listen, the folds of the gown making a crinkling sound as she bent. Elsbeth cupped her hands over Emma's ears, as she had done her grandfather's, and whispered.

"Beauty and the Beast?" Emma clarified. At first, Elsbeth was embarrassed that Emma had said it out loud. She backed away, slowly, catching the heel of her shoe on the carpet. She toppled backward until Emma caught her arms and righted the girl. "Well," Emma smiled encouragingly, "that's a very good musical. I had a friend who was an understudy for it—"

Emma caught herself, her face dropping. It was her now-deceased friend, Clarissa Sauer, who had been in that show. Clarissa had been murdered last year and, for a short while, Emma was a potential suspect in the investigation. It was how she met Officer Dennis. And while she would have given anything to have her friend back, the one bright spot was that the tragedy brought her and Dennis together, something for which Emma would always be grateful. *Well*, she thought, *at least so far.*

Emma found her eyes beginning to well up at the memory. "I should change," she announced to Erasmus, who had finished packing up his tools and was now manually turning the lever of a knob on one of the tall windows behind him to let a little of the crisp New York air in to help rid the room of the smell of harsh oil paints.

She darted past Erasmus before he could see her expression, one that had fortunately been lost on Elsbeth. At the far corner of the room was a doorway that led to a very large private bathroom, which served as her changing area. She closed the door, almost catching the hem of the dress behind her.

"Elsbeth!" A woman's voice yelled from the foyer before bursting into the room like a gale force wind. "Where are you, simple girl?"

Elsbeth ran to hide behind her grandfather. She clung to the back of his shirt with her hands as if to shield herself.

"She's with me, Edwina," Erasmus addressed Elsbeth's mother, his daughter.

Edwina had a short, cropped haircut that almost matched Elsbeth's, except that hers had been dyed brown with streaks of blonde added in strategic places. She wore a white, pin-striped pant suit with a large gold chain that had been double-looped around her neck. At the end of it was a very noticeable, diamond-encrusted, golden cross. Her heavy French perfume was a scent that did not mix well with the smell of paint and solvent.

"I'm sorry, Father," she apologized on her daughter's behalf. "Elsbeth, come out from there and leave your grandfather alone. He's very busy!"

Erasmus' gray brows knit together in a solid line. "I'm never too busy for Elsbeth," he answered simply as he gently nudged Elsbeth toward her mother. "Nice to see you again, Edwina," he answered, formally.

"You too, Father." She took Elsbeth by the hand, just as Emma emerged from the bathroom wearing jeans and an over-sized light pink sweatshirt, a fanny pack wrapped around her waist. Edwina eyed Emma distastefully before turning her atten-tion to Erasmus. "I've instructed Cook to plan for dinner at 6 p.m.," she announced. "I hope that's alright. I know it's late for you, but I need to stay on a strict dietary schedule."

Edwina was a tall, thin woman who didn't really need to stay on any sort of schedule at all. She liked everything just so and felt anxious when life's events were out of her control. Therefore, she attempted to control… everything.

"I'll adjust," Erasmus sighed. Unlike Edwina, who was about thirty-five years younger than he, old Erasmus wasn't put off by little things such as when dinner was served, or if someone interrupted his work. He didn't even bat an eye that his daughter had only just arrived that morning, and she had already taken hold of the house schedule and re-arranged it, even though the house was solely… *his*.

Edwina grasped Elsbeth's hand so hard the young girl winced a little, as she dragged her daughter out of the room, accidentally slamming the door behind her as a gust of wind blew in from the window.

A darkness fell over the room as a few storm clouds blew through Manhattan, casting a shadow over the city.

"She seems nice," Emma bit her lip, sarcastically, and suddenly a laugh erupted from the depths of Erasmus' belly. She had heard plenty of stories about Edwina. Though, surprisingly, few about Elsbeth other than a passing reference.

"She certainly is… something," Erasmus concurred. "Give me a moment, and I'll have Ferdinand meet you out front to take you home." He glanced at the window.

"Thank you, Raz," she agreed. For the first month working for Erasmus, Emma insisted on taking two subway stops from his three-story luxury condo and walking the rest of the way before she finally relented and agreed to be chauffeured to and from her apartment. It was more at the behest of her new boyfriend Dennis. As a cop who'd seen a thing or two in the city, he wasn't comfortable with her having to take any unnecessary risks when Erasmus was perfectly willing to provide a safe escort for her.

At first, she felt funny at the looks she received from her neighbors when she arrived home in a stretch limo, but she didn't even try to explain. She let them think whatever they wanted.

"Same time Thursday?" Emma confirmed.

"Same time Thursday," Erasmus smiled.

Just then, they heard the briefest sound of thunder, followed by a light rain on the roof. Before Emma could close the door behind her, Erasmus hummed pleasantly. Only, the tune had changed to something more sinister, "*No one here can love and understand me... Oh what hard luck stories they all hand me...*"

After years of hob-knobbing with friends in the arts, Emma recognized this song too. Just before the closing line, she jumped in to finish the tune, "*Blackbird Bye-Bye.*"

Chapter 4
Baxter Baker

Two Months Ago in Manhattan; 1998

Emma waited in the front lobby of their building for Erasmus' private driver, Ferdinand, to retrieve her, sitting on a stiff white couch that seemed a poor choice of both color and material considering the foot traffic that must have gone through there regularly. The floor was adorned with gold-trimmed white carpet runners. Overhead hung an over-sized and overpriced crystal chandelier. To amuse herself, she tried to imagine what a carpet and chandelier like that would look like in the entrance of her apartment complex, but decided it was so large that it wouldn't even make it through the front door.

The traffic was heavy on the avenue outside, which meant that it might take Ferdinand a few extra minutes to drive the short distance from the private garage to the front door of their building; but Erasmus wouldn't hear of her actually walking down to the garage to meet him. "That's no place for a lady," he reasoned. He was particular like that.

So, she sat.

"Sit down, you simple girl," a voice barked. Edwina had emerged from the elevator and was now yelling at Elsbeth. They stopped several feet away from Emma. Edwina was now wearing a cream-colored wool walking cape and thin, black-leather gloves. Elsbeth obediently took a seat, not on the next couch over, but rather the opposite end of where Emma sat. Edwina caught Emma's expression and softened her voice. "There's a good girl," she praised her daughter. "Don't move, and I'll be back in a jiffy." She shot Emma a furtive glance before walking back to have a talk with the security guard standing just inside the lobby's entrance. There was another positioned outside too, just under the awning by the front door. It was a well-protected building.

Emma caught the glance but had no idea why Edwina would even care about the opinion of a low-income, working-class girl from the Lower West Side, but guessed that appearances were important to Edwina.

Elsbeth was busy fidgeting with the long coat she had strewn across her lap as she sat, waiting for her mother. Emma caught her glance and smiled. Leaning over, she whispered. "I hope you *do* get to go to the theater this weekend."

Elsbeth returned the smile with a small, close-lipped smirk, appreciatively.

"Is that my favorite cousin?" A voice boomed, startling the women.

Emma looked up to see a tall man with bleach blonde hair parted on the side, hanging in ear-length locks, coupled with a tan complexion too perfect to be real. He wore a striped, long-sleeve polo shirt, black jeans and the swagger of someone with all the confidence in the world.

"H... hi... B... B... Baxter," she stammered, staring at the floor.

He took her by the shoulders and pulled her enthusiastically to her feet. "Here. Give your cousin a kiss." Before she could respond, the man leaned over and planted a kiss on Elsbeth's cheek. She returned with a light peck on his opposite cheek. "Kissing cousins," he joked before noticing Emma sitting on the couch. "It's alright," he reassured Emma. "We're thrice removed." He winked.

Emma didn't find him amusing.

"And who is this charming lady you're sitting with, Elsbeth?" He nodded toward Emma, releasing his cousin's shoulders.

"This is… E… E… Emma… gra… grandfather's… m… model."

Emma was surprised Elsbeth remembered her name. She wasn't sure the young woman had been paying that much attention.

"Oh, really?" His eyebrows shot up.

"She means portrait model," Emma quickly explained. "Her grandfather Erasmus hired me to sit for one of his paintings. I'm Emma." She extended her hand to shake his.

He took her small hand in both of his and just… held it, looking into her eyes. "Well, my grandfather has excellent taste." He looked her over briefly, from head to toe. "Perhaps you'll sit for me one day?"

"Are you a painter?"

"For you, I would become one," he countered, smiling devilishly.

"May I have my hand back, please?" Emma retorted sourly.

"Certainly." He released her palm.

A man in a black suit and driver's hat cleared his throat behind them.

"Ah, Ferdinand." Emma smiled gratefully. "Thank you for giving me a lift." To Elsbeth and Baxter, she said, "Nice to have met you both."

"Just a moment, Emma." Baxter touched the inside of her forearm, careful not to appear too grabby. "Let me take you to dinner tonight."

"Oh." Emma pulled her arm back. Behind her, Ferdinand

stood, rocking back and forth on his heels impatiently. "Thank you, but I have a boyfriend."

Emma felt something in her stomach lurch. Did she, in fact, have a boyfriend? She knew she wasn't dating anyone else, and she didn't think that Dennis was either. He always seemed so eager to see her. But then, she really didn't know for certain. And, since their dating was *mostly* innocent — a few heated kisses at the end of the evening — there was no real reason to push the issue… except in situations like this one. But Emma had dated her share of "Baxters," and they were all the same… self-absorbed, dishonest, charming when they needed to be, and, unfortunately, sexy as hell.

"Should I take your silence to mean you are considering it?" Baxter was hopeful.

"No!" Elsbeth stood and stamped her foot. She was loud enough for a few onlookers to pause. She quickly turned red and retreated inward, casting her eyes to the floor. "Sh… she already t… told y… you. She has a boyfriend. Dennis." Elsbeth crossed her arms defiantly.

It seemed that Elsbeth had been eavesdropping.

"I see… Dennis," Baxter repeated. "And what does your boyfriend do for a living, this… Dennis?"

"What does that matter to you?" Emma demanded.

"He's… a c… cop," Elsbeth answered, lifting her chin. For reasons which Emma could not understand, Elsbeth already seemed to be 'team Emma and Dennis' and definitely not 'team Baxter.'

"Oh, a cop," Baxter smiled. "Must take you on some lovely dates… on a cop's salary. Dinner on the Riviera? Spontaneous trips to the Maldives?"

"There's nothing spontaneous about an 18-hour flight to the Maldives," Emma snapped back. "And what is it that you do, Baxter… exactly?" Emma wasn't sure why she asked, as she really didn't care.

"I'm the Vice-President of Operations for the Vandenberg nutraceutical company. Nutraceuticals are—"

"I know what nutraceuticals are, Baxter. Thank you."

"We have one manufacturing plant in the U.S. and one in Ireland, as well as relationships with over 100 private organizations. I oversee all of it."

"So, you watch *other* people work all day?"

"There's a bit more to it than that," Baxter smirked.

Ferdinand cleared his throat again.

"I'm thrilled for you."

"No need to be snarky, Emma." He shook his head, grinning. "You asked."

"Right." She nodded. "I did."

"I can do better than the Dallas BBQ for dinner," he whispered, leaning toward her.

"I'll keep that in mind." She turned to leave.

"At least…" He stopped her one more time. "Take my card?" He held a business card in front of her face.

Emma didn't move. She just stared at him, her nostrils flaring.

Suddenly, quick as lightning, Elsbeth snatched the card and tucked it into her coat.

"I'll keep it s… safe f… for Emma." Elsbeth dutifully nodded.

"Thank you, Elsbeth." Emma smiled at her new friend before turning to Baxter. "But I won't be calling."

Before Baxter could try again, she darted around him to Ferdinand, who produced an umbrella, seemingly out of nowhere. The sound of thunder erupted outside as the rain came down in buckets. "I parked as close to the building as I could," he explained.

"Don't worry," she told Ferdinand. "I won't melt." Ferdinand let out a laugh. "And, sorry to keep you waiting."

"Not at all, Miss Post." He shrugged as they made their way

awkwardly through a revolving door that forced everyone to stand a little too close for comfort. "It was worth it to see Baxter's face when you turned him down. That doesn't happen often."

Once in the limo that Ferdinand was driving, Emma asked, "Who *is* Baxter, anyway?"

"He's the great nephew of the late Esmee Vandenberg, Erasmus' late wife and great-grandson of her older sister, Katherine."

"Oh," was all that Emma could think to say.

"Oh, indeed." Ferdinand shook his head. "Not my place to say, of course. But Baxter is used to getting his own way. If he bothers you again, be sure to tell Erasmus. He'll put it right."

"Thank you, Ferdinand." Emma sank back in her seat. "But I've dealt with far worse than the likes of Baxter… What's his last name?"

"Baker," Ferdinand answered.

"Well, as I was saying," Emma finished, "I've dealt with far worse than the likes of Baxter Baker."

Chapter 5
Thursday

Two Months Ago in Manhattan; 1998

As promised, Emma returned to the Vandenberg household for her next modeling session. Only this time, Elsbeth was there, too.

"I'm afraid I'll have to miss the theater this weekend, dear Elsbeth," Erasmus broke the news to his granddaughter, who, after having met Emma, decided she quite enjoyed being there during her modeling sessions with Erasmus. Other than Erasmus' random humming, or the rare day when he had classical music playing softly in the background, most times, it was quiet in the room. This delighted Elsbeth because, then, she could hear with crystal clarity the other sounds that normally got overshadowed, such as the gentle movements when Erasmus was mixing oil paints on a palette, or the creak of the couch as Emma made a slight adjustment, and even the crisp rustle of Emma's oversized ball gown when she stood to stretch on her breaks. And the best part of all was sitting behind her grandfather and watching as a blank canvas morphed into art.

"Oh." Elsbeth was pulled from her trance. Her lip quivered a little. She was very much looking forward to seeing a musical with her grandfather. Unlike her mother, who typically hovered over her like a helicopter, criticizing her every move, Erasmus was the typical doting grandfather. To him, Elsbeth was perfect in every way. Elsbeth wasn't sure how her mother, Edwina, had gotten to be so ill-tempered and cross. Her grandfather wasn't like that at all. She assumed that she must have taken after her grandmother, who died long before Elsbeth was born.

"Don't fret, my Dear. I promise we'll go next weekend." Erasmus tried to reassure the young woman.

Elsbeth's face crumpled like a piece of paper about to be thrown in the trash. "W… why… n… not… th.. this w… w… weekend?"

Erasmus stopped and set his paintbrush on the easel momentarily, surveying his granddaughter. "Emergency trip to my production plant in Florida, I'm afraid. It's an urgent matter that can't be handled by telephone. I have to be there in person."

Emma took advantage of the momentary distraction and reached over her shoulder to scratch an itch, pushing on her elbow with her opposite hand so she could reach it more easily. *Finally, relief!* She thought. That had been bugging the hell out of her for the better part of fifteen minutes. Of all the costumes she had to wear, this one was by far the itchiest. *Funny, all the little things we take for granted until they become a challenge to do,* Emma's mind-wandering continued. *Something as simple as scratching an itch, when you have to hold still on the model stand, suddenly becomes the most important thing in the world when you can't do it.* She drew her attention back to the room. Noticing that Erasmus had picked up his brush again, she all but snapped to attention.

"M… m… maybe… I… c… could… g… g o… w… with you?" Elsbeth suggested. Suddenly, her face brightened. "M… maybe w… we c… could g… go to D… Disney… W… World instead?"

Erasmus thought on this a moment. He was getting up in years; he reasoned. Who knows how many more excursions he and his granddaughter would get to enjoy together?

"M… Mother… w… won't… c… care," Elsbeth continued. "S… since I w… was… g… going to be spending the w… w… weekend w… with y… y… you, anyway."

From what little Emma saw of Edwina, Elsbeth's mother, she imagined she'd be delighted to have Elsbeth be someone else's problem for the weekend. It was almost as if Edwina saw her daughter as a burden. And it was obvious that Erasmus did not.

Just then, there was a loud jingle of the tall French door leading into the room, followed by the obvious vibration of someone tugging and pushing the door back and forth, willing it to open. This was followed by a loud knock. "Father, are you in there?"

It was Edwina.

"Yes, just a moment," Erasmus called. To Elsbeth, he said, "Go let your mother in, won't you?" Elsbeth reluctantly nodded and went to unlock the door.

Edwina burst in, all but knocking her daughter over. "Why was the door locked?" She demanded, eyeing Emma on the model stand, as if she had something to do with it.

"I locked it because some people don't know how to knock before entering a room," Erasmus chided, never lifting his eyes from the canvas.

"What?" Edwina grew annoyed. "Hmm… never mind." She thought for a moment. "Now I forgot why I came in here… oh, right," she remembered. "Butler let me know that you and some of the staff are taking the private plane to Florida tomorrow."

"Yes, that's correct," Erasmus confirmed. 'Butler' was his personal companion, Ferdinand. Edwina had trouble remembering their names, so instead she referred to them by their job titles.

"May I ask why?" Edwina crossed her long arms, her deep red lips dropping in a grimace.

"Yes," Erasmus answered simply.

"Yes, what?" Edwina replied.

"Yes, you may ask why," he chuckled.

"You are an impossible man!" Edwina complained. "Fine. Why are you suddenly taking a trip to Florida?"

"It's a business—" Elsbeth started to answer before her grandfather interrupted.

"I'm taking Elsbeth to Disney World. Kind of a spur-of-the-moment thing."

"But I thought you were going to the theater this weekend? I had it on my calendar."

"We were, but then we agreed it would be more fun to visit Belle and the Beast in Disney World instead of seeing them on Broadway."

"Why wasn't I informed of this?" she demanded. "I'm only the girl's mother, after all."

"It w-was m-my f-fault M-Mother," Elsbeth choked. "I asked g-grandfather to take me."

Before Edwina could protest, Erasmus continued. "Grant an old man a trip with his only granddaughter while he's still healthy enough to do it?"

Edwina thought on this a moment, tucking her chin, her sharp nose pointed toward the floor. If Emma wasn't mistaken, she could have sworn the tiniest of smirks crossed the woman's lips and her eyes flashed as if she'd suddenly had an idea.

"Please, M-Mother—" Elsbeth began.

Edwina held up her hand and Elsbeth fell silent. "I agree. In fact, Father, you must let me help you pack. I'll arrange for Chef to go with you too and call in a security guard to accompany you."

"Please, Edwina," Erasmus protested. "Why would I need a personal guard for a simple weekend trip?"

"Because you're one of the richest and most important men

in this town, even bigger than that blowhard, Astor Ellis. And," she added with as much feeling as she could muster, "I worry about you."

Emma cringed at the mention of Astor Ellis. At one time, the young business executive had been secretly seeing one of her friends, before her friend met with an untimely death. It was right before Astor married his socialite fiancé, Portia LaMonte, and stepped into his father Byron's role at B. A. Ellis Industries. *Erasmus was nothing like that family,* Emma decided. She didn't like him even being compared to them.

"Fine," Erasmus agreed. "I'll let you arrange everything, my dear. Just make sure Ruth doesn't forget my health bars and tea. She'll know which ones I like."

"Ruth?" Edwina thought a moment. "Oh, right... Chef." Edwina made a mental note of her name, though she was likely to forget again. Much like Astor Ellis' mother, Gretchen Ellis, Edwina found most people unimportant and quite forgettable. *Must be a strange dementia among the wealthy,* Emma thought, absent-mindedly letting out a snort. Suddenly, everyone in the room was focused on her.

"Ahem," Emma coughed slightly, averting her eyes.

Edwina opened the door and yelled, "Chef!" loudly, before adding, "Ruth! Could you come in here please?"

"Yes, ma'am." A small, rotund woman with gray hair and a large mole on her cheek bounced in the room. Her hair was tucked in a hairnet. She held a wooden spatula in her hand.

"There's been a change of plans," Edwina barked.

"Oh?" Ruth questioned. Emma couldn't help but hone in on the mole as Ruth spoke. It bobbed up and down as Ruth moved, as if it had a life of its own.

"Yes, Father is going on an unexpected business trip. He says you are aware of his preferred health snacks?"

"Oh, yes, ma'am," Ruth answered, shooting Erasmus a pleasant smile. "The purple berry ones at midday, and the green almond cherry bars at bedtime." She tapped a finger on the side of her temple. "I remember everything."

"Thank you, Ruth," Erasmus praised. "Knew I could count on you... Oh," he remembered, "And could you make sure Ferdinand picks up a valerian root tincture for me before I leave? I always have trouble sleeping the first couple of nights after traveling."

"Certainly, Sir." Ruth smiled, awaiting further instruction.

"Eh, Ruth," Edwina paused as if the name were somehow inconvenient. "That will be all."

"Yes, ma'am." Ruth nodded and quietly left the room.

"Elsbeth," Edwina commanded. "Come along so Maid can help you pack your bags." The maid's name was Ivy, but Edwina hadn't bothered to learn her name, either.

Elsbeth nodded, reluctantly following her mother out of the room like a shadow.

"Oh, one more thing, Edwina," Erasmus remembered.

Edwina stopped suddenly, and Elsbeth almost walked right into her mother. Annoyed, Edwina stepped around her.

"Yes, what is it?" she growled impatiently.

"Since you're going through the trouble of packing for me, can you please ensure that Ferdinand compiles my favorite records to bring along?"

"Records?" Edwina was confused, as her mind went toward documents and bank statements.

"Yes," Erasmus confirmed. "Records... Harry James Band, Bing Crosby, and Georgie Stoll... Just ask Ferdinand. He's got them all organized."

"Why on Earth would you need your record collection for such a quick trip?"

"Because I find them relaxing," his voice cracked. "What does it matter to you?" The raised pitch of his voice let Edwina know she had gone too far.

"Very well," she agreed. "But you *will* be back in time for your birthday dinner Monday night, won't you? Chef and I are planning a very special menu."

"Yes, we'll be back in time." Erasmus paused to admire his work. *One of my better pieces,* he mused. Edwina eyed her father, impatiently ringing her hands.

"Can I at least see what you're working on that seems to consume all of your attention these days?" Edwina asked as she shot Emma a look. Something was bothering her. Emma wasn't sure what the woman thought of her, but she suspected it wasn't good.

"Of course," Erasmus answered, surprised. "I didn't think you had an interest. Here it is, then." He backed away so that Edwina could lean over his shoulder for a closer look. "In fact, we should be finished after today's sitting. Probably just need to put the finishing touches on it this evening," he mused.

Emma was crestfallen. It was less about the impact of what not working for a wealthy man would have on her dwindling bank account. She was more disappointed about not getting to spend time with Erasmus, of whom she'd grown very fond.

Edwina eyed the painting critically, peering back and forth between Emma and her portrait. "Lovely," she began optimistically before adding, "You flatter her."

Emma bit back a response.

"No," Erasmus answered. "I don't think I did her beauty justice at all."

That only served to annoy Edwina more. She quickly grabbed Elsbeth's hand.

"Ow!" Elsbeth complained. Her mother ignored her, dragging her out of the room and all but slamming the door behind her.

Erasmus smiled at Emma. "I think we're good for today. But I'm afraid I will need to take a raincheck on lunch."

"That's okay; I understand," Emma answered, standing and stretching her arms over head before twisting from side to side to get the kinks out from hours of sitting in one position.

"Maybe we can plan to meet up when you get back in town next week."

"I would like that very much," Erasmus answered. "And perhaps your gentleman friend will join us, too." Emma nodded as she headed toward the adjacent room to change back into her street clothes. "Oh, and Emma?"

"Yes?" She doubled-back.

"Perhaps we can discuss my retaining your services for a new project... if you have the time?" A sigh of relief rushed over Emma.

"Of course," she beamed gratefully. "I would like that very much."

As she left the room, there went Erasmus, humming again, occasionally breathing out a few of the lyrics, starting with 'Pennies from Heaven' before morphing into 'Bye, Bye, Blackbird'. *"Pack up all my cares and woe, here I go, winging low..."*

"Bye, bye, Blackbird." Emma sang out from the other room.

Erasmus turned back to Emma's portrait and smiled.

Chapter 6
Friday Flight

Two Months Ago on a Flight to Florida; 1998

Erasmus Vandenberg; his personal servant and butler Ferdinand; Elsbeth's private cook and personal companion Ruth; Elsbeth Ions; a contract pilot named Bernie; a flight attendant and licensed co-pilot Vivian; and a security guard named Hugo all boarded Erasmus' private jet at around 4 p.m. on Friday.

Bernie was a pleasant enough, tall fellow who insisted on wearing an official pilot's uniform from his commercial airline days, even though no one asked him to. A man of few words, he settled into the cockpit, and no one heard from him for the remainder of the journey.

Vivian, a medium-sized, Barbie doll-shaped woman with hair tied back into an uncomfortable-looking bun, offered Erasmus an arm to guide him to his oversized seat. Not needing assistance, he grasped her arm because it wasn't often that a woman sixty years his junior took an interest in him. "I'm turning 89 in a few days," he smiled at her.

"Well, happy birthday, Mr. Vandenberg," she smiled sweetly at him, flashing a row of perfectly whitened teeth as she ushered him to his seat.

Elsbeth clunked her carry-on bag, hitting each of the seats on each side of the aisle despite the wide space between them. This included her grandfather's aisle seat, and her own. She finally settled into her spot across the aisle, next to Erasmus. Ferdinand followed behind her with Elsbeth's oversized travel bag and Erasmus' customized rolling record case, followed by Ruth, who actually pushed a serving cart up the ramp and onto the plane so that Erasmus could have a home-cooked meal, even though the flights to and from Florida and New York were only a few hours each way. Ruth liked to be prepared and even had an extra supply of groceries so that Erasmus could stick to his strict diet while staying in his Florida home. The plane's kitchen was tiny for the rather round woman, but she pre-prepped the proteins, grains and vegetables and could make it work. She quickly put all her food items away, with the help of Ferdinand, before the two took their places in seats behind Erasmus and Elsbeth. Ferdinand kept Erasmus' precious record collection, which held a dozen of his favorites securely at his feet.

Then there was Hugo. No one knew anything about Hugo except that he came highly recommended at the Steele Security Service company, and he seemed particularly large and formidable for someone with a small and humble-sounding name. He wore sunglasses on the plane, though it wasn't sunny, and insisted on a place behind all the travelers where he had a clear eye on them, as well as all the plane exits.

Elsbeth took one look at Hugo and furrowed her brows. Everyone else on the plane was very pleasant, but Hugo wore a chronic and intimidating grimace.

Erasmus let out a yawn as he settled into his seat. He smiled pleasantly at Elsbeth, who smiled warmly in return.

Not long afterward, they received an all-clear and departed.

Once in the air, Ruth set to work in the kitchen, making a hearty fish stew with Vivian serving the passengers. Ferdinand, while skilled in many areas, was useless when it came to food prep, and got to sit back and catch up on the latest issue of the *New York Times*. Elsbeth clenched her seat nervously. Despite her apprehensiveness on planes, she couldn't look away and found herself watching the city below, through her window with an odd fascination, as the tall buildings became smaller and smaller.

Not more than an hour and a half later, Elsbeth remembered something and quickly removed her seatbelt. She spun around, kneeling into her seat to address Ruth, who was sitting directly behind her. "You forgot grandfather's snacks," she whispered. Oddly enough, the further away she got from her mother Edwina, the better her speech became.

"Ah," Ruth smiled, remembering. "Got them in the back, along with his nightly tea. Why don't you help me fetch them for him?"

Ruth took no time in preparing his evening tea, held in a small, Japanese-style ceramic cup. She added a few drops of valerian root, just as Erasmus preferred. She unwrapped his nutrient-rich, company branded green snack bar, placing it on a matching plate. Vivian joined them, but Elsbeth insisted, "No, let me." Without the assistance of a serving tray, Elsbeth carefully carried Erasmus' tea and evening snack from the back of the plane to his seat in the front. She paused while Vivian, close at her heals, opened a small, fold-out table for the older man. Elsbeth put the items down carefully before returning to her seat.

"Thank you," he smiled, tugging at a small cotton blanket he had settled around his lap. *Why are planes always so cold?* He wondered.

Within about fifteen minutes of his evening snack, he yawned a second time. Vivian quickly removed the food items, closed the serving table, and helped recline his seat. As if on cue,

Ferdinand produced a small pillow from his seat behind Erasmus.

"Excuse me, Sir," Ferdinand whispered as Erasmus looked over his shoulder.

"Oh, thank you, Ferdinand." Erasmus lifted his head gently while Ferdinand tucked the pillow under his master's head.

"Can I offer you a nightcap, Sir?" Vivian asked. "A martini, perhaps?"

"Oh no," Erasmus shook his head. "Never touch the stuff."

"I'll take one," Elsbeth chimed in. Vivian was surprised, looking to Ruth for confirmation that it was okay to serve Elsbeth a cocktail. People seemed to forget, given her childlike nature, that Elsbeth was in her early twenties.

Ruth nodded. "She'll be less fidgety that way."

"Vodka martini?" Vivian asked.

Elsbeth nodded. "With an olive," she added.

"Certainly," Vivian agreed, disappearing into a small bar area in the back of the plane. She returned minutes later with Elsbeth's cocktail.

Elsbeth took a sip and wrinkled her nose. She wasn't entirely certain she even liked alcohol, but it seemed to calm her nerves, so she endured the unpleasantness of it.

"Elsbeth," Erasmus addressed his granddaughter, tiredly, as she lifted the toothpick housing a large olive and sucked on it. "You won't mind if I close my eyes for a short nap, will you?"

Elsbeth shook her head as she gnawed at the olive. In fact, a nap sounded like a very good idea to her, too. She handed Vivian her now-empty glass and reclined her own seat, settling beneath a cotton blanket similar to her grandfather's.

Bernie's voice suddenly chimed in from the speakers overhead as the plane shook gently. "We're experiencing a few unexpected weather conditions," he explained calmly. "Nothing to worry about, but it may take us a bit longer to land. Might want to strap in with your seatbelts fastened for the next fifteen minutes or so, just to be on the safe side."

Ferdinand and Ruth obliged. Elsbeth, who would have normally been alarmed, nodded off groggily. Erasmus appeared sound asleep across the aisle. Vivian took a free seat behind Ruth. On a commercial flight, she might have asked Elsbeth and Erasmus to return their seats to an upright position during these weather conditions, but she knew how fussy private plane owners could be and silently strapped herself in. Hugo, who everyone almost forgot about, hadn't moved the entire flight, silently keeping watch over the passengers.

In a three-hour flight that took almost four-and-a-half due to bad weather and vying with other small crafts for a runway in which to land, they finally touched down in Florida.

The humidity hit them full force as Vivian opened the cabin's main door.

Elsbeth untangled herself from her blanket, and upon noticing that her grandfather was still asleep, slipped her seatbelt off and bounded to her feet.

"Grandfather," she whispered, touching his arm. "We're here." She recoiled at its stiffness. She shook it again gently. His arm was ice cold. It was only then that she noticed his lips were an odd blue. "Grandfather!" she yelled louder, alarmed.

Hugo pushed his way past the other passengers and shook the older man gently before checking his pulse, just to be sure. "He's dead," Hugo proclaimed in surprise.

The last sound everyone remembered before a swarm of medics and the police arrived was Elsbeth's blood-curdling scream.

Chapter 7
Edgar

Two Months Ago in Ireland; 1998

Edgar Vandenberg had an unusual love of reptiles, amphibians, and arachnids, but not just any kind. He preferred the dangerous ones, such as the Western Taipan snake, the golden poison dart frog, and the Brazilian wandering spider. Sadly, none of them existed in Leitrim. You might stumble upon a false widow, but Edgar didn't find those particularly interesting.

And so, when he was tending to his uncle Erasmus' Ireland estate, he had his collections especially flown in. Most were now well-preserved under glass, having met with untimely deaths years prior, and were of no danger to others. But Edgar enjoyed having his collection with him — some under glass countertop cases and some in shadow box displays he had installed in the wall of the main study. He found them sort of… comforting.

Edgar was only in his early sixties but, between his hunched shoulders and the way he shuffled his feet when he walked, most people assumed he was Erasmus' brother, not his much younger nephew. Edgar didn't care. Appearances meant nothing to him, and he was content to wear the same outdated tweed jacket that he'd had for the better part of four decades. He had a long white beard that he remembered to groom once a month, usually about the time the footman, Isaac, offered to draw him a bath to "relax his weary shoulders from all those long hours in the study." It was Isaac's polite way of telling him that his hygiene habits — or lack thereof — were beginning to offend the other servants in the house.

"Well, Myrna." Edgar went over to a long cage, where the one other living thing in the room resided. "Guess it's feeding time… again," Edgar laughed as he poured a bag filled with assorted dried spiders, crickets and beetles (that he also had especially flown in) into the cage. From its burrow under a pile of dirt, twigs and dried out leaves, a little pygmy shrew emerged, eagerly attacking the delicacies.

Edgar had rescued Myrna after a peregrine falcon accidentally dropped her from a great height on the lawn. Since shrews rarely live more than a year anyway, Edgar saw no need to return her to the wild in her injured state, instead choosing to care for her for the remainder of her days… an oddly compassionate thing to do for someone obsessed with toxic predators.

There was a knock at the door.

"Come in," Edgar called, smiling one more time at Myrna before replacing the lid to the cage.

"Sorry ta interrupt yer work," Isaac said in his thick Northern Irish accent upon entering the room. He was wearing a wool jacket and cap, both soggy from the rain. His coat dripped a little onto the floor, but neither of the men seemed to notice it. Isaac removed his cap and began twirling it uncomfortably.

"That's alright," Edgar replied. "I was just about to break for lunch, anyway." Edgar grew up in New York but spent most of his adult life dividing his time between Leitrim and County Kerry. His accent was a little more subtle than Isaac's. Edgar closed a few dusty books he had open to chapters about the mating rituals of the funnel-web spider. "Care to join me?"

Isaac eyed Edgar curiously. He'd worked for five households in his long lifetime, and this was the only one where the master deigned to dine with the help. Isaac found Edgar's informality both refreshing and slightly uncomfortable. Still, the two men had developed a kind of working-friendship over the years.

"Eh, no, t-ank yew," Isaac replied. "Em… I'm afraid I have some rather bahd news for ya. It's about yer uncle, Erasmus."

Edgar nodded. "He's dead, isn't he?"

His matter-of-factness took Isaac aback.

"Yeah," he answered sadly. "But, how'd yew know?"

Edgar thought a moment. "He's up in years. I suppose by the way you came in here twirling your cap and looking forlorn. I surmised that the news wasn't good when you mentioned Uncle Erasmus by name."

"Are yew, okay, Sir?" Isaac asked, concerned.

Edgar sighed, surveying his collection of reptiles, amphibians, and arachnids. "Yes," he finally nodded. "Uncle wasn't a young man, and—" he tapped the glass overtop the displayed taipan snake, "everything dies eventually."

A small tear formed in the corner of Edgar's eye. He tipped his head and brushed it away, lest Isaac witness his display of emotion.

"Still sahd though, yeah?" Isaac persisted. "He was a gewd man."

Edgar tapped the glass once again and nodded, his back toward Isaac. "That, he was," he agreed. Edgar seemed lost in thought for a few moments.

Isaac cleared his throat uncomfortably. "T-ere's a bit more, I'm afraid," he continued.

Edgar rubbed his forehead. It was much easier dealing with dead insects, reptiles, amphibians, and the like. Feelings attached to people were far more complicated. "What is it?" He turned to face Isaac.

"Yer presence is requested at the reading of ta will," Isaac explained. "It's being held at the end of next month at the Manhattan residence.

"Oh, that will never do," Edgar protested, closing his books. "I have far too much to do here with my research. Erasmus would have understood."

"Erasmus no doubt would," Isaac agreed, scratching the underside of his chin. "But what about yer family, yeah? Your cousin Edwina will be there. So will your cousin Baxter—"

"That boy," Edgar objected, "is *not* part of the Vandenberg line. As for my cousin Edwina… horrid woman. Why can't she just mail out copies of the will instead of being so melodramatic by hosting an official reading?" he scoffed.

"Cousin Elsbeth will be t-ere," Isaac tried again.

Edgar's face dropped. "Oh," he answered quietly. He had a soft spot for Elsbeth. She was a lot like him… introverted, stuck in their own little fantasy world most of the time. He always imagined that if he had had a daughter, she would be quite a bit like Elsbeth. "Poor girl," he mused. "Erasmus was more than her grandfather. In many ways, he raised her when Edwina's deadbeat husband ran off with that hoochie coochie dancer from Vegas."

"Aye." Isaac held back a grin. "But knowing Edwina, could yew exactly blame 'em?"

Edgar snorted. "Do I feel sorry for that Bible-toting, holier-than-thou, control freak cousin of mine? Absolutely not. But he didn't need to abandon Elsbeth. She was innocent in all of it."

"I agree wit yew, Sir," Isaac answered. "But surely you'll go… far her sake?"

"Isaac," Edgar chastised. "When did you become such a softie?" He made his way to the door.

Isaac patted him on the back. "I've always been a softie, Edgar. T-at's why I've put up wit yew for so long."

Edgar laughed. "Well then, I insist that you join me for

lunch. Formalities be damned!" He paused, eyeing Isaac for emphasis. "You'll hurt my feelings if you don't."

"Well, we can't have t-at, Sir," Isaac finally agreed. "Ya know some-tin', Edgar."

"What is it, Isaac?"

"Yer just like yer dad, God rest his soul. And even more like Erasmus."

"Well," Edgar thought it over, closing the door. "That's a fine compliment, indeed."

Chapter 8
Protection Spell

Two Months Ago in Manhattan;1998

"**E**mma." Dennis fumbled with the key to her apartment.

Emma looked up from her place on the kitchen floor as Dennis fought with the copy of the key she had given him 'for emergencies only.' She had forgotten about it. Instead of standing, she crossed her legs under her and buried her head in her hands, sobbing. Around her was a circle of stones that took up nearly her entire kitchen floor: black tourmaline, clear quartz and obsidian. In front of her was a bowl of burning white sage.

"Everything okay?" Dennis continued, finally getting the lock to budge. He swung the door open wide, concerned. "Why did you cancel our date? Why didn't you answer the door? And why—" He stopped when he saw her crying from the center of the room, "are you surrounding yourself with lots of gemstones?" He bounded toward her.

"No!" She stopped him. "Not over the circle," she warned. "Use the entryway."

Off to the side of the circle, nearest the stove, was a small gap in the stones. That was apparently the way in. He crossed the gap, pausing to grab a paper towel from the roll sitting on the kitchen counter. He knelt down next to her, putting a hand on her back. "Em?" he asked quietly. "What's going on?"

Emma sniffled. "What's going on is that I'm a jinx!"

"What are you talking about? Does this have something to do with Erasmus?"

"Yes," she blurted out. "You should stay as far away from me as possible, Dennis… Dennis—" She peered up at him. He handed her the paper towel. Accepting it, she said, "I just realized that in the two months we've been dating…"

"Seven," Dennis corrected.

"Seven?" Emma sniffled. "Has it really been that long?"

"It has definitely been that long," Dennis sighed. He refrained from pointing out that in that time they hadn't gotten much past kissing and some over-the-clothes fondling, but things were going so well otherwise that he didn't want to press the issue. Although, the lack of sex was sometimes agonizing.

Emma seemed unaware of this. "Well," she continued. "In the seven months we've been dating, I realize that I have no idea what your last name is." She wiped her eyes and then nose with the paper towel.

"McCleary," he answered hesitantly.

"Irish?" Emma asked.

"Yes? Are you going to hold that against me, too?" He joked, lightly, considering how much she disapproved of lots of things about him.

"No," she sniffed. "That's fine."

He sat down next to her, folding his legs under him, and hugging his knees to his chest so as not to disrupt the circle of stones, nor accidentally burn himself on the incense burner. "So, what's all this about you being a jinx?"

"Well, Ursula's dead. Clarissa is dead. And now Erasmus! Everyone I get close to ends up dead!"

Unfortunately, they had gotten wind of Erasmus' death nearly two months ago from the tabloids. No one from the family thought to phone Emma and let her know, but maybe that was too much to expect. After all, she was only a contracted art model. Still, she thought it might have been nice of someone to reach out, particularly since she had previously been coming to the house weekly.

The story disappeared as quickly as it came to light. All six people on the flight the night Erasmus died, somewhere between New York and Florida, were interviewed, and his death was quickly ruled as age-related heart failure. He was cremated a month later, and that was that.

Just yesterday, a Mr. Lundy, one of Erasmus' lawyers, reached out to Emma and asked if she would be present for the reading of the dead man's will. No one in the family was privy to its contents and had received no copies prior. It seemed to be something Erasmus had been adamant about when he drafted it. Emma couldn't understand why she would have been included and thought maybe Erasmus left her one of the portraits he'd painted of her over the past six months.

Which would have meant that Erasmus musta amended his will quite recently, Emma thought to herself. *Why would he do that?*

"Em," Dennis reasoned, drawing her out of her thoughts. "Erasmus was nearly 90 years old. Maybe it was just his time."

"Just seems strange that it was not long after he hired me to model for him, is all," Emma reasoned.

"I'm sure that was just a coincidence." Dennis paused as he surveyed the stones. "So, what's all this about?"

"Protection spell," she explained.

"Ah," he nodded. "Well, you see? I'm in the circle with you. We're safe."

"We'll see," Emma answered miserably. Somehow, this new communication from Mr. Lundy sent Emma back into a tizzy.

Dennis put his arm around Emma's shoulders and pulled her toward him, resting the side of his cheek on the top of her head. "I promise you, Emma, everything is going to be okay."

Chapter 9
The Will

Three Weeks Ago in Manhattan; 1998

Finally, the day arrived when family and friends gathered at the late Erasmus Vandenberg's luxury condo in the city for the reading of his will. Emma wore an uncomfortable black business suit over a cream-white polyester shirt, along with a distinctly out-of-place pair of yellow, all-weather boots. Perhaps the woman at the Macy's counter misunderstood that she was looking for something people wear to the reading of a will or maybe a funeral. Instead, the woman set her up with something called a 'power suit.' Emma did not feel powerful. In fact, she felt very awkward. The boots didn't help.

The weather was terrible and unusually muggy for a summer day, even by New York standards. Her face dropped when she saw that everyone else in the room had dress shoes on. There was a neat line of boots in the doorway, along with an umbrella rack filled with soggy umbrellas. She hadn't thought to bring a change of shoes because she didn't really have anything else, other than sandals and sneakers — neither of which would have been appropriate for this setting. She didn't think to ask the lady at Macy's about footwear.

Even Dennis, who had taken the day off from work to support her, had on a pair of faux-leather shoes. He had the good sense to roll up his trousers before they arrived and unroll them before she rang the bell to Erasmus' suite. Save for a few wrinkles around his ankles, it didn't look *too* bad.

Ferdinand eyed her curiously as she wiped her feet on the doormat before entering, and then quickly snapped to attention. "Good to see you, Emma," he greeted her. "You must be Dennis," Ferdinand smiled. "Nice to meet you… though, I wish it were under better circumstances."

Dennis' eyes brightened as he glanced at Emma. It was nice to know that she had been talking about him. She shot him an annoyed, *Don't let it go to your head or nothin'* look.

"Nice to meet you." Dennis put out his hand.

Ferdinand eyed it, bowed slightly, and said, "Right this way."

Dennis dropped his hand. Coming from a blue-collar family, he had no idea what to expect from the upper crust of society, particularly people who had their own year-round servants.

Emma and Dennis followed Ferdinand quietly into the room. It was the library, just at the other end of the hall of the spacious room where Emma used to model for Erasmus. The library was set up with several long couches, armchairs, and a few upright dinner chairs that had been relocated from the kitchen and dining area to accommodate the more than a dozen family members in the room. The walls were lined from side-to-side and top-to-bottom with books, along with a sliding ladder on each wall, making the books on the highest shelves accessible.

Emma and Dennis took a seat next to the least intimidating person in the room… Elsbeth. She furrowed her eyes slightly before moving over to give them space on the couch beside her. Elsbeth rocked nervously back and forth. She didn't like this many people in one place and kept staring at the clock above the mantle on the opposite wall, as if counting the minutes until it would all be over.

Her eyes brightened when her second cousin, Edgar, arrived. She was about to rise to greet him when her mother clamped a hand on her arm.

"Stay where you are," Edwina hissed from her high-backed armchair situated right next to the young woman. "Don't make a scene."

Elsbeth nodded and dropped her eyes. She had no idea how getting up to give her cousin a hug was a 'scene,' but, as usual, she found it best not to argue.

Edgar, accompanied by Isaac, shuffled into the room and spotted Elsbeth sitting there with down-turned eyes, flanked by her mother and two people he didn't know. Isaac motioned toward a seat on the couch adjacent to them, and the two men sat. Edwina eyed Isaac as if to protest. After all, there was a clear order of things — at least in her mind. The primary family came first and branched outward based on blood relatives versus relations by marriage only, and how far removed people were from her father, Erasmus Vandenberg. Friends sat behind the relatives. The 'help,' however, stood behind those who were seated. Or, if they were getting up in years, they took a seat far behind the family circle. By Edwina's estimation, Emma and Dennis should have been at least two rows back, but she was trying not to make an already uncomfortable situation worse. That was exactly how she described the death of her father in her mind, too... uncomfortable. She fidgeted with the gold cross around her neck.

Ferdinand took his place next to Ruth, the chef, and Ivy, the housekeeper. There were other servants standing behind various relatives, but Emma didn't know who they were nor what function they served.

Several whispers ensued as family members eyed Emma curiously. Finally, one rotund woman leaned forward and asked, "Forgive me, my dear. But who are you?"

"Emma Post," a boisterous voice called from the entryway. Everyone's eyes shot up, startled. There stood Baxter Baker, next to a tiny twig of a woman wearing a low-cut, skin-tight, wrap black dress that hung about mid-thigh, with three-inch heeled shoes and a ridiculous fascinator hat that should only surface during the Kentucky Derby, at Royal weddings or on Halloween. The woman eyed Emma suspiciously and wrapped a tiny hand around Baxter's arm, gripping it possessively.

"Who's she?" The woman asked, flicking a strand of her long brown hair over her shoulder with her 'non-possessive' hand.

"That's what we were wondering," another older man in the room answered before squinting his eyes at her. "Lisa?" he asked.

Baxter cleared his throat. "No, Uncle Morris," Baxter explained. "This is Rachel. Surely, you've heard me talk about her... many times."

Morris cleared his throat. "Oh yes," he played along. "Now I remember. Nice to see you."

Baxter and Rachel took a seat in chairs across from Elsbeth, Emma and Dennis and behind Morris and the woman who was presumably his wife.

"We still don't know who this woman is," another young woman sitting behind Edgar said, "nor the man sitting next to her. Were you a friend of our dear Erasmus?"

"Yes—" Emma began.

"This is Emma," Edwina interrupted. "She was Erasmus' art model... a protégé of sorts."

"Protégé?" Morris's wife eyed Emma suspiciously. "Are you an aspiring artist?"

Emma's face grew warm as everyone in the room turned their gaze in her direction. Dennis took her hand and squeezed it supportively.

"No," she admitted. "At least I have no plans to become an artist at this moment."

"Then… why are you here?" The woman asked.

"Stella, please," Morris whispered. "Leave it alone."

"Why should I leave it alone?" his wife answered. "I'm a member of this family, aren't I? Certainly more than this protégé of Erasmus'! Why shouldn't I be able to ask questions?"

Dennis clenched his jaw angrily, fighting back a response. In relationships past, he would have attempted to defend his partner's honor. But Emma was different. She preferred to fight her own battles, and he knew it.

"She's here because I asked her to be here." A very large and formidable looking man, wearing a three-piece suit and carrying a briefcase, entered the room. A younger man, also in a suit, stood at his heels.

"Mr. Lundy," Edwina acknowledged. "Thank you for coming."

"Of course." He tipped his head slightly to one side. "And may I present Mr. Adani? He is assisting me today with the reading of the will."

"Oh!" Stella's eyes widened. "Your Erasmus' lawyer. Is that it?"

"One of them, yes," Mr. Lundy answered simply.

Ferdinand sat Mr. Lundy and Mr. Adani on two upright dining chairs sandwiched between the couches where Emma and Edgar sat. Mr. Lundy set his briefcase on the glass coffee table and clicked to open it.

"As I was saying." He motioned his head toward Emma. He seemed to make a lot of gestures using just the nod of his head. "I asked Miss Post to be here as today's reading of the will pertains to her, too."

Once again, the attention fell on Emma. Elsbeth eyed Dennis holding onto to Emma's left hand for support and watched as Emma clenched it in return, sucking in her breath. It was then that Elsbeth did a curious thing. She took Emma's right hand in hers and squeezed it. Emma looked at the young woman, surprised. But Elsbeth merely pursed her lips and nodded at her, as if she understood exactly how Emma was feeling. Emma's heart lifted slightly as she gripped Elsbeth's hand lightly and smiled.

Edwina slapped Elsbeth's arm, motioned toward her hand, and Elsbeth quickly retrieved it, setting both her hands in her lap. She looked apologetically at Emma, who merely smiled warmly back and furrowed her brow as if to say, *It's okay. I get it.*

"If everyone is ready?" Mr. Lundy asked, retrieving the will from his briefcase.

"Not just yet, Mr. Lundy." Edwina stood. "We are a God-fearing family," she began.

Edgar rolled his eyes. Baxter stifled a grin, covering his mouth so no one could see. He then turned his gaze toward Emma with eyes that suggested he was thinking less than godly thoughts about her. Rachel pinched her fingers into his arm until he winced, returning his gaze to the small woman at his side. To Edwina, Rachel nodded, removing one hand from Baxter's arm long enough to make the sign of the cross.

Edwina smiled approvingly. She wasn't Catholic, mind you. But the girl was behaving acceptably. *She can be molded,* Edwina thought.

"Everyone, join hands." Edwina insisted, and like it or not, those in the room attempted to join hands, as well as they could sitting in varied circles. Edwina took Elsbeth's hand, and Elsbeth, once again, took Emma's. This time, her mother did not protest. Her mother had a strange order of things, Elsbeth decided.

"Dear Lord, we come to you as humble servants, here to carry out your will—" Edwina began. Most in the room bowed their heads. Edgar's knee bobbed up and down uncomfortably. Elsbeth resisted rocking back and forth lest she hear about it from her mother later. Dennis bowed his head and closed one eye, using the other to glance at Emma, gauging her reaction. Emma stared straight ahead, expressionless. "We know we are sinners who do not deserve your mercy—" Emma shifted in her seat but remained silent. "But through your grace, we will move through this darkness and into the light."

After what seemed like an eternity, Edwina ended the prayer with an "Amen."

Everyone in the room said, "Amen," except for two people: Edgar, who sort of grunted, and Emma, who didn't even attempt to mouth the words. Everyone dropped their hands.

"I didn't hear you say Amen, Emma," Stella pointed out. "Are you an atheist?" she asked.

"No," Emma answered. "I have my beliefs."

"And what does that mean?" Stella challenged.

"It means just that," Emma answered simply.

"But are you a friend of Jesus?" Ruth leaned over Emma's shoulder, whispering helpfully into her ear as if encouraging the woman.

Emma glanced back toward Ruth. "Can't say that he and I are acquainted, no," she answered flatly.

There was a collective gasp from the room.

"Then, what are you?" Stella persisted.

Baxter fought back a laugh. Unlike Dennis, he *did* feel the need to intervene. "Oh, come on, people! Are we really here to interrogate this poor woman and find out her religious perspective, or are we here to find out what's in Uncle Erasmus' will?"

Emma looked at Baxter gratefully before casting her eyes toward the floor. Inside, Dennis' heart boiled. *Should he have said something?* It now bothered him that Baxter had come to her rescue when he had not. Emma was unaware of Dennis' internal struggle.

"Now, may I begin?" Mr. Lundy asked tiredly.

"Of course." Edwina motioned to him. "Please go on."

"I, Erasmus Vandenberg, being of sound body and mind—" Mr. Lundy began.

For the next several minutes, the family sat, mesmerized. Mr. Lundy began with the charities to which Erasmus was leaving some of his fortune, and how much.

"Such a generous man." Stella nodded at Morris, approvingly. Several nodded in agreement.

Then, they reached the critical part...

"Now, I'll read the rest of the will, leaving out sensitive information, such as personal social security numbers, and such—"

Edwina nodded in understanding.

"I leave my New York estate to my granddaughter, Elsbeth Ions, along with a trust fund in an amount to be disclosed on her twenty-fifth birthday. I name Edwina Vandenberg the executor over my New York estate until the time she decides to turn over such executorship to Elsbeth Ions, or when Ms. Ions reaches her twenty-fifth birthday — whichever comes first."

Edwina clenched her jaw but said nothing.

"To my nephew, Edgar Vandenberg, I leave my Leitrim estate in Ireland, along with $500,000 dollars to renovate the property in any way he deems necessary." The lines around Edgar's eyes softened, his face dropping in a way that suggested he was both surprised and touched. Isaac touched his arm supportively. Then, upon seeing several people eye the gesture quizzically, he pulled his hand back.

Edwina put her arms on each side of the armrests on her chair and dug her fingers into them like talons.

"And finally, to my cherished friend, Emma Post, I leave my St. Petersburg, Florida estate and all of my remaining wealth, including all property, vehicles, money, and assets in my name."

"What the hell?" Morris, Stella, and several family members stood angrily. Rachel, who was not even a family member, looked at Baxter, infuriated. Baxter merely shrugged his shoulders.

"What did you do?" Stella pointed an accusatory finger at Emma. "Were you sleeping with him?"

Emma's face grew red and contorted. "No! I most certainly was not!"

"Then why else would Erasmus leave the bulk of his estate to you?" Morris challenged. "Why not Edwina?"

Edwina wondered the same thing, though, she had her suspicions. Elsbeth and Edgar looked up at each other briefly. Elsbeth was terrified, but Edgar merely gave her a gentle smile. She took in a deep breath and sat back in her chair.

"There's a bit more," Mr. Lundy explained as his assistant, Mr. Adani, handed him another paper.

"More?" Edwina asked. "I assume this has something to do with Vandenberg Nutraceuticals?"

"It does," Mr. Lundy agreed. "Ms. Post is now the primary shareholder of the company and technically in charge of both manufacturing plants and their operations."

Baxter sat up, a look of surprise and amusement across his face. He and Emma locked eyes for a long moment, something that escaped neither Dennis nor Rachel.

"I can speak with you privately about the best way to proceed," Mr. Lundy assured Emma, who now had a lump in her throat that felt so large she assumed it was visible on the outside of her neck. "But my law firm and all of Erasmus' personal accountants and advisors are at your disposal. You might also want to speak with Mr. Baxter Baker over there about company operations." Baxter, upon hearing his name mentioned, smiled in Emma's direction. It was as if he were thinking, *Looks like I'm getting that dinner date with you, after all, Ms. Post.*

Emma's eyes widened in fear. Mr. Lundy leaned in and whispered, "Don't worry, Ms. Post. It'll be all right."

At that moment, an unusual hush fell over the room. It was as if they all realized something at the same moment. They could contest the will if they wanted to, but for the time being, this stranger, Emma Post, had access to nearly all of Erasmus' fortune and, consequently, their future.

"Well," Edwina finally stood and addressed the room. "We

did open in prayer and put our faith in the Lord," she smiled. "And we know he works in mysterious ways."

Outside of what was now Elsbeth's condo, several reporters hovered, snapping photos of the black limousines that lined up out front. They swarmed Erasmus' family and friends as they emerged from the lobby of the high-rise.

"What happened?" One reporter shoved a microphone into Mr. Lundy's face, who merely answered, "Client-lawyer privileges, I'm afraid." Mr. Adani swatted at the reporters like flies, trying to get them to back away. He clearly wasn't as polished at dealing with the press as Mr. Lundy was. Mr. Lundy glanced over his shoulder, watching as Emma and Dennis slunk away to the parking garage around the corner. He smiled to himself, satisfied, before getting into one of the limos. No one recognized the two, and so blending in with pedestrians on the busy sidewalk at midday was easy.

One reporter spotted Edwina as she purposefully strolled toward Ferdinand, who opened the door for her. "Edwina Ions!" He shoved past the others and blocked the entrance to the passenger seat.

Her eyes narrowed. "It's Vandenberg," she hissed. "Ions is my ex-husband's name, and he's dead to me."

"Sorry, Ms. Vandenberg," he corrected before pressing on. "Can you tell us what happened today at the reading of your father's will?"

A short distance away, Morris' indignant wife whispered, "How did they know what was happening today?"

"I dunno. Maybe the limos out front gave it away?" Morris shrugged.

Baxter walked slowly behind them, giving Rachel ample time to tiptoe along with her tight dress and impossible-to-walk-in heels. She eyed her companion curiously. Sure, he was handsome, but somehow not as handsome now that he seemed far less affluent at this moment than he was before the reading. Baxter glanced at her and grinned, as if reading her thoughts. Her face grew pale. Baxter turned his attention momentarily toward Edwina. Baxter Baker was more than a pretty face. He was far shrewder than anyone gave him credit for, assuming he got by in life on his looks and his family's money… or his late aunt's money, as relatives were so fond of pointing out.

He knew exactly who alerted the press. He turned his back on Edwina as soon as she began her obviously practiced reply to the media, "Obviously, some members of our family were surprised. However, given Erasmus' generous spirit, and how much he cared for the less fortunate, we couldn't be happier for Ms. Post…" Baxter helped Rachel into one of the limousines, shutting the door after she'd finally settled inside. "Yes, that's right." He could hear Edwina clarifying. "Emma Post… spelled just as you'd expect… P… O… S… T."

Chapter 10
Murder?

One Week Ago in Florida; 1998

Ortega wasted no time reviewing the case that Emma and Dennis had now dropped into his lap, all of which began after that unexpected phone call from Dennis just a week prior. But he had to tread carefully. After all, he'd promised Nancy that once he'd retired, there'd be no more late nights, no more abandoning her on holidays and special occasions, and particularly no more pacing the house drinking and smoking a cigar while he berated himself over what clues he may or may not have missed. Most importantly, he promised to be there for her.

On the other hand, he reasoned to himself, it hadn't escaped his attention that Nancy had managed to fill up her social calendar quickly once they'd moved here. At first, she tried to include him, but he wasn't particularly interested in bridge games, golf, cocktail parties… or people, in general. He liked his solo lifestyle with one or two people he could reach out to if he ever felt lonely… which was almost never. After a while, Nancy just stopped inviting him. He would have been fine with that, except there was something distant about her lately. He couldn't put his finger on it.

Well, he decided. *I think a special moonlit dinner on Anna Maria Island might be just the ticket.* He made a mental note to phone a bistro he knew and make reservations.

But for now, he justified his agreeing to help Emma and Dennis. After all, he wasn't supposed to officially retire for at least another six years. So, there should be some easing into retirement, he felt. Plus, he wasn't technically a detective anymore, either. This was just a one-off instance where he was helping a young couple out.

He just had to make sure Nancy didn't find out about it.

Ortega poured himself several ounces of bourbon on the rocks, while he reviewed the notes he'd fervently taken following the newest and rather arduous phone call, this time between both Emma and Dennis. He laughed as he recalled bits of the conversation just one hour earlier…

"Would you give me the phone?" Emma had protested. "That's not what I said at all!"

Dennis reluctantly handed her the phone, only to interrupt a second later. "I don't want you anywhere near Baxter Baker!" Dennis grumbled at her suggestion, grabbing the phone and stretching it over his head so Emma couldn't reach.

"Oof!" Ortega heard Dennis proclaim as something clattered to the floor. There was a shuffle before Emma returned to the call after she had presumably punched him in the gut in order to retrieve the phone.

"Detective Ortega," Emma huffed into the phone. "Wouldn't you agree Baxter is the best person to shed light on this situation?"

From Ortega's perspective, the couple was approaching this

case like amateurs. He would have expected this from Emma but not from Officer Dennis. *The boy is letting his Johnson get in the way of solid police work,* he thought to himself.

"Listen," Ortega interrupted them. "Put me on speaker phone," he ordered.

"Uh," Emma replied. "This is a landline, and I have no idea if it can even do that. I'll have to call you back on the cell phone thingy."

"You do that," Ortega suggested. "Then, call me back." He didn't wait for a reply before hanging up. Moments later, his cell phone rang.

The first thing he heard was Dennis' impatient voice saying, "Not that one, this one." Eventually, both Emma and Dennis had figured out how to use the speakerphone feature on Dennis' still relatively new cell phone.

"Can you both hear me?" Ortega confirmed.

"Yes, we can hear you," the two answered.

"Good, because I'm only going to say this once. If I'm going to help you, I need to glean as much information as I can from the both of you. Therefore, we're treating this like a formal investigation."

"Well, that's good—" Dennis began.

"Let me finish, Officer Dennis." Ortega reverted to the old days. It worked. Dennis fell silent. Ortega continued. "I want to interview one of you—and I mean only one of you — at a time. While I do that, I want the other of you to go somewhere else, someplace out of earshot."

"My apartment is a studio," Dennis complained. "And it's raining outside!"

"I don't care where you go… hide in the bathroom with the fan on for all I care," Ortega raised his voice in annoyance. "All I care about is taking a statement from each of you without the other interrupting."

Dennis sighed. "I'll go first," he relented. He shut the speaker phone feature off and handed his phone to Emma.

"Call me when it's my turn." Dennis retreated into their bathroom, turning on both the fan and the shower radio. Once Emma was certain he was out of earshot, she told Ortega everything she knew.

The call took more than an hour, but Ortega refused to hang up until he was certain he'd gleaned every possible bit of information about Erasmus and everything surrounding his death.

Erasmus Vandenberg was as healthy as a horse and scheduled to turn eighty-nine just three days after he died. He had no known cardiovascular issues, no diabetes, nothing.

The coroner ruled the cause of death congestive heart failure given his age, and since he had fallen asleep at such a high altitude, no one would have noticed if he had any breathing issues. Therefore, the informal ruling was that he, quite simply, died of old age.

There had been no formal investigation and no autopsy.

"So, who would have cause to off old Erasmus?" Ortega said to himself. "And why?"

On his short list of possible suspects was someone from the Vandenberg family. Edgar and Elsbeth were named in the will. *What if they knew they stood to collect a lot of money once he was gone? But why chance it at Erasmus' age? And what about Edwina Vandenberg? How was she to know she had been left out of the will? Or did she? Even worse, what if she had an inkling it was going to be amended, but she got to him too late?*

"I'm missing something obvious," he chastised himself aloud, taking another sip of bourbon. "Why on a plane?"

He heard Nancy's car pull up the drive. He quickly hid his notes in his desk drawer and left his office to head out to the kitchen to greet her.

"And what have you been up to, my dear?" Ortega smiled at the assortment of shopping bags Nancy carried in, all from the nearby Ellenton Outlet stores. He gave her a peck on the lips.

"I needed a new tennis outfit and bathing suit," she answered. "And I know what you've been up to," she laughed. "Already hitting the booze?" She set the bags down. "You're not working on a case, are you?" She teased.

He let out a cough. "No, just pacing the floor until my lovely wife returned home… Didn't you just buy a new tennis outfit last week?" He eyed the purchases curiously.

"Yes, Mr. Nosey Pants." She touched his nose playfully. "But Dominic says I have real potential if I practice, so I've added in a few more lessons. You don't mind, do you?"

"Potential for what?" Ortega wanted to know. "Are you trying for Wimbledon?"

Nancy rolled her eyes. "I know it may not mean much to you," she answered. "But I wouldn't mind competing in some local tennis matches, just for fun. Gives me a sense of purpose."

"The whole raising a child and having a husband doesn't give you purpose?" He stopped himself before pointing out that she had made him give up his purpose when he was forced into retirement. Ortega saw the look on her face and instantly regretted it. "I'm joking, my Dear." He wrapped his arms around her and gave her a kiss on the cheek. "Of course, I support anything that makes you happy."

"Did you remember to pick up some lettuce and chicken breast at the store today?" She broke from his grip and walked over to the refrigerator.

"Uh," he tried to cover. "I'm sorry, I forgot."

"Well, what have you been doing all day?" She eyed him suspiciously, opening the refrigerator and finding it in the same condition, with the same contents, as when she left.

Ortega thought quickly. "Actually, I didn't forget. I was going to surprise you later, but the truth is… I was hoping to take you to that French bistro on the island tonight."

"Well, that will never work," she answered. "You have to

book well in advance for that place." Ortega knew that too, but it was that or admit he was working on a case. "Besides, what's the occasion?"

"Can't my loving you be occasion enough?"

"You're hiding something." Nancy squinted at him.

"Nancy, I'm wounded." He gripped his heart melodramatically.

"Never mind." She waved a hand at him, chuckling. "Let's just order a pizza and watch a little TV tonight. There's a new *Sex & the City* on."

"Gre-e-at," he answered unenthusiastically. He couldn't understand why Nancy, who was so adamant about getting out of New York, was enthralled with a very unrealistic show about single women living in Manhattan, who could afford very large living accommodations and an ostentatious lifestyle on what — a writer's salary? At least, he seemed to remember one of them was a writer. But then, Nancy was born into money, so it's likely she never did have a clear sense of what 'normal' people could or could not afford.

Ortega picked up the phone to dial for a pizza. He eyed one of Nancy's many bags, one of which had 'factory outlet' written on it.

"That's it," he accidentally said out loud. "It had something to do with his visit to the factory."

"What was that, Honey?" Nancy asked.

"Er, nothing," he lied. "Just thinking about a story I read in the newspaper."

Someone didn't want Erasmus visiting his Florida factory, but why?

Chapter 11
The Disagreement

Present day in Manhattan; 1998

"**I**f there's nothing going on, then why am I not invited?" Dennis grumbled loudly so she could hear him on the other side of the apartment.

"Because," Emma explained, inserting small pearl earrings into each of her pierced ears. "You're a cop. He's not going to speak freely if you're there."

"Right, that's why Baxter Baker specifically asked you to come alone." Dennis crossed his arms, leaning into the counter in Emma's kitchen while she finished getting dressed on the other side of the divider that led to her bedroom. "What makes him think you wouldn't just come home and fill me in on everything that happened?" Emma emerged from behind the screen. Dennis' eyes widened when he saw her. "And *that's* what you're wearing?"

She looked down at her jeans questioningly. "What the hell is wrong with what I'm wearing?"

"You don't need to dress so… provocatively," he accused.

"Dennis," she chastised, "I'm wearing stonewashed jeans and a black t-shirt. And look," she pointed to her feet. "Flats… I don't even own heels… which you probably already have noticed. How is this provocative?"

"It's just in those jeans, you look a little…" Dennis struggled to find the right words. "Curvy."

Emma snickered, swaying her hips seductively as she sauntered over to him and gave him a playful kiss on the lips. "You are cute," she said.

"And you're trying to distract me." He touched her nose with his forefinger. Although, if he were to admit it to himself, he was suddenly having trouble catching his breath.

"Did it work?" she asked.

"No." He was adamant. "Okay." He blushed. "Maybe a little… But that's not the point. I don't trust him."

"Then we agree on something," Emma pointed out. "I don't trust Baxter Baker either, but he's the best person to shed some light on the Vandenberg family business and why the hell Erasmus left me most of his fortune."

"What makes him the best person?" Dennis challenged.

Emma pursed her lips. "Because he's the only one who will talk to me, except for Elsbeth, but I'm not sure she'll be much help. And he said there's stuff I should know about the family."

"Fine," Dennis relented. "But at least take this." He handed her a large, handheld cassette recorder. "What the hell am I supposed to do with that?" She looked at her outfit.

"Well, don't you have a purse you can hide it in?"

"And what, leave it sitting in my bag, recording the entire time? Not sure how that'll work getting a good audio recording, and besides…" She hit the record button and waited while it beeped loudly. The gentle whir of the cassette wheels turning could be heard. "Kind of obvious. Anyway, even if you follow us, you still won't be able to hear what's going on inside."

"Fine, then we go back to my original plan. I like that one better, anyway."

"Sitting in a van outside and listening in?" Emma's voice went up in pitch. "What's with the cloak and dagger bullshit? And don't you think a wire is a little extreme?"

"You said yourself, you think Erasmus was murdered. I would much prefer to be close by in case anything happens. And the wire was Detective Ortega's idea. You *were* the one who asked me to reach out to him.

After multiple telephone calls over the course of the week, it came to light that while the Vandenberg family may have publicly praised Erasmus' decision to leave most of his fortune to her, they completely shut her out of their life. The closest she got to them was the lobby of the suite, now owned by Elsbeth Ions.

"W… what does she w… want?" Elsbeth's voice could be heard over the intercom.

"Elsbeth," Emma had leaned over the counter, while the concierge eyed her with a mixture of surprise and annoyance. "I need Baxter's number."

"Why?" Elsbeth demanded.

"If you let me come up and see you, I can explain."

Suddenly, Edwina's voice boomed through the intercom. "That won't be possible, Ms. Post," she answered curtly. "We don't even have Baxter's number and couldn't give it to you if we wanted to."

That wasn't entirely true, and later that evening, Emma received an anonymous message on her landline. The voice was disguised. It told her to stop by the lobby in the morning and that Baxter Baker's business card would be left with the concierge, along with instructions to give it to her. Sure enough, his business card, the one he had tried to give to Emma, but that Elsbeth had intercepted, was waiting for her at the counter.

Well, at least one member of that family likes me, she thought.

Though she couldn't understand why Elsbeth felt the need to disguise her voice. But who else might have phoned her? Emma chalked it up to the young woman's fear of her mother finding out.

Meanwhile, Dennis tried to voice his concerns to the police detective that replaced Ortega, but the response was that there was simply not enough evidence to support opening an investigation. Dennis made the mistake of suggesting that this is exactly the reason for investigations… to find the evidence, and nearly got himself suspended.

Instead, he asked for a temporary transfer and made plans to move with Emma to her new estate in St. Petersburg, Florida.

Baxter Baker appeared to be the only family member willing to talk to her and only if she agreed to a date. Ortega suggested the wire and that Dennis be close at hand. Ortega wasn't fond of potentially putting Emma in harm's way, but she was adamant. He had to admire her for this. After all, why not just take the money and keep your mouth shut? She had a level of integrity that few possessed.

Dennis waited for an eternity for Emma to respond to his question.

Emma sighed, "Okay. Okay. I'll wear the damn wire. We'll at least be able to play the audio for him afterward… assuming I get anything useful. So how do we do this? Better get moving, so I'm not late for my 'date with destiny.'"

"That's not funny, Emma," Dennis sulked. "And, as far as the process…" He blushed again. "Er…"

"What?"

"I'm gonna kind of need you to take your shirt off?"

"And you think Baxter Baker is a player? This is the best line I've ever heard." Before Dennis could protest, she stripped her black t-shirt off to reveal a lacy matching bra.

Dennis paused for a moment, staring at her. His chin nearly dropped before he caught himself.

"Hey, Dennis McCleary." Emma snapped her fingers at him. "My eyes are up here!" She bit back a grin as Dennis, very *uncomfortably*, taped a wire to her. She giggled. "That tickles," she complained, squirming a little.

"Sorry," Dennis answered, trying to focus. "Kind of hoped my first time seeing you in lacy underwear would be under different circumstances."

"Don't worry, Dennis," she smirked. "There will be plenty of time for that soon enough."

Chapter 12
Date With Destiny

Present Day in Manhattan

Frankly, Emma was expecting something a little more upscale for her 'date with destiny' with Baxter Baker, particularly after he made such a point of bragging about his money and influence when she'd first met him. Instead, they sank into the booth in the corner of a very ordinary Irish pub in lower Manhattan.

He'd told her to dress casually, but somehow she expected to be whisked away on a private boat or something. She was mildly disappointed. Somehow, that made her feel guilty, as if Dennis could hear her thoughts from the police car he had parked outside. He would have rather used an unmarked van, but the car was the only way to ensure he could stay in one place for any length of time on the busy New York strip without causing suspicion.

Meanwhile, inside, Baxter asked her to meet him early and, as such, the pub wasn't crowded, save for a few early drinkers at the bar and several men playing cricket, occasionally arguing as they scratched out numbers on the chalkboard. There were hundreds of holes in the wall around the dart board from players who thought they played better drunk instead of sober — they were wrong. A small, skinny man with an oversized guitar case strapped across his back paused at the bar to grab a few unshelled peanuts. He glanced in their direction momentarily before turning his attention back toward the small stage in the corner. It was only a foot high and barely large enough to fit more than about five musicians on it at a time. He cracked open the peanuts and popped them in his mouth and then dropped the shells directly on the floor before stepping on stage.

Emma looked at the shell-covered, dusty floor distastefully. No one but her seemed to notice or care, except for Baxter, who merely slunk back into the corner of the booth, covering his mouth so she couldn't see him grinning at her.

A server came by with menus and to take a drink order. Baxter settled on a Guinness on tap.

"Iced tea," Emma ordered, just as the guitarist launched into an acoustic version of Eric Clapton's *Change the World*.

"Long Island Iced Tea?" the server confirmed, talking above the music.

"Wow," Baxter nodded approvingly as the server dropped the menus on the table. "I like your style, Emma Post."

"No," Emma corrected, "regular unsweetened iced tea." The server looked visibly disappointed. Non-alcoholic drinks and non-drunk patrons rarely led to overwhelmingly high tips.

Baxter waited patiently as Emma eyed the menu. Between the burgers, Shepherd's pie, bangers and mash, there was nothing on the menu that she could actually eat. Even the salads were smothered in turkey and bacon.

"Excuse me a moment," Baxter said. "You look at the menu. I'll be right back." Emma nodded as he slid out of the seat and approached the bar. He whispered to the bartender as he slipped something across the counter. The bartender nodded, turned quickly and retreated to the kitchen behind him.

"What was that about?" Emma asked accusingly.

"Oh, nothing," Baxter replied innocently.

"You should know that I have a lead stomach and strong constitution," she answered fervently. "So, if you're trying to sneak liquor, or worse, into my drink—"

"I'm not." Baxter held up his hands. "I promise."

Moments later, the server arrived with Baxter's Guinness and Emma's iced tea. She silently grabbed the menus and left.

"Why did she do that?" Emma asked. "We didn't even order."

"And what off that menu would you have ordered?" Baxter asked.

"Iceberg lettuce, hold the… everything," Emma admitted.

"Give me a little credit, Ms. Post. I chose this location for anonymity, not for the cuisine. And I promise you, if given the chance," he leaned in and whispered, "I can do better."

At that moment, the server returned, setting down two plates. "Cauliflower and potato soup," the server announced, "soda bread and a side of hummus. Anything else?" she asked.

Baxter shook his head. "I think that will be all, thanks." She turned on her heels and walked away.

Emma looked up, surprised. "This wasn't on the menu."

"I know," Baxter smiled, adding a pinch of salt to his soup without even tasting it first. If it had been Dennis, she would have chastised him for his salt consumption, and for adding it without checking first to see if the dish even needed more salt. But Baxter wasn't Dennis, so she bit her tongue. "Again, give me a little credit, Ms. Post. I specially requested it based on what I assumed they'd have in the kitchen. You're vegetarian, correct?"

"Yes," Emma's eyes narrowed. "But how did *you* know that?"

"Unfortunately," Baxter confessed. "I probably know a lot more about people than is good for me, yourself included."

"What is that supposed to mean?" Emma asked, finally taking a sip of her soup. She hated to admit it, even to herself, but it needed more salt.

Baxter leaned in for his quiet confession. "It means that I'm taking a big risk in being here with you, Emma Post."

Emma eyed him suspiciously. "Is that a line?" she finally asked.

"No." He leaned back, once again pressing his forefinger against his mouth to hide his amusement. "But I wish it were."

"And what is *that* supposed to mean?" She tried again, agitated.

Baxter took a moment to slide his hands underneath their table, as if searching for something. He even bent his head awkwardly to survey the underside.

"Did you misplace your chewing gum?" Emma asked sarcastically. "Saving it for later?" But she knew why he was looking. He was searching for a bug or some other listening device. She fidgeted slightly, absentmindedly touching the left side of her shoulder, where the wire was taped to her, recording everything for Dennis, and eventually Ortega, to hear. Baxter eyed her curiously, his gaze falling on her shoulder. Emma sucked in her breath, worried that she'd given herself away.

"Erasmus went to Florida to shut down the production plant for Vandenberg Nutraceuticals," he finally confessed, averting his gaze.

"Why on Earth would he do that?" Emma was curious.

Baxter leaned back in the booth, taking a long breath in and out before continuing. "Because he suspected that our biggest client, the Church of Infinite Love, was taking Vandenberg health bars, beverages, and other snacks and infusing them with their own…" he cleared his throat, "special sauce."

"Special sauce?" Emma asked.

Baxter sighed. "Think, Emma," he chastised. "What do you *think* I mean?"

"The Church of Infinite Love," Emma thought a moment. "Didn't they have a show that aired on Sundays? Seemed to have a stadium-sized audience."

"Yeah, and that was filmed during one of their 'Holy Days'

where members from nearly a hundred locations across the United States and Europe met at a rented-out arena in Texas."

Suddenly, images of the church's early-morning TV broadcasts, which often featured people magically being healed of pain from old war injuries, flashed before her eyes.

"You mean, like… drugs and potentially mind-altering substances?"

"Now the witch is catching on," he smiled. "Thought that, given your bent for magic, you would have figured that out sooner."

Emma huffed as she used a spoon to scoop some of the hummus onto a piece of bread. "Why the heck does everyone assume I would — obviously — know about such things?"

"Well, being a pagan and all—"

"Kind of a broad category," she explained. "Just cuz I don't fit into the Judeo-Christian belief systems, doesn't mean that I necessarily smoke peyote, drink ayahuasca or take hallucinogens. And it certainly doesn't mean I'm a witch."

"Well, are you?" Baxter asked curiously, taking a sip of his beer.

"I prefer the term animist."

"And what does it mean to be an animist, exactly?"

Emma took a bite of her food, careful not to chew too loudly, given that the microphone was so close to her mouth.

"It means I have respect for the natural world and see all energy as sentient."

Baxter knocked on the table. "Even this table?"

"In a way… look, Mr. Baker, while I'd love to talk at length about my fundamental beliefs, don't you think it's best if we focus?"

"My apologies," he offered, taking a sip of his soup. "I can't help it if you're fascinating."

"Why shut down the plant?" Emma ignored him, instead, changing the subject back to the reason they were both there. She ignored the flushed feeling in her face, hyper-aware that

Dennis was on the other end of the microphone, probably turning red with anger and fit to be tied. "Why not just cut them off as clients, if his morality was getting the better of him?"

"I'm not sure," Baxter confessed, rubbing his forehead tiredly, before taking a sip of his soup. "Most of the churches were clean… I mean, as clean as a money-hungry cult *can* be. Erasmus himself used to make large donations at the end of the year… I assumed for tax purposes," he smirked. "To my knowledge, there were only a few locations with questionable practices. Maybe it was penance, or maybe he wanted to ensure that his legacy wasn't marred. Whatever the case, Erasmus was taking no chances that we would continue to turn a blind eye to the church's practices. He even went as far as to publicly denounce the church."

"Continue?" Emma asked, biting into her soda bread.

"You are very curious, Emma" He shook his head. "I'd be lying if I said I didn't have the tiniest inkling of poor practices… easily justified as we, technically, had nothing to do with what happened to our product *after* it sold."

"And that didn't bother you?" Emma questioned.

Baxter paused for a long time, as if sizing Emma up as a person. Finally, he answered, "I am exactly what you think I am, Miss Post. Did it bother me? Yes. Was it enough to turn down a fortune? No. Turning a blind eye is easy when it doesn't affect you personally."

"So, what changed?" Emma asked. "Why are you telling me this now?"

He leaned toward her, taking one of her hands for emphasis. "Because now? Now it affects me personally."

Emma slipped her hand out of his. "I believe I told you, Mr. Baker, that I have a boyfriend." The heat in her cheeks rose enough to where she was sure it was visible.

"I meant, Elsbeth," he grinned, leaning in toward her shoulder. "And I'm aware of your relationship with the flatfoot." His eyes lifted to meet hers… he knew.

"What about Elsbeth?" Emma asked, blushing.

"Surely you've noticed that she's… different?"

"Yes, I assumed she had some sort of developmental or neurological disorder?"

"She might," he admitted. "But no one knows for sure because Cousin Edwina refuses to have her tested."

"Really? Why?" Emma was surprised.

"Because the Church of Infinite Love frowns on pesky little things like doctors and scientists." Baxter suddenly pulled a cell phone from his back pocket, glanced at it momentarily, and cringed before putting it away again. Emma recognized it because Dennis had acquired the same Nokia variety at the behest of Ortega. She really didn't understand the need to have a phone attached to one's hip at all times.

"You mean Edwina is—" She drew his attention back to the conversation.

"A very high-ranking leader within the church," he finished. "No doubt she feels she is being judged for having a daughter with mental challenges. She either failed as a mother, failed as a Christian, Elsbeth is possessed by a demon, or a combination of all three."

"Are you being serious right now?" Emma asked. "Demon possession?"

"I'm afraid I am," Baxter sighed. "Listen, as it turns out, I can't stay long. So, here's what you need to know. And if you speak to the authorities, remember that none of this… I repeat… *none of this*… came from me."

Emma leaned in. Baxter did the same. She could smell his aftershave… *Damn it!* She thought to herself, annoyed. *He smells… really good.* She pushed the thought away.

"Erasmus denounced the church about a month ago and, no doubt, stopped making 'charitable donations' to them. There's a good chance Erasmus was also planning to shut down *both* factories, the one in Florida and the one in Dublin. But it's the factory in St. Pete that you want to look into. That's the one selling to select congregations of the church… all of which happened to be under Edwina's district."

"Quite a coincidence." Emma shook her head.

"Indeed," he agreed. His eyes fell to her lips for a moment before he lifted them to meet her gaze, holding it there for a little too long.

"Well, should be easy enough." Emma tapped her fingers on the table. "Since I'm the main shareholder now."

Baxter shook his head, "Oh, Emma… Adorable, Emma. It's not going to be that easy. You're not going to be able to waltz right in and ask to see the books nor the facilities. You'll need to be a bit more discreet than that."

"Well, aren't you the Vice-President of Operations? Surely, you can help me."

He leaned in even closer, his face only inches from hers. "I'm afraid I can't."

"How are we doing over here?" The waitress returned with a paper bag filled with, presumably, take out.

"Ah, thank you. We're just fine — a check when you have a moment." He eyed Emma's half-eaten plate. "Did you want to take the rest of that with you?"

Baxter appeared to be in a hurry, suddenly, because he checked his watch… twice, only seconds apart, just to confirm he'd gotten the time right.

"You don't worry about me," Emma answered. "If you have somewhere to be."

To the server, Baxter confirmed, "Shepherd's Pie and a side of sausages to go?"

"Yes, that's right," the waitress nodded, handing him the bill. Without looking at it, he pulled a large wad of cash from his pocket and sandwiched it between the billfold. "I believe that should cover it."

The server's eyes grew wide and then immediately narrowed. Without leaving the table, she pulled out a marking pen and began checking off each bill now in her possession, as if looking for a fake. When she was satisfied, she smiled enthusiastically, flashing a large mouth with seemingly very thick teeth. "Well, thank you very much!" After a dramatic pause, she finally added, "Have a good night!" And all but ran away before he could change his mind.

"Shepherd's pie and sausage." Emma eyed him coldly.

"As I've already told you," Baxter explained. "I am exactly what you think I am. I've never tried to hide that from you."

Emma had no idea what to make of Baxter. He was a conundrum. He flaunted his money and then took her to the most mediocre pub in the city — a place that had not a single vegetarian dish, so he could gallantly order up something special for her — only to leave with a meat on a meat takeout platter. If he was trying to woo her, his courting methods were the oddest she'd ever seen.

Baxter leaned in. "Oh, don't take it personally, sweet Emma." He caught her gaze again, as if reading her thoughts. "I just need to make a hasty exit for a while." He paused a moment before adding, "I don't think you realize the risk I've taken talking with you this evening."

He slid out of the booth, brown paper dinner bag in hand. Before Emma could say anything, he leaned over and pressed a soft kiss on her lips, lingering for a moment. Emma was so surprised she didn't react. At least, that's what she told herself. If she were being honest, she would have admitted that, while he caught her by surprise, she leaned into it and kissed him back… and liked it. It was a momentary lapse of judgment that someone like Emma rarely made.

"Please be careful, Emma," he whispered earnestly, pulling away. "I don't think Erasmus' death was due to natural causes any more than you do, and I wouldn't want anything to happen to you."

She nodded dumbly. *Exactly how much of that had Dennis picked up on?*

"If things don't work out with your cop friend…" Baxter put

his mouth near her shoulder, where he knew the wire to be. She shuttered a little as the warmth of his breath sent a few chills down her spine. "You give me a call."

For once in her life, Emma was speechless.

Before leaving, Baxter whispered, "You'll be the death of me, Emma Post."

Chapter 13
The Second Disagreement

Present Day in Manhattan

"What the hell was that about?" Dennis angrily removed his gun and holster, all but tossing them on the kitchen table of Emma's apartment.

"Hey!" she complained. "Be careful with that. I'm not exactly keen on having guns in this place to start with."

"Oh, I'm sorry." Dennis' face turned red. "Was I insensitive? Like you, when you were sucking face with some rich guy born with one silver spoon in his mouth and another up his ass."

"That's not at all what happened!" Emma protested.

"Then what did happen?" Dennis challenged.

"He leaned in to kiss me, and—" Emma paused.

"And what?" Dennis spat, sweat beginning to form around his brow. "Please don't give me the 'I was just playing along' crap!"

Emma had to think quickly. She wasn't keen on lying, but she was worried about what would happen if she told the *exact* truth. The *exact* truth was that Baxter Baker had kissed her, and

— despite her better judgment — she liked it… a *lot*. But when she kissed him back, she remembered that she wasn't chronically single anymore. In fact, she most definitely… probably… had a boyfriend. This was a relatively new phenomenon for the fiercely independent Emma, so that exhilarating moment was coupled with… guilt.

"No," she answered carefully. "He kissed me… on my cheek," she lied. "I didn't push him away, which I probably should have. But, I was trying to get information from him so—"

"So… what?"

"So, I let him kiss me on the cheek and did my best not to flinch." She paused to gauge Dennis' reaction. "That's what you must have heard over the wire… his ridiculous breathing in my ear." She smiled, as if she and Dennis shared an inside joke.

He took the bait, which only made Emma feel worse.

"Okay." He put his hands in the air. "I'm sorry. I'm not the jealous type, it's just—"

"Just what?" Emma asked.

Dennis rapped his knuckles lightly on the table before looking up at Emma seriously.

"What are we Em?" he asked, sincerely.

"What do you mean?" Emma knew. A lump formed in the back of her throat. She wasn't ready for this conversation, and it had nothing to do with Dennis. She was gripped by a sudden fear that made her worry that she might never be ready.

"I mean…" Dennis hesitated. "Are we boyfriend and girl-friend? Are we exclusive? What are we? I heard you tell him you had a boyfriend, but you've never actually let *me* in on this small detail."

Emma thought fast, pulling from her mental directory of all the excuses men had given her over the years until a few helpful nuggets surfaced.

"Do we have to give it a label?" she finally asked.

"I'm sorry… what?" Dennis was confused.

"Why do we have to be confined to everyone's definitions of what relationships are? Can't we just enjoy each other's company?" The words flowed easily, but they didn't come from her. She couldn't remember which past love interest they came from, but they were definitely not *her* words.

It took Dennis a moment to gather his thoughts and harness his emotions. Finally, he answered, "Listen, Em. I don't want to rush you into anything you're not ready for. But the truth is, I *like* those labels." He moved toward her and pushed a strand of her hair away from her face and traced the line of her cheek with his finger. "I want nothing more than to be your boyfriend, exclusively." He paused to gauge her reaction. Dennis sensed fear. "But if you're not ready, I understand. I just hope that someday you will be."

Emma opened her mouth, but no words came out. She was having a difficult time understanding the heart-pounding rush of emotions she felt when Baxter kissed her, unexpectedly, to the warm, safe glow she felt every time Dennis was near her. The energy was different. That much she knew. But she didn't understand *how* or *why*.

"I should go," Dennis finally said, picking up his gun and holster. "I'll go through the recordings tonight and forward them to Detective Ortega… Er… Jo." Emma nodded as Dennis opened the door to her studio apartment. She opened her mouth to say something, but finding herself at a loss for words, she shut it again.

"Goodnight, Em," Dennis whispered. He leaned in to kiss her. Emma kissed him back. She wasn't trying to compare his kiss to Baxter's… she really wasn't. But she couldn't help it. Baxter's had this electric, lusty… let's-do-this-now vibe. But Dennis' kiss was different. His lips were warm, fleshy, and lingered in a comforting and warm way that said, "I'm in this for the long haul. And I'm here for you, no matter what."

Emma had never experienced this kind of kiss before.

Chapter 14
Rue and Emma

Present Day in Manhattan

Emma wasn't happy about meeting up with Rue Brennan and Darwin Fennec at their condo in Midtown Manhattan, any more than Rue was interested in having Emma Post in both her home and workspace. Rue Brennan and her former boss-turned-partner, Darwin Fennec (an unlikely love interest, cyber forensic consultant, and private investigator) were once again having issues with their official place of business in Battery Park. This time, there had been an electrical fire. Darwin was beginning to suspect that the landlord was planning these little emergencies for insurance purposes, but he couldn't be sure.

Rue met Darwin back when her then-boyfriend, Spencer Hargrove, hired Darwin Fennec to investigate a tech company that was competing with his own, unexpectedly dragging an unsuspecting Rue into the middle of a murder case in which she had been the primary suspect.

Under normal circumstances, Darwin might have requested

that Emma and Dennis meet him at a new, up-and-coming co-workspace on the Lower East Side. It was one of the first of its kind and promised to be a great solution for small start-up companies and those displaced because of workplace disruptions, such as the one he and Rue were currently experiencing.

However, he'd developed an unlikely friendship with the newly retired Detective Ortega over the last year. While older and decidedly more jaded about life, Ortega had grass roots skills and powerful deductive reasoning that few could match. Meanwhile, Darwin understood the value of new technology to compensate for human error and had this chameleon-like ability to adapt to people and environments. Darwin had connections to, let's just say, the seedier side of town with people who would talk to him but never let a former cop in their confidence.

Had Nancy not convinced her husband to move to Florida, Darwin and Ortega would have been an unbeatable team. Therefore, when Ortega made a special request for Darwin and Rue to help Emma Post in her time of need, Darwin found it impossible to say, 'no.'

Rue was hoping for a redemption of sorts, as she was reminded that Emma still blamed her, in some way, for the death of two of Emma's closest friends. Even though Rue was an innocent in the events, she still felt the need to prove herself.

"Please, come in." Darwin welcomed Dennis and Emma into their home and make-shift office.

"Thank you, Mr. Fennec," Dennis acknowledged, pausing for Emma to enter the room first.

Emma bristled when she saw Rue.

"Please, make yourself comfortable." Rue motioned toward the couch, clenching her jaw ever-so-slightly.

Emma eyed the room hesitantly, wondering exactly how much one would have to earn to get to live in a place like this. She settled on *a lot.* Finally, she sank into the dark plushy couch. It was comfortable… much more so than the small, hard mini-malist chairs in her kitchen and the bean bag sack in her bedroom. *Heck,* she thought. *It was even more comfortable than her twin bed.*

Most times, Emma didn't feel insignificant, not even when modeling for multi-millionaire Erasmus Vandenberg. But today was one of those days. If she'd only realized that less than a year ago, Rue had lived in a place that was only moderately nicer than Emma's current digs, she might have felt less insecure. Emma was also aware that money would be forthcoming, but she didn't entirely trust the news — at least not until some of it actually hit her bank account. Dennis took a seat beside Emma and placed one hand over hers. She usually disliked public displays of affection, but given her emotional state lately, first at the reading of the will, and now, she allowed it.

"Can I get you some coffee?" Rue asked with forced politeness.

"I dunno. Is it poisoned?" Emma retorted.

"Not usually, but I can add some if you like," Rue smiled sweetly.

"That's enough, kids," Dennis chastised in a joke that didn't land quite as well as he'd hoped. The two women glared at him. He coughed a little. "Uh, no coffee for me, thanks. I'm good."

Rue wasn't particularly fond of Dennis either, after his one investigation where he confiscated her clothes, sending her home scantily clad in a costume and oversized shoes from a modeling gig that got interrupted. *Boy,* she thought. *Emma can sure pick the winners.*

Darwin was too busy retrieving the audio recording from Emma's date with Baxter, while also setting up the Tandberg camera and video conference with Ortega, that he'd missed the exchange.

"I think we're about ready," Darwin announced.

Suddenly, the former Detective Ortega appeared on Darwin and Rue's oversized plasma TV like the magical Wizard of Oz.

He was in his living room, sipping what appeared to be a

tumbler of bourbon. He was also smoking a Cuban cigar. Dennis found this amusing.

"Can you see and hear us okay, Ortega?" Darwin asked, lining up his webcam to capture the sitting area in the condo.

Rue took her seat in an easy chair beside the couch, crossing her legs and leaning forward, curiously. She still couldn't quite fathom how you could have a video conversation with someone hundreds of miles away. To her, it was as if she were having a conversation with one of the actors from a movie. This was only the second time she'd experienced this phenomenon, as Darwin was still working out the bugs in the system.

"I can see and hear you just fine." Ortega took a puff of his cigar. "Especially you, Officer Dennis." He pointed a meaty finger toward the camera. "I can see the judgment in your eyes to see me drinking on the job. But may I remind you, I don't technically *have* a job anymore. Mr. Fennec is taking the lead on this case. I'm just here to support when possible."

"I wasn't judging, Jo," Dennis protested. "It's nice to see you relaxing a little, for once."

"Well, I dunno about relaxing." Ortega fidgeted in his chair. He was going stir crazy with all this retirement crap. "But let's just say, I'm trying not get as wound up about things as I used to."

"Well, that's just fine, Sir." Dennis smiled pleasantly. Somehow, a face-to-face video call, while not in person, had a deeper connection for Dennis than a disembodied voice on the phone line. Despite having multiple conversations recently, this was the first time that he felt truly connected to his ex-boss.

"What say we begin with a replay of Emma's conversation with Baxter Baker, a nephew by marriage and the VP of Operations for Vandenberg Nutraceuticals?"

Emma and Dennis exchanged glances. At Emma's behest, Dennis edited out the last part, where there was a kiss that was less innocent than what Emma let on.

Just then, the buzzer rang. Darwin, the only one in the room still standing, went to open the door. "Ah, Monique," he greeted one of his assistants. "You're just in time. We're about to review the audio from Emma's meeting with Baxter Baker last night. Please, come in and have a seat."

Monique was dressed demurely by 'Monique standards' wearing black slacks and a white blouse with a bright red scarf wrapped around her neck that matched her high-heel shoes. Before taking a seat beside Rue on the couch, she peered at the plasma screen and blew Ortega a kiss.

"Is that really necessary?" Ortega replied gruffly. Monique merely winked.

This was the first time Emma and Dennis had ever met Monique, so they didn't realize that on alternate days, he went by 'Monte.' He dressed according to his gender preference for the day, switching it up only when necessary for undercover work. All Emma knew was that something was different about Monique, but she couldn't quite figure out what. Monique sensed her confusion and found it highly amusing.

"Bi-gender," Rue leaned in and whispered, saving what she thought might be a considerable waste of time.

"You take the fun out of everything," Monique pouted.

"Don't start, Montgomery," Rue chastised, using his given name — which he hated.

"Trollop," Monique retorted.

Emma mocked, "Well, Rue Brennan, you appear to make friends everywhere you go, don't you?"

"Oooh." Monique flicked a wrist at Emma, showing off a perfectly manicured set of candy apple red nails and enough sparkly bracelets to light up Central Park at night. "Feisty! I love it!"

"Ahem," Darwin cleared his throat. "Shall we?"

Darwin replayed the audio from Emma's meeting with Baxter. Ortega pulled out a notepad and pen and began fever-ishly jotting down details of the call. Rue and Darwin had already logged their observations on their private server, and so they waited patiently for Ortega to finish.

"Thoughts?" Darwin finally asked. If he didn't know any better, he could have sworn that Ortega's eyes lit up at the prospect of a new case.

"Lots," Ortega answered, taking a sip of his drink before continuing. "Obviously, Junior here is afraid of what might happen to him for talking with Emma… Do we have any idea why he was suddenly in such a hurry to leave, though? Seemed rather abrupt."

"No," Emma answered. "He pulled a cellular phone out of his pocket… like the one Dennis carries. I'm guessing he saw the number of someone calling or received a text message? Anyway, he looked at his watch seconds later and then rushed us through dinner."

"Hmm," Ortega thought.

"Maybe whomever was on the call was letting him know they were on to him?" Darwin suggested. "After all, he was pretty convinced Erasmus Vandenberg was murdered, and was essentially outing the company for unethical practices."

"Or maybe he had a getaway plan in place, and once he was told it was time to go… he went?" Rue added.

"Maybe," Ortega nodded. "Or maybe someone was looking out for him and trying to warn him."

"Well, he knew I was wearing a wire," Emma offered. "But that didn't seem to bother him."

"What?" Dennis sat up abruptly. "Why didn't you tell me that?"

"Because," Emma lowered her voice. "You were already mad. Besides, what does it matter?" Dennis' face turned a little pink. He sucked in a deep breath and sank back into the couch, hands balled into fists and resting on his knees.

"Strange," Ortega furrowed his brows, "that he'd be fine with being recorded, but suggested that he was putting himself at risk being there."

"Not if he planned on vanishing," Darwin reasoned. "If this ever turns into an official case and it goes to trial, and we can't find Baxter to testify, then this is all we've got."

"Same is true if someone offs him," Monique suggested, sucking on a nail.

Something in Emma's stomach dropped. She didn't like Baxter Baker, but she somehow didn't like the idea of something happening to him even more.

"So, where do we go from here?" Dennis asked. He was all about the practical next steps.

"May I?" Darwin asked Ortega.

"Please," Ortega handed the proverbial floor to Darwin.

"I think we start off visiting one of the main Northeastern branches of the Church of Infinite Love. It's located in a small town in rural Pennsylvania. Rue and I can manage that. Then, perhaps when Emma and Dennis make it to Florida, your team can investigate the main nutraceutical factory that Baxter suggested… undercover, of course."

"Wait," Monique protested. "Then what am I supposed to do?" She pouted a little. "I could go undercover at one of the church's special healing ceremonies they are so fond of sharing on Sunday morning television. They would love me," Monique smiled seductively. "I can ask them to pray the gay away and then transform into Monte, right before their eyes!"

"While we all appreciate your flare for the dramatic," Darwin answered. "I've got research I need you to do."

"Boring," Monique sighed. "But fine. I'm the best researcher you've got at the moment, since your sister-in-law, Ashley, got herself preggers again."

Rue bit her tongue. She was mighty fine at investigative research herself… though no one had Ashley's mad ethical hacking skills. But after giving birth to twins, she ended up pregnant again soon afterward, leaving her little time to support the team at the moment.

Darwin ignored the 'preggers' remark and continued. "I

need you to see what you can dig up on the church. Specifi-cally, if they were adding a 'special sauce' to their supple-ments, drinks, and energy bars. We need to find out who was affected by it, any legal troubles, illnesses, lawsuits, that sort of thing."

"I'm on it, boss," Monique agreed.

"What am I missing?" Darwin asked Ortega.

"Not much, from what I can tell so far," Ortega answered. "Except one vital question."

"What's that?" Darwin asked, surprised. He thought he'd been thorough.

"Why take him out on an airplane to the factory?" Ortega asked. "Why not at home or in Florida?"

"To cast suspicion on the passengers on the flight?" Rue suggested.

"But no one suspected foul play," Darwin replied.

"To make it harder to investigate? You'd be looking at a federal investigation versus a state one." Ortega offered an answer to his own question.

"But wouldn't that draw more attention?" Darwin suggested.

"Ahem," Monique coughed politely. "May a gal offer an opinion?" Both Rue and Emma found this mildly annoying. None of the other gals in this room felt they needed to ask for permission to speak.

"Spit it out," Ortega answered brusquely.

"Only sometimes," Monique winked. Ortega's expression let Monique know he was not amused. "Well," she continued. "Maybe that was the only time the murderer would have had access to Erasmus."

"Actually, that's good thinking," Ortega had to admit.

Suddenly, keys could be heard jingling in a lock from a door behind where Ortega sat. "Shit!" he exclaimed, snubbing his cigar out in an ashtray sitting on the table in front of him.

"Are you smoking again?" A woman's voice asked as Nancy

could be seen entering the main doorway and now stood behind Ortega in their kitchen.

"Yes, but it was a special occasion," Ortega lied. "Darwin and Rue are expecting. We were just having a celebratory smoke. You remember I told you about Darwin Fennec and Rue Brennan — the last case I was on before our move?"

Nancy peered over Ortega's shoulder and smiled into the camera. "I remember," she answered. To the camera she bellowed, "Congratulations guys!" But then the corners of her mouth dropped. "Why are you the only one smoking, dear?" She shot a suspicious glance in her husband's direction.

"Uh, Rue has terrible allergies, and we thought the second-hand smoke might be bad for the baby," Darwin lied in an attempt to cover for Ortega.

"Hmm, interesting," Nancy answered. "And here I thought that was a ritual saved for men pacing outside of a hospital nursery."

"Well, times are changing?" Darwin tried again, the pitch in his voice shifting slightly.

"Oh, Darwin. Stop covering for my husband. I know when he's full of shit." She paused. "So why are you really on this call… It's not a case is it, because you promised—" her voice raised as she squeaked out the last bit.

"No, Honey," Ortega tried to calm his wife. "It's not like that. Officer Dennis just asked me to share a bit of knowledge with him based on my experience. It's for a case *they're* working on… has nothing to do with *me*, I promise. Come here." He pulled Nancy into his lap. Sitting on one of Ortega's thighs, she peered into the camera and asked, "Is this true, Dennis?" She leaned so far forward that her face took up the entire screen. "I know you wouldn't lie to me."

Dennis cleared the lump that was forming in his throat. This time, Emma took his hand for support. Technically, it was *mostly* true. He had been hoping Ortega would take the lead on the investigation, at least on the Florida side. But since nothing much had happened yet, he wasn't *exactly* lying. "That is true, Mrs. Ortega," Dennis nodded emphatically. "This is my fault. I asked for Detective Ortega's advice."

Nancy squinted at Ortega and wrinkled her nose at him. "That better be all you're doing," she warned, before playfully giving him a kiss on the bridge of his nose. "I'll leave you to it, then." To Ortega, she added, "I'll be upstairs if you need me."

Once Nancy was safely out of earshot, Ortega continued. Beads of sweat now formed on his brow. Instead of wiping them away, he took another sip of his quickly dwindling bourbon. Little of the ice remained frozen.

"As I was saying," Ortega whispered loudly. "There's not much missing except… you might wanna find out more about Baxter's relationship with Elsbeth. Seems to have a soft spot for her. Curious if his sudden change of heart is truly related to her, or someone or something else."

"Good thinking," Darwin answered.

"And I'd like to find out why no one I contacted from the precinct in Manhattan agreed to investigate his death. They were convinced it was simply 'his time' and not the least bit open to the fact that it might not have been. I'm also befuddled as to why no one in the family is contesting the will."

"Let's gather what we can first," Ortega suggested. "Give them a reason to pay attention."

Dennis nodded.

"I'd like to propose one more question," Emma piped up. "Seeing as I'm the reason we're all here?"

Always about her, Rue thought. Though that wasn't entirely true, and she knew it. Rue was just feeling disagreeable.

"Of course," Darwin answered.

"Why is it you two," she pointed toward Darwin and then Rue, "are the ones visiting the Church of Infinite Love instead of sending Dennis in undercover before we head to Florida? Are you worried someone will connect him to me?"

"That's part of it." Darwin shot Rue a glance. "But, there's something else."

Rue sighed. She knew this was coming. She just wished she could have stalled a bit longer. Finally, she explained: "I happened to have spent nearly the first three decades of my life living at the Church of Infinite Love campus in Pennsylvania as a member before finally escaping to New York. And that was only because the police stormed our campus one night back in '96 after two young women went missing. I know exactly what to do, when we get to the church, and how to do it." After a long pause, she added, "I'm counting on Darwin here to make sure I don't get stuck there again." Even as she said it, chills ran up her spine. The thought of returning made her nauseated, but she had to go. In her mind, she had a strange sense of duty. She felt a duty to help Emma out of guilt over what happened to the woman's friends and a larger mission. She hoped her actions might help other women break free from the church, too. Rue's nausea was coupled with dizziness, so she let go of her thoughts for a moment and forced her attention back into the room.

For once, Emma was dumbfounded. Somehow, she had this story in her head about Rue that included having life handed to her on a silver platter. It certainly didn't include growing up in a cult known for its less-than-stellar treatment of women.

"I'm sorry," Emma finally answered. "I didn't know that."

And for the first time, Rue and Emma shared a look. It was one of mutual respect.

Chapter 15
Nyla Sprightly

Present Day in St. Petersburg, Florida

Emma and Dennis arrived at Erasmus' mansion on Treasure Island in St. Petersburg after a ridiculously long flight because of unforeseen weather and mechanical issues. *Correction: It was now Emma's mansion. Something she needed to remind herself of regularly.*

Not two days after their visit to Darwin and Rue's 'fox den' to discuss a game plan for investigating Erasmus Vandenberg's likely murder, they were addressing part two of that plan... getting Emma set up in her new home and working out the details of her inheritance. Frankly, she was surprised that no one asked what she thought would have been a logical question. "How do we know you didn't murder Erasmus yourself, Emma, after learning of his will?" But she wasn't aware of the will. Nor did she have the means to kill him. And, even if she had both, why risk it when there was a good chance that he was going to die of old age soon enough, anyway? But somehow, it never occurred to them she could have been responsible. This unearned trust only made her that much more motivated to figure out who killed her friend, Erasmus. In her heart, she knew it wasn't old age or 'just one of those things.'

Emma paused in front of the two-story waterfront property, surrounded by royal palms and an entranceway paved with polished stones leading up to a set of blue and white-painted, double-wood doors. For the first time since learning of her inheritance, she felt woozy, and stopped to take in a deep breath. Dennis caught her as she swayed from side to side, wrapping one long arm around her shoulders.

"You okay?" he asked.

Emma nodded. "Quite a bit different from my old digs, huh?" She eyed the two suitcases and carry-on that the taxi driver dropped next to her before making a hasty exit. Storm clouds were rolling in, for what promised to be a miserable, rainy night. "Half my life so far can fit into one of those cases. How sad is that?"

He hugged her tightly. "Not sad, at all." He motioned across the expansive property. "Look at this as the beginning of a new life for us… er, you." He corrected himself, not wanting to be presumptuous. He was just thrilled that she was letting him accompany her and that his request for a temporary transfer at the precinct had been approved.

"I've never had a lawn before," was all that Emma could think to say, daunted as she eyed the property. "I don't even know how to take care of it. Have you ever mowed a lawn before?"

Dennis laughed a little. "Pretty sure I can manage. Hey," he motioned to the sky. "Let's get inside before the floodgates open, huh?"

Emma nodded.

After fighting with the two keys for the upper and lower locks of the front door, Emma eventually pried it open. She barely had time to breathe a sigh of relief when a shrieking alarm began to sound, reverberating through the house, piercing through the air like an ice pick.

"What the hell?" Emma covered her ears.

Dennis cringed, squinting as if walking through a blizzard. "I don't suppose the property manager said anything about an alarm code, did they?

"No!" Emma yelled. "I'm sure I would have remembered."

The shrill was so loud, it began feeling as if the very pulse of it replaced their heartbeats, and the high-pitched tones pierced their brains. Emma felt a dull pain forming behind her eyes.

At that moment, Emma witnessed a slim, ebony arm reach past her and punch a few numbers on the keypad next to the front door. Moments later… silence.

With the noise, neither Emma nor Dennis heard a slim, dark-skinned young woman wearing a patchwork sundress and brown, spaghetti-strap sandals slip past them and disable the alarm.

"Uh, thanks—" Emma turned to the woman, startled, as she spun around to find the woman's face not three inches from her own. She tried to back up, almost tripping over the threshold of the now open doorway. The woman flashed a large toothy grin, so wide it caused her eyes to crinkle around the edges. She looked at Emma as if expecting something. What, Emma had no idea.

From Emma's best guess, the young woman couldn't have been more than in her early twenties, tops… probably Elsbeth's age.

"Hi! I'm Nyla," the woman declared enthusiastically. "But my friends call me 'Sprightly.' Nyla-Sprightly seemed to carry with her a lot of pent-up energy. She looked as if you took her by the shoulders and gave her a good shake, she would take to flight like a rocket.

"Why do they call you—" Emma paused, watching as the girl restlessly swayed from side to side, swinging her arms. One of them almost slapped Dennis in the abdomen, but he side-stepped just in time. The wide-eyed grin remained plastered on her face as if frozen that way. "Never mind. Nice to meet you, uh…" Emma's head was still throbbing from the alarm and the effects of a long travel day. "Nyla Sprightly."

"Oh," Nyla corrected. "Sprightly isn't my last name, it's—" Suddenly, the gears in Nyla's brain clicked into place. She decided she rather liked her new name. In fact, the more she thought about it, it was much nicer than her actual last name, and it wouldn't require her to give up the pet name people seemed to use around her. "That's right," she finally answered. "Nyla Sprightly, at your service!" She saluted.

"I'm sorry, I don't follow," Emma confessed.

"Oh, didn't Erasmus tell you?" She seemed surprised. "I'm the house manager slash house sitter." She made a cutting motion in the air to represent the slash between her two job titles.

"And what exactly does a house manager slash house sitter do?" Emma asked, repeating the slashing motion in the air, for emphasis.

"Well," Nyla Sprightly thought a moment. "I do a few overnights here, every once in a while, to make sure there's no funny business with burglars… to give the place a presence, you see."

"I see," Emma answered. But she really didn't. She'd heard of pet sitters and babysitters, but never house sitters. But then, Emma never really owned a house… or much of anything, for that matter.

"And I make sure the lawn service comes weekly to mow and trim the trees and bushes, and that the bug people spray regularly."

"Bug people?" Emma asked.

"Yeah, you know, so you don't get overrun with roaches, ants, and spiders… this is Florida, after all. Plus, you're near the water, so if you see any snakes, don't engage. Just call me, and I'll take care of them for you."

"I promise you," Emma smirked. "I won't be engaging with any snakes, that's for sure."

"Well, good." Sprightly swung her arms from side to side again as she shifted from one foot to the other. "Sorry about the alarm, by the way. Erasmus only recently had it installed. Guess not everyone knows about it, yet."

"Don't worry about it," Emma answered, jiggling her pinky finger in her ear as if washing water out of it. It still rang, slightly, from the piercing noise just moments ago.

Dennis began lifting one of the suitcases. Sprightly rushed to his side. "Oh," she smiled. "I can help you with that."

"No," Dennis protested. "That's a man's job, I can—"

He stopped when Emma shot him an, *Oh no, you just didn't* look.

"Fine," he corrected. "But it should be the job of the strongest and most capable."

Before he had a chance to lift a single suitcase, Sprightly already had them stacked inside the front door.

"I agree," Emma chuckled. "It should go to the strongest and most capable." She turned to follow Sprightly inside the house.

"Now that was just mean," Dennis complained.

"So, how long will you be staying Miss—" Sprightly's eyes grew wide. "Oh! I just realized that I don't even know your name!"

"I'm Emma, and this is my—" She paused, trying to find the right words. "Dennis."

Sprightly curtsied. Emma raised a curious eyebrow.

"Well, it's nice to meet you, Miss Emma and Mr. Dennis." She nodded approvingly. "I'm also available to run errands, schedule appointments, and do light housekeeping, though when Erasmus is here, he usually brings people with him." Sprightly paused again, the wheels in her head ticking. "Come to think of it, no one told me you were coming. Usually, Mrs.

Edwina has her secretary phone me to let me know who in the family is on their way. So… who are you?"

Emma tried to ignore her pounding head. All she wanted was a long hot bath and to maybe to have a veggie pizza delivered. "I'm the new caretaker of this home," Emma finally said.

Sprightly was crestfallen. "Oh." She rolled her eyes away, embarrassed. "I see. Were my services unacceptable?"

Dennis realized the confusion and stepped in, putting out a hand as if to calm her. "No, you misunderstand," he explained. "Emma is not replacing you. She's the new owner of this house."

Sprightly brightened for a moment. "Oh! Er… but what happened to Erasmus?"

"He's dead, I'm afraid," Emma blurted out.

Dennis shot her a *What is wrong with you?* look.

It was too late. Sprightly's face crumbled like a discarded piece of paper. Her lips began quivering, and soon she began sobbing uncontrollably. "Dead?!"

Dennis put a supportive hand on her shoulder. "I'm sorry," he explained. "If we had been told you'd be here, we would have made sure you were informed."

Sprightly's shoulders shuddered as she continued sobbing. "Such a nice man!"

Dennis patted her shoulder. Emma, feeling like a jerk, rubbed the girl's back in as comforting a way as Emma knew how. Her bedside manner needed work. Empathy was Dennis' area of expertise, she decided.

"There, there," Dennis continued. "He had a long and good life."

Sprightly nodded. "He was rather old. Did he die in his sleep… natural causes?" She looked up, hopefully.

"Exactly," Dennis confirmed. He had his doubts about the *natural causes,*' but he figured this shock was about as much as Sprightly could handle in one day. "Didn't suffer a bit."

Sprightly sniffed back a few more tears, absentmindedly

grabbing the hem of her dress to wipe her eyes. Dennis dutifully looked away so as not to accidentally see the woman's unmentionables as she hoisted the fabric up to her face.

"I can't believe Ms. Edwina's secretary didn't call to tell me," she sobbed.

"I'm sure she meant to," Dennis offered. Sprightly nodded.

"Sprightly." Emma dropped her hand. "I hate to be rude, but we are exhausted. Could we pick this conversation up another day?"

"Oh." Sprightly's eyes grew wide. "Of course, Miss Emma. I can be here bright and early tomorrow at—"

"How about Monday?" Emma suggested. "It will give me a chance to settle in and figure out exactly what I need here."

Sprightly nodded. "Of course. Whatever you need." She thrust a hand into her dress pocket and pulled out a plastic card-holder with a mini pen attached to the side. The woman yanked a card from the case and scribbled something on it with the pen. "Here." She handed it to Emma. "Good thing I always keep these handy. I've added your alarm code on the back for next time. Also, I run a small concierge business and manage a few houses in the area. It has my direct phone number on it." She pointed to the number on the card. "If I don't pick up, it means I'm working, but just leave me a message and I'll call you right back as soon as I can. I've got one of those fancy new answering machines built right into the phone… so I can check my messages from almost anywhere." She beamed proudly.

Emma had no idea what the young woman was talking about. She had a landline that she hardly ever used and couldn't be bothered with answering machines. If it was important, she reasoned, people would call back. Dennis had tried to persuade her to use a cellular phone, but at the moment, it was still in its original casing, nestled in one of her suitcases.

"Thanks." Emma accepted the card and waited for Sprightly to make her exit.

Instead, Sprightly stood there, kicking the edge of the door frame.

"Is there something else?" Emma asked.

"Ohhh, no… it's just—"

"What is it?" Dennis encouraged.

Sprightly wrinkled her nose uncomfortably. "It's just that it's payday."

Emma sighed. She knew money was coming soon, but she didn't have her inheritance yet — aside from the house. She had no idea how to pay the woman.

Dennis chimed in. "And how much are you usually paid?" he asked.

"Well," Sprightly answered. "My going rate is $11 an hour, but Erasmus always insisted on paying me $18 dollars an hour. I put in about 20 hours over the past two weeks, so… $360?" She cringed. "If that's too much—"

"No," Dennis answered. "It's not that. We've just arrived and don't have any money on us at the moment."

Sprightly's eyes shifted back and forth from the house, back to Emma and Dennis as if mentally trying to get them to notice something, but it was apparent to no one except for the young woman.

Emma crossed and uncrossed her arms. "What? What are you motioning toward?"

"Erasmus keeps cash in the cookie jar in the kitchen. He usually just tells me to pay myself and then, when Miss Edwina or another family member arrives, they refill it and make sure I didn't pinch more than I should… which I'd never do," she reassured them.

"Then why don't we see about paying you?" Dennis led the way inside. To Emma, he whispered, "I can take it from here if you want to have a look around."

Emma sighed gratefully. She wasn't used to having support in domestic matters, and she kind of liked it.

Dennis marched through the main entryway, past the living

room and down the hall into the kitchen, as if he'd lived there all his life. In truth, he was pretty much just guessing. He eyed the layout of the kitchen with interest. It was the first he'd ever seen with an island in the middle for prepping food, not to mention stainless steel appliances.

Sprightly reached for a colorful tin on the counter. Apparently, Edwina had refilled it recently, because it was full to the brim with cash in a variety of bills.

"I can just take $220 and give you my normal rate, if you prefer," Sprightly offered. "Seeing as this is an unexpected change of events and all."

"No," Dennis insisted. "Take what you're usually paid."

"You can check with Mrs. Edwina," Sprightly offered. "She can confirm I'm telling you the truth."

"I don't have to check with anyone." Dennis crossed his arms. "I have a pretty good sense about people."

"Really?" Sprightly asked, counting the bills and tucking them into her dress pocket. "How's that?" She wanted to know.

"I'm a cop," he confessed. "It's my job to have a good sense about people."

Sprightly's eyes grew wide. "Do you carry a gun and all?"

"Sometimes," he confessed.

"Ever shoot someone?" Sprightly was fascinated.

"No." He shook his head. "See you in a few days, Nyla Sprightly," he smiled. Dennis knew that Sprightly wasn't her last name but saw how Nyla's eyes lit up when Emma referred to her as such.

Sprightly's wide, toothy grin returned.

"Sure thing, Mr. Dennis."

"Just Dennis," he answered, showing her to the door. "'Mister' is my dad's name," he laughed.

Sprightly laughed as he escorted her out. He watched her all but skip down the driveway and climb on a little green bicycle that was sitting by the curb. Nyla Sprightly waved and hit the bell on it as she pedaled away.

Later that evening, Edwina Vandenberg was plagued by two annoying phone calls. While Dennis claimed to have a 'good sense about people,' Emma was not as trusting. She phoned Edwina to confirm that Sprightly was who she said she was, and that she could be trusted. Edwina, who couldn't be bothered with the woman who, in her mind, stole the family fortune, barked messages to Ferdinand, who calmly delivered them as if echoing Edwina.

"Tell her that—that girl has been with us for several years now, and her mother took care of the Florida home for two decades before that," Edwina called over Ferdinand's shoulder, forgetting Nyla's name as quickly as Emma read it from the business card.

"Miss Nyla has been with us for several years now—" Ferdinand began.

"Thank you, Ferdinand," Emma interrupted. "I got that." She bit her lip.

"Tell her that I trust that girl more than I trust a woman who ran off with the Vandenberg fortune!" Edwina added, bitterly.

"Madame Edwina says—" Ferdinand tried, again, reluctantly.

"I heard her, Ferdinand," Emma answered, a hint of sarcasm creeping into her voice. "I just wanted to make sure Nyla was truly the property manager. Thank you for confirming."

Not ten seconds after Ferdinand hung up the phone, it rang again.

"What does everyone want from me?" Edwina complained loudly from the couch as Ivy brought the woman her nightly cream sherry and the latest copy of *Vogue*.

This time, it was Sprightly on the other end.

Ferdinand listened with a mix of confusion and patience

while the hyperactive woman explained. "I didn't even think about it until after I'd let them in that maybe I shoulda made sure they were who they said they were—" Nyla began.

"Miss Nyla—" Ferdinand tried in vain to gently interrupt.

"I would just feel awful if I let strangers into the house and, come to think of it, maybe I should go back there now and check on the place—"

"Miss Nyla—" Ferdinand tried again.

"I mean, they seemed trustworthy, with Mr. Dennis being a cop and all… assuming that was even true! What if it wasn't—"

"Miss Nyla!" Ferdinand all but yelled into the phone.

"Yes?" Sprightly answered softly.

"Miss Emma was telling you the truth. She is the new owner of the Florida estate. Perhaps you should consider contacting her for all future concerns related to the property."

"Oh, I see. Okay," Sprightly acknowledged. "Could you at least tell Miss Edwina that it was lovely working with her and—"

"I will do that, Miss Nyla," Ferdinand cut the girl off once again. He knew if he didn't, she would keep talking non-stop for another twenty minutes. "Good night."

Chapter 16
The Church of Infinite Love

Back in Pennsylvania

Rue and Darwin swerved through the twists and turns of the mountainous road in upstate Pennsylvania. Darwin was at the wheel of the rental car. Meanwhile, Rue was clenching both the hand-rest and her teeth, trying not to be ill. Her face was visibly sallow.

It had nothing to do with motion sickness.

Rue was afraid.

"Talk to me, Rue." Darwin glanced at her and then back at the road as he expertly maneuvered their rental car along the long and winding road. "Are you okay?"

He knew she was nervous about returning to a church that took her so long to flee from. But there was more to it than that. He was certain of it. Darwin suspected it had to do with her family… a topic that, even after being together for nearly a year now… was a touchy one, and largely off limits.

"It's just that—" she began.

"Yes?" Darwin encouraged.

"I know it's silly, but — whenever I'm back in this neck of the woods, I get all panicky."

There was a long pause while Darwin waited for an explanation that didn't come. "Why?" he finally asked. He suspected he knew.

Rue let out a labored sigh. He was going to figure it out sooner rather than later, anyway. "Because it took me so long to escape from this town, that being back here sets off an irrational fear that somehow I'll get sucked back in and won't be able to leave."

"Do you mean that they'll imprison you? Not let us leave?" Darwin asked, alarmed.

"I don't think they'll physically detain us, no," Rue answered. Though she wasn't a hundred percent sure this was correct. "But it doesn't stop the fear."

The two pulled into the parking lot of the Church of Infinite Love.

There was nothing spectacular about the church itself. In fact, the building looked like a large, gray wooden barn about to collapse in on itself. The most remarkable features were the new white sign that had been recently placed by the roadside with an arrow to the church, and a large, red glass heart that someone hung on the front door of the entryway. It looked like one of those old sun catchers that people painted for fun… it probably was.

"I would never let that happen," Darwin reassured her. "Besides, Monique outdid herself with your makeover. Any members there who knew you back then aren't likely to recognize you."

It was true. Monique helped her sift through their hall closet, where Darwin kept an assortment of costumes and disguises at the ready for cases requiring they go undercover. Monique fitted her with a passable auburn wig that was long and curly. "Don't mess it up," she cautioned. "It's my favorite." Rue knew that. She wore it all the time. Since she remembered that the church didn't permit women to wear makeup (it was deemed a sign of vanity), but she needed some to adequately change her appearance, they settled on a self-tanning cream, green contacts and oversized, prescriptionless glasses. For the pièce de résistance, Darwin suggested a brown corduroy skirt that reached her ankles and an ugly white polyester blouse with ruffles around the neckline that furrowed down the front where the buttons were.

"Perfect," Monique praised. "You look hideous."

Now at the church, Rue unlocked the passenger side of the car and pushed the door open, sticking a leg out and stepping to the ground. "We'll see," Rue shrugged. "Let's go."

As they approached the doorway, it swung open, as if they were expected. Rue couldn't help but think this was the setup to a bad horror movie. Her stomach lurched a little.

A pear-shaped, middle-aged woman with hair that ran the length of her back (about a foot of it, a tangled mess of split ends) greeted them. "Welcome," she smiled, reaching into a shallow straw basket that she was holding and producing a brochure. "Are you here for today's service?"

"We are," Darwin answered simply, accepting the brochure. "Thank you."

The woman cautiously looked them over. "I don't believe I've seen either of you before," she confessed. "Is this your first time at the Church of Infinite Love?"

Darwin opened his mouth to answer again, more out of habit than anything else. Rue put her hand out and touched his chest to silence him, as if to say, *"I've got this."*

"Haven't been here since I was a kid," Rue explained. "But we regularly attend the sister church in Hoboken."

"Oh," the woman nodded. "The one in New Jersey?"

Rue nodded. *Was there any other Hoboken in the world?* Rue wondered.

Just then, a family made their way to the door, waiting for their turn to enter. The woman wore an all-white cotton dress, while the man wore a light tan suit with a fat, burnt orange tie. The two kids, one boy and one girl, were dressed in similar colors, with a matching yellow dress and ruffles for the girl and a white suit with a wide yellow tie for the boy.

"Right this way." The woman motioned toward the rows of chairs. "Take a seat anywhere."

"You let Monique know our exact location, right?" Rue whispered.

"Yes," Darwin tapped his cell phone. "Tracker," he answered simply. Rue wasn't certain she completely trusted the tracking feature on Darwin's cell phone out in the middle of nowhere. She hadn't used one long enough, and thus, she doubted their effectiveness, despite the fact that his friend Bristol had used it to rescue her one fateful night outside a nightclub in Manhattan some months prior.

Inside the church, Darwin expected to see a series of church pews lined up in front of a podium. Instead, there were rows and rows of ordinary folding chairs. The floor appeared to have old basketball patterns on them, now worn away and scratched. The most interesting aspects of the room were the high, V-shaped ceiling with interlocking wooden beams, and the tall stage in the front of the room where the podium stood. In front of the podium was a large gold medallion featuring a lion, a leopard, a young lamb, a wolf, and a small child. It was probably the most ornate object in the room.

Rue planted herself in the back row, in the farthest corner where she could survey the entire room. Darwin took her cue and sat next to her, eyeing the room curiously. "Have you never been to a church before?" Rue whispered.

"Oh, I have," Darwin answered. "It was a cathedral, actually. And I was only there once… on my wedding day."

Rue's chest dropped. "Wedding day?!" she whispered back, visibly shaken. After all, they had been living together now for the past four months. She even gave up the lease on her apartment. Why had she not heard of this sooner?

Several people a few rows up turned to look at them, puzzled by the noise. But instead of saying anything, they merely smiled politely, in a way that suggested, *"You know you're in a church, right?"*

Rue sat back and crossed her arms while Darwin finished surveying the room. It was only when he glanced at her to say something that he saw her expression. "Oh," he realized his mistake. "That was over a long time ago, decades really."

"You didn't think it pertinent to mention that you were married before?" Rue leaned toward him. A few more people looked in their direction. Rue smiled back sweetly.

By now, dozens more people had arrived, and the seats in front of them began to fill up quickly. A few sounds of babies crying and children being fussy echoed against the high ceilings as their parents tried to hush them.

"Not really," Darwin admitted. "I don't pry into your past because I know you don't like it. Didn't seem to make sense bringing up mine." Rue let out a huff. "But if you want to discuss it later, we can. It was a mistake that only lasted a few years."

"So, you're divorced?" Rue confirmed.

"Yes," Darwin answered. "Have been for quite some time. Wasn't in a hurry to do *that* again," he joked, saw her expression, and promptly fell silent.

Rue wasn't sure how to take this news. On the one hand, it further disrupted her previous beliefs that Darwin was a playboy afraid of commitment, as he was committed enough to marry someone, and then went on to invite Rue to move in with him. So, that's something. Still, there was a childlike part of her that didn't like to think that there had ever been a 'someone else' even though he was in his early forties, and it stood to reason that there had been many 'someone elses' along the way. *Come to think of it*, she thought. *I don't even know exactly how old Darwin is or even when his birthday is. We've known each other nearly a year now, and the topic has never come up? Did it pass without him mentioning it? It must have!* It was becoming increasingly clear to Rue that the two might consider spending less time working on cases and more time actually getting to know one another.

Just then, a woman stepped from behind a black curtain that hung on each side of the stage and stepped slowly, rhythmically even, toward the podium. "Welcome friends," she smiled sweetly. "Please rise." The congregation stood. "I invite you to turn to page 137 in your hymnals. A second woman stepped from behind the curtain and made her way to the far corner of the stage, where an old upright piano stood. Once seated, she opened her hymnal and placed it in front her, set her right foot on the sustain pedal and began plunking the ivory keys.

The church sang, *"A mighty fortress is our God…"*

The pianist hit the piano chords angrily, as if trying to adjust to the fact that the congregation didn't get the timing right on their words, so she kept modifying her rhythm.

Rue felt flushed and her hands began trembling. She handed the hymnal to Darwin, who quickly grabbed it out of her unsteady hands. Holding it open with one hand, he circled his free arm around her waist for support. "You okay?" he mouthed. Rue nodded.

Darwin didn't know the song, of course, so he just mouthed the words and occasionally emphasized an end note as attendees around him smiled and nodded.

"Please be seated," the woman at the podium said, after the song had finished.

The congregation sat. The woman was shorter than Darwin had first realized, concealed by the fact that she was on stage and wearing very high, chunky-heeled shoes. Her peach dress flowed down around her ankles, and the collar was cut high around the neck. The gossamer sleeves reached all the way to her wrists and were tightly buttoned on each arm. It was clear that the dress was going nowhere and was revealing nothing.

"For those who don't me, I am Deaconess Frances. Before Reverend Simon gives his sermon for today, I'd like to welcome out-of-town guests and first-time visitors. I'll begin with first-time visitors." Her gaze honed in on Darwin. "If you are a first-time visitor, would you stand, please?"

Darwin was about to stand, but Rue grabbed his arm and shook her head. He stayed firmly seated.

Frances seemed a little unnerved. "In that case, any out-of-town visitors?" This time, she stared directly at Rue. That was their cue. Rue motioned for Darwin to stand first, and she followed. Rue dutifully tucked her head shyly and allowed her gaze to fall to the floor. "Ah, welcome," Frances called. "Which church are you visiting from?"

Darwin waited for Rue to answer. Instead, she elbowed him in the ribs. "Hoboken," he coughed out.

"Hoboken." Frances' smile remained plastered to her face. "One of our… newer churches, no doubt. Please, share your names with us so we may greet you properly."

Darwin thought a moment. "Mr. and Mrs. Swift," he answered simply.

To the congregation, she said, "Let's give Mr. and Mrs. Swift," as she eyed Rue again, "a warm welcome."

"Welcome Mr. and Mrs. Swift," the church droned.

After what seemed like an eternity, Reverend Simon took to the stage. He was a tall and bulky man with a broad chest and belly. He wore a black suit and tie, and had his hair slicked back with what looked like men's hair cream that went out of style in the '50s.

"Where will you be on that fateful day?!" Reverend Simon boomed. Rue slouched in her chair and did her best to tune it out. Darwin, on the other hand, found the entire experience completely fascinating. He choked back a laugh somewhere in the middle where Simon reminded the wives to obey their husbands, and husbands to cherish their wives as the 'weaker vessel.' Darwin glanced at Rue, who uncrossed her arms as soon as she saw him, and instead rested her hands lightly in her lap. She smiled lovingly back at him, holding his gaze just long enough for her to witness a few church goers smiling approvingly in her periphery.

Weaker vessel? Darwin laughed to himself. *And good luck getting Rue to do any obeying. That woman has a mind of her own, and I prefer it that way.*

"Now it's time for the healing ceremony," Reverend Simon announced. "If there is any among you feeling physical or emotional pain, please come forward so that we may pray over you."

Finally, Rue thought. This is why they were here. The healing ceremony was a double-edged sword. On the one hand, there were a small group of people who actually believed in faith-healing. For some newcomers, it was their last option when they had exhausted all others. Mixed in were those with a victim mentality, who showed up for every service with a recurring injury or a new ailment-of-the week. They claimed to feel immediately better after each prayer circle, but the effects didn't always last as long as they'd hoped. And then there was the *other hand*. If you admitted you had any physical or emotional pain (and really, who doesn't?), then you were clearly doing something wrong spiritually. So, many would clam up and feign perfect health. Meanwhile, the martyrs had no trouble admitting their 'weakness,' and paying a weekly financial offering to the church in the hopes that *this* time would be the time they were cured of all ills.

Rue turned to Darwin, rolling her eyes at the number of people lining up in the long row down the center of the church. It was only then that she realized he was no longer sitting next to her. *Where did he go?* She peered around frantically for a moment before she saw him in line, limping slightly as the line progressed. *What was he up to?*

The young woman in front of Darwin approached the front of the stage. Deaconess Frances motioned for her to walk the steps that led to the podium where Reverend Simon stood. "What ails you, my daughter?" Reverend Simon asked, having retrieved the microphone from its stand on the podium and holding it in front of her. The young woman rung her hands, embarrassed. "It's okay, you're among friends."

"I've been feeling… sad," she answered simply.

"Really?" Reverend Simon peered at her sympathetically. "And why are you sad?"

"I just—"

"It's okay." He touched her shoulder. "We're all here for you."

"I just feel like my life is pointless," she finally admitted. "And then I feel guilty for even thinking that because, after all, I am one of God's children." She began to tear up.

"Indeed, you are, my daughter." He motioned for Deaconess Frances to bring over a cup and plate. She placed them on the podium. "And you are among the chosen," he continued. "God has a special plan for you, and today we shall pray that he reveals it to you." He handed the deaconess his microphone. She, in turn, offered him a tiny vial, opening it and placing a few drops of oil into his palms. He rubbed his hands together before placing them on the young woman's bowed head. Without the microphone, the congregation could only hear mumbling. And it was quite possible that it was gibberish. Although onlookers would have asserted that he was speaking in tongues.

After a moment of prayer, Frances handed him a small yellow plate with what looked like a cookie. He held it up, and the young woman opened her mouth as he placed it on her tongue. "Let this morsel represent manna from heaven, blessed by God." She chewed whatever it was and swallowed before he followed up with a small yellow cup. "Let this holy water complete your healing." She drank the water and smiled.

"Better?" Reverend Simon asked gently.

She nodded gratefully as the church said in unison, "Amen." The woman was quickly escorted offstage by another church attendant.

Frances returned the microphone to Reverend Simon.

Darwin was next. When he reached the front of the stage, he, too, was invited up the steps to the podium. The minister asked, "What is troubling you, my son?" Reverend Simon thrust a hand-held microphone in front of Darwin's face.

It should be noted that Reverend Simon was at least a decade younger than Darwin. Darwin bit the inside of his cheek lightly to avoid laughing. He let out an awkward cough. "It's my knee, you see." Darwin pointed. "Old sports injury. Doctor says I need surgery."

There was a gasp from the audience. Rue crossed her arms and pursed her lips, shrinking into her chair. Surgery and doctors were generally frowned upon, and the church had to make special allowances for those with cancer who needed chemotherapy or radiation. But it was always mixed with a bit of judgment. After all, it was easier to blame the cancer patient for not being right with God. Otherwise, you might have to admit that God wasn't listening or, even worse, that he didn't care.

"I can assure you, my son," Reverend Simon furrowed his bushy brows. "That won't be necessary. Deaconess—" he addressed Deaconess Frances.

Once again, she returned with the small bottle of anointing oil. Given his height, Reverend Simon had to all but stand on his toes to reach the top of Darwin's head. The minister went as far as to push Darwin's head forward roughly, encouraging him to bow his head a little further.

After the prayer, Frances handed Darwin a small, macaroon-shaped morsel that sat on a green plate. It was larger than the one offered to the young woman, so Reverend Simon suggested, "Perhaps you could put your palms out, my son."

"Certainly," Darwin obliged, placing his cupped palms out in front of him. Once handed the macaroon, he took a bite before coughing awkwardly. He pulled a handkerchief from his pocket and spit the morsel into it.

"Is something the matter, my son?" Reverend Simon touched Darwin's arm, concerned, and possibly a little annoyed.

"Forgot to mention a peanut allergy. There aren't any peanuts in this, are there? Should have thought to mention that first. Sorry." He slipped the handkerchief back into his suit jacket.

"No peanuts," Reverend Simon confirmed. He waited while Darwin ate the remainder of the macaroon.

Next came the beverage in a matching green cup, except when Reverend Simon went to offer it to Darwin, he sipped it so fast that he spilled half of it on his shirt.

"Geez, I'm sorry. I'm such a klutz." He looked down at his stained shirt, laughing awkwardly. "Oh, and sorry for swearing."

"That's quite all right," Reverend Simon reassured him, motioning for Frances to bring over another cup... another green one. "You seem to be having a rough day, aren't you?" He joked.

"I'll say," Darwin laughed, again, jovially. This time, he downed the beverage without incident. It tasted like the sugar water they give small children when they have the hiccups.

Reverend Simon repeated the ritualistic words he had used for the woman who stood for healing before Darwin.

"And how is your knee?" Reverend Simon finally asked.

Darwin played along, shaking out his leg, surprised. "Better!" he proclaimed.

"Amen!" the congregation called enthusiastically.

Darwin was escorted off the stage and made sure to limp, just slightly, on the way back. After all, he didn't want to oversell it.

The healing ceremony continued for a good thirty minutes before they were called to pray once more and close with another hymn.

After the service, a few members of the church politely stopped to greet Rue and Darwin.

"Hello, dear," an older woman wearing an enormous hat

said. "So lovely to meet you." She put out a hand. Rue tried to shake it, but it went limp in hers. Instead, they held hands for an awkward moment while Rue answered, "Nice to meet you as well, Mrs.—"

"Grail," she finished. "Mr. and Mrs. Harold Grail." Apparently, the women didn't get a name of their own. Rue felt a chill up her spine and neck. It took her a moment, but then she recognized the longtime member, Mrs. Grail. *Let's hope she doesn't remember me,* Rue thought.

Harold was a boatload of enthusiasm. "Hope you'll both join us in the reception room for fellowship," he stated. It seemed more a command and less a request. He eyed Darwin's soiled shirt and let out a chuckle.

"Yes," Rue quickly answered, before glancing downward, embarrassed. "After I visit the ladies' room, of course."

"Oh, it's just through there." Mrs. Grail pointed toward an archway on the side of the stage. "We'll catch you both in a few minutes, then?"

"Of course," Rue lied. She had no intention of fellowship. In fact, after they had gotten the information they came for, Rue planned to be back on the road and heading straight to New York.

"You know," Mrs. Grail paused. "There's something about you that is familiar to me. You've never been to our church before, you say?"

"No," Rue interrupted. "Never been to the Pennsylvania campus before today."

"Oh," Mrs. Grail nodded. "Well, then you have a twin somewhere. Your voice is just so familiar." The woman mulled on this for a moment. Finally, at Mr. Grail's hurried request, they made their departure. He seemed to be in quite a hurry for refreshments.

Damn it! Rue thought to herself. Somehow, she'd never thought to adopt an accent or in some way disguise her voice.

Just then, the rumble of thunder could be heard outside.

The congregation quickly dispersed to the reception room, where coffee cakes and fresh brew awaited. Lightning flashed through one of the small, square windows at the top of the church. It was as if the Red Sea were parting as people moved aside. And that's when Rue saw her. Deaconess Frances now standing directly in front of them, as if appearing out of thin air. She smiled sweetly and waited until the room was empty, and she, Darwin and Rue, were the only remaining people.

"Hello, Rue." The woman eyed Rue up and down, almost amused. She wasn't fooled by the disguise. "It's nice of you to visit."

Rue swallowed hard before answering, "Hello, Mother."

Chapter 17
Private Quarters #5

Present Day in Pennsylvania

"You might have told me she was your mother," Darwin whispered as he and Rue were led down a long hallway toward Frances' private quarters.

After Rue and Darwin's unexpected encounter with Rue's mother, the deaconess excused herself, but not before requesting the two meet with her in private after she'd been given 'a few minutes to collect herself,' following the shock of her daughter's unexpected visit.

"I wasn't sure she'd be here, and by the time I saw her, it was too late," Rue whispered back.

"Still, a little heads up in the car would have helped."

The usher, who escorted them, politely walked in front of them, pretending not to eavesdrop.

"Could we talk about this later?" She nodded toward the woman leading them.

Darwin nodded. Between her mother and his undisclosed divorce, the list of things they needed to discuss was adding up.

The attendant rapped on the door at the end of the hall in a very distinctive pattern… three rapid hard knocks, followed by a pause and then two very light taps. It was one of many doors they passed, but this one was labeled, 'Private Quarters #5.' Across the hall was a door labeled, 'Private Quarters #6.' From the looks of it, this particular wing appeared to have about a dozen or so such rooms.

"You may enter," Frances' voice called from inside the room, recognizing the knock.

The attendant quickly opened the door and motioned for Darwin and Rue to follow. Like the deaconess, this woman was also covered from neck to ankle, with little skin showing, but was wearing a stiff black blouse and a long black dress. She had gray-brown hair, no makeup, and a mole that was almost as dark as the dress. Had they not been opposed to doctors, Rue might have suggested that the woman have that looked at by a dermatologist.

"You may go," Frances addressed the attendant, and waved at her as if to shoo her away. The woman merely nodded and, despite Rue's hope that the door would remain open, she shut it quickly, and from the sound of it, locked it behind her.

Darwin heard it, too, and found that quite curious. He let out a yawn, oddly tired after the service, coupled with a strange sense of calm. *Maybe I should give this faith healing thing more of a chance?* He thought to himself.

Frances was still in her church dress, sitting at a small round table off to the side of the door, and motioned for them to sit in the two upright, uncomfortable-looking chairs across from her. Glancing behind the woman, Rue could see a small single bed and pillow, with a nightstand and lamp next to it. There was a thin clothing rack on the far wall.

"Can I offer you some tea?" she asked. "Or perhaps a snack? We have our own signature nutrient-rich fruit and nut bars that I'm sure you'll like. Rue, you remember?"

It was then that Rue noticed that her mother had what

looked to be a small efficiency kitchen behind her, with a utility sink, mini refrigerator, and even a tiny stove and oven. *I guess the deaconess role comes with privileges,* Rue thought.

She remembered her parents having to share a room smaller than this one at their old campus, but there was no private kitchen. Everyone ate together in a common area, and no food was permitted in the private quarters. She learned that the hard way when she and her three roommates, sharing a room about this size, but with matching bunk beds, tried to sneak extra fruit snacks back from dinner. As punishment, they were all sent to the infirmary and forced to drink something that made them vomit. They were then given lots of water to re-hydrate but denied a regular breakfast the next morning… only a slice of whole wheat bread and a glass of water for each of them. And none of the other children were permitted to speak with them for 72 hours.

"Something the matter, Dear?" A rumbling could be heard outside, the signal of a storm brewing.

"No, Mother," Rue answered, "just taking a private stroll down memory lane."

Darwin stood next to her awkwardly. His head felt a little muddled, as if he were standing in the middle of a dream.

After an inordinately long pause, she asked, "Aren't either of you going to sit down?"

"I think I'll stand, if you don't mind, Mother. We won't be long."

"Oh." Frances seemed surprised. "So, this isn't a social visit? How disappointing. I was going to have rooms prepared so that you could both stay the night."

"We definitely won't be staying the night," Rue announced, not realizing that she was now shouting above the rain and thunder that began violently pounding the roof.

"Unfortunately, you may not have a choice," Frances answered.

"You can't keep me here, Mother." Rue growled.

"*I* have no intention of keeping you here." She pointed to the ceiling. "But given the weather, perhaps *He* does." She was, of course, referring to God. "Listen to that storm. The roads here are prone to flooding, and do you really want to be driving on a winding mountain road in this weather? I wouldn't advise it."

She looked at Darwin. "Please have a seat, Mr. Swift. You look very uncomfortable."

Darwin eyed Rue apologetically, really not wanting to be caught between whatever it was that was happening between Rue and her mother. All he knew was that it was big enough where neither woman felt the need to even hug one another nor share more than the most basic of pleasantries upon their reunion.

He finally concluded that he could win more bees with honey, and if they were going to get any information out of Frances, he should attempt to be amenable, particularly if Rue was not. Plus, he was feeling a little groggy and sitting seemed the best option.

As he sat, Frances added, "Or should I call you Darwin Fennec? That is the name you are going by these days, isn't it?" She flashed a devilish smile at him.

"How did you—" Rue began.

"Oh, hush my dear. I'm a mother; I worry. When you left the sanctuary again, in the middle of the night, without telling anyone where you were going, I had to send some of our protectors to find you."

"Protectors?" Rue asked. "Is that what you're calling your prison guards these days?"

"You're being overly dramatic. Are you sure you won't have some tea? It always relaxed you when you were anxious, which —" she laughed as she looked up at Darwin, as if sharing a quaint childhood story, "… was all the time, it seemed."

Darwin didn't laugh. Nor did it escape him that Frances referred to her leaving 'again.' *Exactly how many times had she tried to leave and failed before?* He rubbed his forehead, forcing himself to focus.

"No thank you, Mother. And that was two years ago. Once you'd discovered where I was, which it seems that you clearly did, why did you keep tracking me? You could see that I was alright."

Frances cleared her throat. "If by alright, you mean living in that little hovel of yours and posing nude, then I suppose you were alright—"

"Now she sounds like Spencer," Rue joked to Darwin.

"Well now, that man had potential—"

"What do you know of it?" Rue retorted angrily. "And my hovel was a lot better than the cramped dorm rooms the church had me in."

"Well," Frances explained. "If you had worked your way through the ranks as I did, or not run away when you did, that would have changed." Rue opened her mouth to speak, but after seeing her mother's eyes narrowing as if to challenge her, she closed it again. "After all," her mother continued, turning to Darwin. "Off she went into the night, and on the eve of her wedding—" Frances paused to witness Darwin's surprised expression. She was enjoying this.

"That's enough, Mother," Rue interjected, shooting Darwin a look, as if to say, *"Add this to the things we need to discuss later."* Thunder boomed again as the lights in the room flickered, as if threatening to go out at any moment. "We're here because we need to ask you some questions. But perhaps you already know that, too."

"Questions?" Frances appeared surprised, but it was nearly impossible to tell whether or not she was acting. "Whatever do you mean?"

"Darwin and I are investigating a murder."

"Murder?" Frances' eyebrows lifted in disbelief. "Who was murdered?"

"Erasmus Vandenberg," Rue said loudly, waiting expectantly for a horrified reaction that didn't come. A slight shuffling could be heard on the other side of the door as someone passed by.

"Is that name supposed to mean something to me?" Frances blinked innocently.

Rue repeated his name. "You know... Erasmus Vandenberg... wealthy nutraceutical and vitamin tycoon who made his fortune by largely selling custom-branded products to churches such as yours."

Frances thought a moment. "Oh," she finally answered with a start. "You mean the teas and snacks and such?"

"Yes, Mother," Rue answered blandly. "That's exactly what I mean."

"It's *his* company manufacturing our healthy foods? I had no idea. I always assumed the church made them in house."

"Really?" Rue was suspicious. "You, who know where I live, who I date, and what kind of work I do, and yet you were unaware of who made the 'miracle' foods that you pimp out to the congregation at a pretty penny for cures for everything from arthritis to depression?"

"First of all," Frances corrected, "I resent your suggesting that I'm pimping anything, particularly coming from you. And second, I trust the church and have no reason to look into their business dealings. That's none of my concern."

Rue crossed her arms and all but stamped her foot. "In other words, you don't trust me and... what the hell do you mean by that 'pimping' remark, anyway?"

"Well, you were never known for your sound decisions... except maybe for Spencer, but you screwed that one up, didn't you?"

"He was a liar and a cheat!"

"Judge not, lest thou be judged," Frances retorted.

"That's rich coming from you, one of the most judgmental people I have ever met!"

Darwin sat up, alarmed.

"Keep your voice down, Dear," Frances hushed her daughter. "Noise travels here."

"About the pimping?" Rue couldn't let that one go.

"Just seems odd to me that your boss suddenly became your lover, is all. Is that part of your work arrangement?"

Rue was about to respond, telling her mother exactly what she thought of her when Darwin held out his arm, as if to say, *"Just wait a moment."*

"Frances—" he began.

"I'd prefer it if you addressed me as Deaconess," she replied. Darwin bit back a response. He was beginning to share Rue's sentiment about her mother.

"Deaconess," he tried again. "I am not your daughter's boss. It may have seemed that way at first—" Darwin tried to frame his words carefully. After all, it was Spencer that commissioned him to hire Rue on the pretense of a job to keep her out of the way while he pursued other work and personal interests — a fact that Darwin discovered too late. "But we are currently business partners who run our investigative agency together."

"Oh, is that so?" Frances nodded.

"Yes," Darwin confirmed. "That is so."

"But you are lovers?" Frances asked.

"Darwin and I are dating, Mother," Rue explained. "So, yes. I wouldn't have put it as crudely as you just did. But we are, in fact, intimate."

"Who live together and work together?" she confirmed.

"What does that matter?" Rue demanded.

"It matters not at all… if you don't mind living in sin and potentially being cast out into the Lake of Fire and damned for all eternity."

"With all the murderers, pedophiles, and abusive people in the world, I hardly think any God will give a rat's ass if I, a grown woman, am having sex with my boyfriend out of wedlock."

Darwin cringed. He really didn't enjoy being in the middle

of this. Frances turned to him. "Do you have any intention of marrying my daughter?"

"You don't have to answer that, Darwin," Rue told him.

"But I want to," Darwin replied calmly. "Yes, Deaconess. While it's still early in our relationship, that thought has crossed my mind."

Rue's expression froze, as if someone had just slapped her in the face. She had no idea he was that serious about her, and the thought was both electrifying and terrifying, all at once…the idea of being a Mrs. Fennec. But then her face dropped when she thought about it. *That would make me Rue Fennec or Rue Brennan Fennec. Both of those sound like terrible names!*

"My husband and I married two months after we met," Frances explained to Darwin. "There's nothing wrong with early." After pausing for a moment, she eyed Rue up and down. "Of course, why buy the cow when you can have the milk for free?"

"Am I supposed to be the cow in the scenario?" Rue all but yelled.

"Once again." Frances motioned with her hand to indicate Rue should lower her voice. "Please keep your voice down."

"And may I remind you, Mother," Rue whispered vehemently. "That Father *did* buy the cow *and* still got his milk for free?"

"And you saw where that got him." Frances waved her hand, as if this were old news. "Excommunicated and paying child support for some poor bastard." Frances' eyes drifted away for a moment as she curled her nose distastefully. "Ah well," she returned with a small grin. "He'll get what's coming to him, and at least he brought me two things." She touched Rue's hair in what felt very fake and very forced. "You and the church."

"Mother," Rue said, as she tried returning to the subject at hand. "That's all very sweet, but we still have a crime to solve. Can you help us?"

"I don't see how I can possibly be of any help to you." She eyed the two of them quizzically.

"We have reason to believe that Erasmus Vandenberg's death has something to do with the Church of Infinite Love," Rue stated emphatically.

"Why on Earth would you think that?" Frances asked, surprised.

"Because Erasmus Vandenberg was not only selling large quantities of his nutraceuticals, and protein bars, and vitamins, etc., but he was also a large donor to the church."

"Oh, I hadn't realized he was a member." She thought a moment. "Funny, I've never heard his name mentioned before now."

"Well, he was," Darwin chimed in. "But just a month before he died, he denounced the church and cut off funding. And, we have reason to believe he was trying to cut off all ties with the church, even though it meant giving up Vandenberg Nutraceuticals' most prestigious client."

"The Church of Infinite Love," Frances finished quietly. Rue could see her mother putting connections together in her mind, and it appeared that she was not happy with the results. "That couldn't be—"

Thunder and lightning struck again, and the room went dark. Rue sucked in her breath, realizing that she was having trouble inhaling. She started panting in and out like a small dog overheating in the sun.

"Rue, are you alright?" Darwin stood, knocking his knee against the small table. "Dammit!" He rubbed his knee, which ironically, hadn't been sore before today's service, but now it was. He felt his way through the dark until he reached her, wrapping an arm around her.

"She's fine," Frances answered flatly. "She just gets like that sometimes."

Rue continued to pant rapidly.

"I've never seen her get like this!" Darwin hissed. To Rue, he said calmly, "Slow breaths… calm down. The power went out; that's all."

"We're not… staying… here… tonight," Rue forced out.

"No," Darwin promised. "Definitely not."

"Well, where are you planning on going with weather like this?" Francis was incredulous.

"We'll sleep in the car if we have to," Darwin reasoned. The lights flickered back on. Rue's knees started to buckle under her. Darwin wrapped his other arm around her waist, pulled her up, and drew her tightly into his chest, adrenalin now coursing through his veins, replacing the earlier grogginess. She sank into him, her hands and the side of her cheek pinned against his chest. "Don't worry," he whispered. "I've got you." Rue's breath slowly returned to normal. To Francis, Darwin said, "It's been lovely meeting you, Deaconess. We'll just be going now."

"Rue," she interjected. Rue raised her eyes slowly to meet her mother's gaze. "Do you mean to tell me that you'd feel safer sleeping in a car in a flooded parking lot, during a major storm with dangerous thunder and lightning, instead of a comfortable room, not unlike the home you spent nearly your entire childhood in?"

"Yes, Mother," Rue answered quietly. "That's exactly what I'm suggesting." Their eyes locked for an additional moment. Rue saw a flicker in her mother's eyes. It was the tinge of an emotion she couldn't quite place — at least, not coming from her mother. It almost felt like… regret.

Darwin began guiding Rue carefully to the door. He grasped the knob, only to remember that the door was still locked — from the outside.

"Oh, just a moment, Mr. Fennec." She stood. Frances darted over to the efficiency kitchen and rifled through her cabinets. She plucked two different snack bars from the shelf and walked over to Darwin, quickly stuffing them into his pocket. "In case the two of you get hungry later," she whispered. "The red one is good for energy in the morning. The purple one is best before bed. It has valerian root, used for calming purposes." She held his gaze several seconds longer than necessary. "Both contain very powerful nutrients, so space them out by at least six hours…" Frances deliberated on something before adding, "They're different from the macaroon you ingested earlier. We're not typically supposed to have snacks outside of the common area, but it will be our little secret." Darwin wasn't sure how that explained the miniature kitchen behind her, but nodded, nonetheless. To Darwin she added in a whisper, "The walls have ears."

She then turned to Rue, and said, "You'll come back and visit me again, won't you Rue? After all, you are my only child."

Rue felt a sudden flash of heat, and her heart sped up again, just for a moment. It triggered a memory, the one where she was talking with her friend Midge under the most unpleasant of circumstances. She pushed the thought aside.

Francis pulled on a chord hanging next to the door, summoning the same attendant who, once again, purposefully rapped on the door in her signature pattern.

Frances unlocked it. "Please escort our friends to the front door," she instructed.

"But it's raining cats and dogs out there!" the attendant protested. Maybe the deaconess didn't realize that.

"Then give them an umbrella," Frances responded curtly.

"Yes, Deaconess," the woman replied meekly, biting her lip as if fighting back a response. To Rue and Darwin, she said, "Right this way."

After Darwin made certain that Rue was settled as comfortably as possible in the back seat of their rental car, he climbed into the front, stripping off his suit jacket and shirt.

"Aren't you going to be cold in just an undershirt?" she protested.

"I'll survive," Darwin answered, rolling up the pieces of clothing and tucking them under the front passenger seat side. "Besides," he grinned into the rearview mirror, "I can always climb back there with you if I need to warm up."

Rue forced a groggy smile. The evening was turning out to be cold, damp, and anxiety-producing. She tugged off the itchy wig that was now beginning to lose shape and stick to her cheeks in a damp mess. Rue fluffed her hair underneath and combed it with her fingers.

"Probably best to remove the contacts, too," Darwin reminded, reaching into the center console and retrieving a small contact case. "They're not really meant for long-term use."

A clap of thunder and the boom of a tree getting struck by lightning sent them both jumping toward the ceiling of the car. Darwin nearly dropped the case before Rue snatched it with both palms as he leaned over the backseat.

Rue caught her breath before settling in again, curling up on the seat and wrapping her arms around her for warmth. "Can you put the heat on?" she suggested. "Just for a few minutes?"

"Yeah, I can do that," he agreed. "But we can't leave it running too long or we won't have enough fuel to get back into town in the morning."

"Darwin?" Rue yawned.

"Yes, Rue," Darwin answered.

"Why didn't you tell me you were married?"

"Probably the same reason you didn't tell me you ran away on the eve of your wedding."

After a long pause, Rue asked, "Do you think I'm crazy?"

"No, of course not." Darwin was surprised. "Why would you think that?"

"Well, because of my panic attack, running out on my fiancé, and then disappearing to New York."

"No," Darwin reassured her. "I don't think you're crazy." After a pause, he added, "Why don't you try to get some rest, and we can talk about it during our long ride back to New York in the morning?"

Rue let out a groan as the rain pelted the roof of the car and fogged up the windows. "Darwin?"

"What is it, Rue?"

"Now I really *do* have to go to the bathroom," she whined.

Chapter 18
Long and Winding Road

Present Day in Pennsylvania

Rue was so hungry by morning that she was tempted to eat one of the snack bars her mother had given them. But she couldn't. She knew they were evidence. What she didn't realize was that Darwin had a little evidence of his own tucked under the passenger seat that she now occupied.

"We can stop for a quick bite to eat," Darwin reasoned. "But we have to get these samples to the forensic scientist Ortega recommended. I forget her name—"

"Penelope," Rue offered. "She was on the scene when one of the art models died before my session at the Atelier school." Rue remembered that while Ortega and Dennis were being… well, very stereotypically male and seemingly unfeeling… Penelope had been kind, advocating for Rue. That type of kindness somehow didn't match with her work investigating potential homicides.

"That's right," Darwin nodded. "Penelope."

"But what's the hurry? There are just two snack bars for her to send to the lab to analyze."

"That's not all," he smiled, glancing at her. "Under your seat are the remains of that spilled sugar water on my shirt and a half-eaten macaroon in my suit jacket."

"You devil," Rue laughed, sitting back and shaking her head.

"Oh, you don't know the half of it." He wriggled his eyes suggestively.

"I have some idea," Rue smirked.

After a long silence, with nothing but the sound of the windshield wipers going back and forth, cutting through a light drizzle, Rue finally asked, "So about that marriage?"

"Yours or mine?" Darwin's eyes remained on the road.

"Yours, obviously," Rue answered. "I've never been married."

"Right." Darwin tapped the steering wheel. "So, what would you like to know?"

"Uh, the usual… Who was she? How did you meet? Why didn't you stay married?"

"You're missing one vital question in that," Darwin replied.

"And, what's that?"

"Why we got married in the first place?"

"Well?" Rue motioned for him to continue.

Darwin thought a moment. "I was around twenty-three at the time. She was a bit younger."

"How much younger? What was her name?" Rue interrupted.

"Twenty-one, and why does it matter?"

"Just curious."

"I was in Ireland at the time—"

"Really? Why?" Rue sat up.

"If you'd stop interrupting me, I'll tell you," Darwin chastised.

"Well, excuse me for living," Rue pouted. "Go on."

"Let's just say I had fallen in with some bad people — story for another time. But the point is, I was about to get my proverbial goose cooked were it not for a young lass that took pity on me."

"What did she do?"

"She prevented her very influential father from feeding me to the fishes on a grift gone bad."

"You? And here I thought you were a pillar of society," Rue mocked. "But, that sort of explains Bristol."

Bristol was a contractor Darwin hired periodically for his special skills as a bodyguard, 'project manager,' and getaway car driver. He owned a chop shop in Jersey that posed as a car repair and detail service center. Now married with kids, he appeared to be making a slow transition into respectable living. She was still waiting on the 'origin story' of how he and Darwin met. But, one reveal at a time.

"Well, funny you should mention Bristol," Darwin laughed.

"Why is that?" Rue wanted to know.

"Cuz I married his sister."

"What? How did I not hear about this sooner?" Rue leaned so far forward, she all but hit her head on the windshield.

"Careful," Darwin warned. Rue sat back, folding her arms. After a moment, Darwin relented. "I was orphaned at a young age but discovered I had the gift of gab… managed to support myself by small grifts here and there. By the time I was seventeen, I had several mates working for me."

"Bristol being one of them?" Rue asked.

"Ours was more of a collaboration. Only, we chose the wrong mark."

Rue put the connection together. "The 'mark' being Bristol's dad?"

"Exactly," Darwin confirmed. "The man had more money than God, and we thought if we could nick a bit of it, we'd have enough to flee to America and start a real enterprise."

"Only you got caught."

Darwin nodded. "Only, we got caught. His dad let him off with a warning, but I wasn't about to be so lucky."

"Until Bristol's sister took a shine to you?"

"Er, something like that."

"What does that mean?!"

"It means we sort of had a… thing… before that."

"What kind of 'thing'?" Rue wanted to know.

"C'mon Rue. I was a young lad with nothing in this world who suddenly had this pretty red-head making googly eyes at me. What do you think?"

"Oh." Rue was somewhat disappointed. "I see."

"Don't look so disappointed. That was over two decades ago!" Darwin could sense her doing the math. "I'm forty-four," he finally answered.

Rue shook her head. "How is it that we're living together and still know so little about one another?"

"Maybe neither one of us is particularly proud of our pasts?" Darwin offered.

"Hmmm, maybe," Rue agreed. "But so far, your past sounds far more exciting than mine. So, let's skip ahead to the marriage part."

"Not much to say after that." Darwin confessed. "I was adopted into Bristol's family and became part of a larger grift. Molly got pregnant."

"Her name was… is… Molly?"

"You were right the first time," Darwin sighed, pushing back emotion.

"She's dead?" Rue confirmed.

"Yes. I'll get to that," Darwin paused for several minutes as he swerved carefully down the mountain road toward the Pennsylvania Turnpike. "She got pregnant. We were convinced that getting married was the 'right thing to do,' even though we soon learned that we had almost nothing in common. She had a miscarriage, but we decided to try to give it a go for a few years."

"And then got divorced," Rue confirmed.

"Yes… stayed friends though. It was just one of those things."

"How did she die?"

"Like me, she decided to go it on her own. Only, I wasn't there to save her like she did me. Got in with the wrong crowd… ended up dying of an overdose at age thirty-three."

"Shit, Darwin." Rue folded her arms. "And here I am feeling sorry for my life."

"Yeah, but it didn't need to be that way," Darwin answered. "I mean for Molly, not you. Like you, she was born into the family's… way of thinking. But Bristol and I did our best to protect her. But we were too late."

"I'm sorry," Rue answered quietly.

"Well, the silver lining, if there is one, is that it convinced Bristol that he and I should try using our talents for good. I arrived in the States first, changed my name and set up my business as a private investigator. Been on the straight and narrow ever since… mostly."

"That explains my mother's comment about the 'name you're going by these days.'"

"You caught that, huh?"

"Yup. So, what *is* your name?"

"Could we just leave it as 'Darwin Fennec' for now?"

"Sure," Rue answered.

After another long pause, they approached a roadside diner.

"Wanna grab some breakfast here?" Darwin asked.

"Works for me. I'm so hungry, I could eat a horse."

"I've never heard that expression said where somehow it didn't disgust me," Darwin confessed.

"But eating chicken-fried steak with a side of ham is okay?" Rue challenged.

"I didn't say it was logical," Darwin confessed.

"Besides, you know as well as I do, you're going to settle on granola and yogurt.

"You are probably right, Ms. Brennan," he joked, reverting to a time when they used to refer to one another by their surnames. After parking the car, Darwin and Rue made their way to the entrance of the Red Eagle Diner. He opened the door for her to pass first. "Why, thank you, Mr. Fennec."

"So," Darwin asked when they'd finally slid into a cracked red vinyl booth, "When do I get to hear about the time you skipped out on your fiancé and escaped to New York?"

A waitress wearing a pale blue dress and white apron and bonnet handed them menus. "Howdy folks," she boomed pleasantly. "Start you off with some coffee?"

"Sounds great," Rue answered. After the server had nodded and disappeared, Rue leaned over to Darwin. "Soon. Story for another time?"

Darwin nodded. He felt a little exposed, though he hated to admit it. But then, Rue had just faced her mother, and a cult she tried for years to get away from, and a panic attack that she was embarrassed about and would rather forget.

"Story for another time," Darwin agreed.

The ride back to the city was an uneventful one… until the last leg when they were about three miles shy of the Lincoln Tunnel.

Darwin had been sulking, just a little, about the realization that he knew so little of his now live-in girlfriend. More unsettling was the fact that he had been so forthright about his past, always answered her questions honestly, and yet, when it was Rue's turn, she'd always clam up. Having met her mother and visited the church, he was beginning to understand why, but what would he have to do to earn her trust? *Time,* he thought to himself. *Maybe she just needs a little more time.*

Suddenly, a deer leapt into the road. Surprising for this time of day. Darwin hit the brakes, except the peddle felt mushy, as if he were stepping into mud or melting snow. He swerved, just missing the beast, who — after stopping in terror — seemed to regain its wits and scamper away. Car horns blared as he pulled off the road to avoid getting hit from behind. The car behind him jammed on the brakes while the car in front was smart enough to speed up, avoiding a near collision. Meanwhile, Darwin's rental spun around 180 degrees and stopped roadside, facing the wrong direction. Thanks to last night's storm, the car got stuck in a thick pool of mud. He quickly pulled the key from the ignition and sucked in a breath.

He looked over at Rue, who stared straight ahead of her as if in a trance.

"Rue?" he asked, touching her shoulder. "Are you okay?"

Rue blinked several times before turning her head toward Darwin and muttering, "I hate Pennsylvania."

Chapter 19
Penelope

Somewhere in Brooklyn

It was half-past one when Darwin and Rue finally arrived at forensic scientist Penelope Washburn's Brooklyn apartment complex.

"Sorry," Penelope sniffed as she let the two into her home. "Seems the elevators are chronically out of order in this place."

Rue was used to it from her former life living in a Lower East Side walkup. Darwin, on the other hand, was a little out of breath. "That's okay," he huffed. "Just a reminder that my green smoothies are not going to do my cardio for me."

Penelope didn't understand the comment and decided to nod politely but otherwise ignore it. She shut the door behind them.

It was only from the glow of the hallway light that they could see that her eyes were puffy. She had been crying.

"Are you alright?" Rue asked sympathetically. She, herself, was exhausted from the encounter with her mother and the church, spending all night sleeping in a car, and almost dying in

149

car accident near the Lincoln Tunnel. Frankly, she felt she could really use a shower. But Penelope's worn-out expression pulled Rue out of her own feelings of self-pity.

"Mmm, hmm," she lied. Penelope used the back of her hand to wipe away a few tears. That seemed to bother her, so she darted behind her kitchen counter to grab a paper towel from the roll. She blew her nose, threw the paper towel in a foot-operated trash can, and then quickly washed her hands. Years of collecting data from a crime scene made her highly aware of fingerprints, germs, and why one should not stick one's fingers near their eyes. Just then, the phone above the counter rang. "Excuse me a moment." Penelope grabbed the phone while Rue and Darwin stood awkwardly in the entranceway. Darwin was still holding his balled-up shirt and suit jacket from the church service just the day before.

"I can't talk now, Gareth," Penelope whispered. "I have company." She paused while they could hear the muffled sounds of a male voice on the other end. "None of your darn business. Don't call me again tonight. Goodbye." She hung up the phone, abruptly, despite protests on the other side. Moments later, the phone rang again. Penelope lifted the receiver and quickly hung it up again. Then, she unplugged the phone from the wall.

"Sorry about that, too," Penelope said, eyeing the clothes in Darwin's hands. "Whatcha got for me?"

"A shirt stain from some kind of sugar water, a half-eaten macaroon in the right jacket pocket, and two snack bars from the Vandenberg Nutraceuticals company… any or all of it may be laced with something. What? I don't know."

"Fascinating." Penelope's eyes lit up slightly. Ortega had notified Penelope that Darwin might need to stop by, but she didn't know the details. It was better that way in case she got caught using the crime lab for outside private cases.

Penelope reached under the counter and pulled out what looked like an oversized plastic freezer bag and a pair of blue latex gloves. After putting the gloves on, she pulled open the bag and stood in front of Darwin. "Here, drop them in the bag for me."

He obliged, and she quickly sealed the bag, removed the gloves, and grabbed a permanent marker that was attached by a magnet to the side of her refrigerator. She quickly scribbled a few letters on the bag before setting it on the counter with lightning speed.

"Wow," Rue commented. "Efficient."

"I try to be," Penelope answered modestly. "I'll phone Detective Ortega with the results, if it's all the same to you?"

"That's just fine," Rue answered. "We can check in with him about next steps. In the meantime, thank you for letting us barge into your personal home on your day off. We appreciate the help."

Penelope wasn't risking her neck and her job for them, and they knew it. But, she was ever-polite, nonetheless.

Rue opened the door. "We'll just see ourselves out. Thank you." She motioned for Darwin to go first. Before closing the door, she turned and whispered to Penelope, "Whomever they are, they are an idiot for making you cry and don't deserve you."

It was only then that Penelope recognized Rue. "Wait a moment." She waved a finger into the air. "You were the gal at the Artist Atelier school during our investigation months ago. The one wearing that weird costume… Oh!" The lightbulb went off in her head.

"Yes, few recognize me when I'm not dressed as a scantily clad Electra," Rue joked.

"I knew the name Darwin was familiar when José mentioned it, but I didn't piece it together until just now. Funny—"

"What is?" Rue was curious.

"That you both went from being suspects in a murder investigation to investigating murder." Penelope thought a moment about the irony. "Oh," she finished. "And you're right, Gareth is an idiot who doesn't deserve me." Penelope held her chin up proudly.

Rue didn't know who Gareth was, but she nodded supportively. After all, Penelope seemed the kind sort. And in this world, that breed of human is sometimes hard to find.

A burner phone rang just as Darwin and Rue entered their condo after a harrowing couple of days.

"That was quick," Darwin greeted Bristol pleasantly, as he answered. It was someone from his team who towed Darwin's car after the near-accident in Pennsylvania.

"Who'd you tick off?" was all that Bristol could say in a down-played Irish-turned-New York City accent. "I've seen a lot of funny 'mess with the breaks' situations, but this here was a little too clever for me."

"What do mean by clever?" Darwin wanted to know.

"They didn't slash the brakes. That would be too obvious," Bristol answered. "They drained the brake fluid just enough to where you'd have troubles an hour or so down the line but not immediately, and—"

"And?"

"You did say this was a rental car, right?"

"Right," Darwin confirmed.

"The brake pads are so worn thin they might as well be rice paper. What rental company would send a car out in that condition?" Darwin could feel Bristol shaking his head from the other end of the phone line. Meanwhile, the sound of welding and a chainsaw could be heard in the background. Darwin decided not to ask why.

"So, we're presuming someone messed with the brake fluid and pads while we were attending Rue's old stomping grounds?"

Bristol let out a huff loudly into the receiver. "It's an easy enough job - they probably only needed an hour or so, tops.

Whoever did this, well, if they didn't wanna kill ya, they certainly wanted you messed up a bit."

"Well, thank you, Bristol. Do I need to come and get the car to take it back to the rental agency?"

"Nah!" Bristol answered, as the sound of grinding in the background continued. "I'll take care of it for ya."

"I don't know what that means, Bristol," Darwin answered.

"Probably best that way," Bristol answered, hanging up the phone before Darwin could ask any more questions.

Moments later, the phone rang a second time… It was Ortega.

"Please tell me your day is going better than mine," Darwin greeted.

"Why? What happened?" Ortega demanded.

Now out of harm's way and safely back at their condo, Darwin filled Ortega in on the day, ending with their near-accident.

"Shit!" Ortega answered. "I don't like this. I don't like this at all."

"I wasn't too fond of the idea of dying either," Darwin joked.

"Want me to make some calls at the precinct?" Ortega offered.

"Absolutely not," Darwin answered. "Ever since you and Officer Dennis left, we've been hitting nothing but brick walls. Between the Church of Infinite Love and the Vandenberg Family, the two seem to have their fingers in many pies. Seems hard to find support from law enforcement in Pennsylvania and New York."

Ortega sighed. "Running into the same deal in Florida," Ortega confessed. "But I've got a few tricks up my sleeve. You and Rue need to lie low for a couple of days. I'll follow up as soon as I a can."

"What are you going to do?" Darwin asked, before catching himself. "Never mind, don't tell me. Probably shouldn't have had told you as much as I did over the phone." Time for Darwin to bust another burner phone and set up a replacement. While security on cell phone calls had gotten better over the past year, he still wasn't taking too many chances.

There was a long pause on the line. Darwin could hear Ortega breathing unsteadily.

"You okay?" Darwin asked.

"Uh, yeah," Ortega answered. "Listen, I have a favor to ask outside of the case. Do you mind?"

Darwin was intrigued. Ortega wasn't one to ask for help and was somewhat flattered that he trusted him for it. Finally, he answered, "What do you need?"

Chapter 20
Ortega and Nancy

Back in Florida

Nancy arrived home to witness her husband slamming the house phone down, only to pick it up and slam it down a second time.

"Rough day?" Nancy asked, swinging her tennis racket slightly from side to side.

Ortega began to pace angrily. "I used to be able to snap my fingers and get what I needed to do my job. Now that I'm retired, it's like I'm invisible and powerless. I have to ask 'Mother, May I?' for every blessed thing!"

She glanced at the cell phone on the counter quizzically. "So, you're resorting to violently attacking our landline?"

"Somehow, pushing the little button on the cell phone is not as satisfying when you're trying to hang up on someone," Ortega huffed. "Call it… catharsis."

"Oh, I'd call it something all right," Nancy chuckled. "But that wouldn't be the 'c' word I'd have chosen."

"I'm sorry, Honey." Ortega gave Nancy a peck on the lips. "How was your day?"

"Obviously, better than yours," Nancy retorted. "This is why I didn't want you wrapped up in detective work anymore. Look at what it does to you."

"I couldn't tell Officer Dennis 'no,' not after all our work together."

"Bullshit," Nancy answered. "I could see the gleam in your eye the other day on that video call. You were champing at the bit to get back into solving crimes."

"Is that so terrible?" Ortega challenged. "I was actually a useful, productive member of society before moving to Florida. Now I'm just—"

"My husband?" Nancy offered. "Maybe if you were a little more social… volunteered somewhere—"

"But this is what I love," Ortega protested.

"Can't you try loving something else, for once?" Nancy all but yelled, before catching herself. She set down the racket, defeated. "Fine."

"What do you mean, 'fine'?" Ortega asked angrily.

"Tell me about your case." Nancy waved her hand at him.

"I told you. It's not my case. I'm just helping Officer—"

"Tell me about your case," Nancy tried again. "You're up to your eyeballs in it. So, what's the problem?"

Ortega paused for several moments, assessing whether she was serious. Finally, he answered, "Might want to have a seat." Ortega guided his wife over to the couch, where files were strewn everywhere on the coffee table in front of him.

Ortega took the next half hour getting Nancy up to speed on everything he knew so far. When he was finished, he waited, expecting Nancy's eyes to be glazed over with boredom. But it was just the opposite. She had a fire in them the likes of which he'd never seen before.

"I can help you," Nancy proclaimed suddenly.

"Come again?" Ortega was certain he'd misheard her.

"I can help you," she grinned from ear to ear. "Our next step is to snoop around Vandenberg Nutraceuticals, right? We can ask my father. I'm sure he's got connections with someone there—"

"No," Ortega shook his head fervently. "We're not dragging your father into this. Besides, it's got to be undercover, otherwise, they'll just hide the evidence before we get there." Suddenly, Ortega realized something. "And what's this 'we' all of a sudden."

"If you're not going to take an interest in my life, then, let me take an interest in yours." Ortega was about to protest both her involvement in the case and the fact that she'd assumed he had no interest in her day-to-day goings on. She held up a hand, "I'm not taking 'no' for an answer, José." After a dramatic pause, she added, "I can go undercover."

"What?! No you can't!" Ortega barked.

"Why not? I did a little theater in college."

"Did a little theater in college? Nancy, would you listen to yourself?" Ortega stood, and went back to pacing across the living room floor. "There's been a murder—"

"*Alleged* murder," she corrected him.

"Pretty sure it was murder." He tilted his head, sideways. *Alleged my ass*, he thought. "And you're not a trained agent!"

"But it seems that since Officer Dennis can't get the New York or Florida police departments to look in on the case, trained agents are in short supply, wouldn't you say?" Nancy raised an eyebrow, the one she always raised when she knew she had won.

"And if I did enlist your services, how exactly do you plan on getting in?"

"Well, you said yourself," Nancy rummaged through his files, pulling up one that outlined a map of the Vandenberg factory and security procedures for getting in and out of the place, "someone has to go in undercover. Perhaps a new employee? I can do that."

"When have you ever work—" Ortega caught himself under Nancy's fiery gaze. She hadn't ever had a traditional job, from what he could tell. Ortega was her third husband. Nancy had gone right from graduate school to marriage and motherhood, volunteered here and there, but she always had her father's money and two exes who made significantly more than Ortega ever did. Both paid her a decent settlement to end their marriages quietly and without media attention. Frankly, Ortega wasn't sure why Nancy had even picked someone like him in the first place. He certainly didn't fit into any of her social circles, something that had become increasingly evident with their move to Florida.

Ortega tried a different tactic. "You'd be willing to perform tedious factory work for eight hours a day, for an indeterminate amount of time, just to potentially dig up clues?"

"I know what's going on in that brain of yours, Honey. And yes, I am fully capable of handling a job. Plus, it sounds exciting! I've never worked on a case with you before!"

"Yeah, well it's not nearly as romantic as you think it is," Ortega reasoned.

"Well, you seem to love it," Nancy retorted.

"And, how do you suggest we get you past security with any recording devices or tracking equipment?" Ortega asked. "Even if we manage to get you on the payroll, you'd have to go in clean." *Once Nancy makes up her mind about something,* he thought to himself, *there's no changing it.* One of the things he loved the most about her was her fierce determination and strength. Unfortunately, also, on occasion, these were traits that he liked the least.

"Don't you worry about that." Nancy winked, standing and tossing his thinning hair as he paced by her. "I've got a plan. Theater, remember?"

"Yeah, no problem, Jo," Dennis told Ortega, who phoned the officer not long after his conversation with Nancy. "Let's plan on meeting here tomorrow, if that works for the two of you. Say, 8:00?"

Dennis heard a quiet shuffle behind him as he assumed that Emma had returned from a grocery store run. The two were pleasantly surprised to find that waiting in the garage at their new residence was one of Erasmus' 'old' cars, a sleek, shiny black Porsche 959. But this one had a customized upgrade… an automatic transmission. He was surprised he hadn't heard the garage door open or the rev of the car's engine, but he had been a little distracted today.

Dennis listened to Ortega's remarks on the other end of the phone line, nodding to no one but himself as he moved around the house, visiting each indoor plant with a watering can. "I agree. We need to send someone in undercover, but I'm hesitant to use civilians. Let's talk about it tomorrow. Maybe, then, we'll get closer to understanding what really happened to Erasmus."

Dennis ended the call, tucking the cell phone in his pocket and setting the can above the kitchen sink. He swung around and all but body slammed Sprightly, who stood right behind him with a fabricated grin plastered on her face that didn't match the concern in her eyes.

"What really happened to Erasmus?" Sprightly asked.

"Sprightly, how long have you been here?" Dennis enquired.

"For about three minutes," Sprightly answered honestly. "Right about the part where you said you needed to investigate Vandenberg Nutraceuticals to get to the bottom of Erasmus' death."

"Well, I'm sorry you heard that, but you shouldn't go sneaking up on people. What are you doing here, anyway?" Dennis demanded.

Then he saw her, a small woman standing silently in the open doorway… Elsbeth.

"Have you guys met?" Sprightly motioned toward the girl in the doorway and then to Dennis.

"Yes," Dennis answered. "Elsbeth, nice to see you again." He began grinding his teeth nervously. To Sprightly, he said between grit teeth, "Sprightly, remind me that you and I need to discuss your letting yourself in and out of the house unannounced. That may have been okay before, but it's not okay now."

"Roger that," Sprightly saluted unapologetically. "But it seems Elsbeth is here for the same reason you're having a meeting tomorrow."

"Is that so?" Dennis asked cautiously.

"Yes," Elsbeth answered simply. "S… s… someone m… murdered Grandfather Erasmus. And, I'm here t—t-to help find out who."

Dennis was taken aback by her response. Far from the timid young woman he met at the reading of Erasmus's will, this one appeared like a solid block of granite at his doorstep. She had clearly set her intentions and would not be moved.

A car could be heard coming up the drive, followed by the electric whirring of a garage door opening. Moments later, Emma appeared carrying two large brown paper bags.

Sprightly immediately went to retrieve them from her. "I coulda gone shopping for your, Emma. But I was picking up—"

"Elsbeth?" Emma was surprised. "What are you doing here?"

"Nice to s… see you, too," she mumbled. At that moment, the facade broke, and the girl began sniffing back tears.

"Oh, Elsbeth," Emma's voice softened. While not as good at the whole touchy-feely thing as Dennis, she rushed to the girl's side, wrapping her in an awkward hug that was not returned by Elsbeth, who valued her personal space. This hug was not on her terms. Elsbeth stood there coldly, save for a single tear that trickled down her cheek. Eventually, Emma caught on, smiled awkwardly, and released the girl.

"As I was saying," Sprightly set the bag on the kitchen counter, "I would have gone shopping for you, but I got a call from Ferdinand about picking up Elsbeth from the airport."

Emma looked around the young woman. "Elsbeth?" she asked. "If you just flew in, where is your luggage?"

"On it!" Sprightly circled a finger in the air as if whipping up some magic. "Got it in my car."

Emma had wondered who was driving the unsightly beater car sitting to one side at the end of the driveway. She'd almost hit it accidentally when turning, with great speed, heading toward their garage. Emma was having a little too much fun with her newly acquired vehicle.

"Elsbeth, why don't you sit down in the living room and I'll get you something to drink. An iced tea, perhaps?"

"Got any vodka?" she asked abruptly, gently wiping her eyes with her fingertips.

"Well, no," Emma answered.

"Too bad," Elsbeth replied, marching into the living room and sitting on the edge of one of the couches.

Moments later, Sprightly returned with her single bag. "Shall I put this in one of the spare bedrooms?" she asked.

"Uh, yes," Dennis chimed in quickly. "The first one on the left, just next to the main bedroom." He didn't want her wandering into his room at the far end of the hall, lest she, for one thing, see how messy he was, and secondly, notice that he and Emma were sleeping in separate bedrooms. He had a reputation to uphold... for some reason.

"Sure thing," Sprightly called, as she made her way down the hall. "By the way, I'm in!"

"In?!" Dennis called back. "In for what, exactly?"

Sprightly bounced back in the room. "The coup you're planning at the factory. I'll go undercover for you. No problem."

Emma and Dennis glanced first at Sprightly, then at each other, and then at Elsbeth, who was now eyeing them all with odd fascination. She saw Dennis and Emma exchange glances once more.

"I know w-w-hat you're thinking," Elsbeth answered. "I m-might be a s… suspect. But if you w-w-ant to get into that f… factory, you are going t… to have t… to t… trust m… me."

Chapter 21
The Plan

Florida

It was almost as if the word "ragtag" was invented after seeing Ortega's team gathered at Emma and Dennis's residence the morning before their 'factory coup.' Sprightly was the first to arrive, wearing a paisley-patterned, spaghetti-strap dress and flip-flops. She also donned a hat and sunglasses, furtively looking around, as if to make sure no one in the neighborhood noticed her arrival, even though her telltale blue bicycle was sitting out front.

"Coffee?" Dennis offered, once Sprightly had made her way to the living room inside their home.

"No thanks." Sprightly rocked back and forth on her heels, excitedly. "Makes me too jittery."

Ortega arrived with Nancy next. Dennis had only met Nancy in person, briefly, on two occasions, one was at a station Christmas party thrown when Ortega was still a detective with the precinct. The other was the time she stopped by their station to drop off Ortega's lunch one day. (Though many suspected it was really so she could see what Penelope, Ortega's old flame, looked like.) She has gained a bit of weight since he first met her several years ago. Her hair was also now dyed a dark red and cut short.

"Nice to see you again, Mrs. Ortega," Dennis greeted. "Coffee?"

"No thanks," Nancy answered. "We brought our own." She held up a thermos that was hiding behind her back. "And you can call me Nancy."

"Decaf," Ortega whispered to Dennis, shaking his head sourly.

"I heard that!" Nancy answered. "Caffeine isn't good for your nerves. You're lucky I don't make you drink herbal tea."

At that moment, Emma made her way down the hallway carrying a small plate of cookies.

Ortega almost didn't recognize her. Her usual sweatshirt and jogging pants had been replaced with a short-sleeved red blouse and flair skirt that covered her knees. Her hair was now a curly bleach blonde that she somehow pulled off despite her olive complexion. Emma still wore red running sneakers though, he noticed.

"Nice house," he said absentmindedly.

Nancy hit him in the arm. "Where are your manners?" To Emma, she said, "I'm Nancy Ortega. It's nice to meet you."

"Likewise," Emma greeted. "Won't you sit down?" The words felt funny coming from her mouth. She'd never had enough furniture to invite guests to sit down... or to even entertain.

"Are we waiting on anyone else?" Nancy asked.

As if on cue, Elsbeth arrived in the room, appearing almost out of thin air. Nancy was taken aback. Despite her small frame, it was almost as if Elsbeth was a vacuum and could suck the energy out of the room just by her presence. Today, she wore an all-black blouse and slacks, a stark contrast to her excessively pale complexion.

"Everyone, this is Elsbeth Ions, granddaughter of Erasmus Vandenberg," Emma quickly introduced her.

"Elsbeth, why don't you have a seat next to Nancy?" Emma suggested. With the stealth of a ghost or quiet ninja, she floated across the room and sat down. Nancy was confused by Elsbeth, looking to her husband for clarity. Ortega seemed unaffected by the woman's odd behavior. Nancy sighed. Ortega seemed emotionally unaffected by lots of things. So, there she sat, with Elsbeth to her left and Ortega to her right. *I'm surrounded by emotionally unavailable people*, Nancy thought. *Story of my life.*

"Shall we begin?" Dennis offered pleasantly, standing at the front of the room. "Jo, do you want to lead this or should we?" He motioned to Emma, who had been leaning up against the wall, arms folded. She stood upright, taken aback. She wasn't used to being a 'we' and wasn't entirely certain how she felt about it. Meanwhile, Ortega cringed at his new nickname. *Surely Officer Dennis could come up with something better?* He thought.

Ortega was used to leading, barking orders for everyone else to follow. Frankly, he was surprised Dennis had even questioned who was in charge. But then, he was retired now, and one sidelong glance at Nancy reminded him that she was only there trying to be supportive but wasn't really keen on him taking a case. This was a departure from her excitement just yesterday. Ortega was beginning to recognize that, after more than a decade of marriage, he didn't seem to know Nancy very well at all.

"Why don't you kick it off, Dennis," Ortega finally answered. "And, I can just fill in where necessary."

"Uh, okay," Dennis was surprised. "So, Elsbeth arrived yesterday insistent on…" Dennis reconsidered his words, "… convinced that her grandfather's death was suspicious, and she wants to help use her influence as a member of the Vandenberg family to get her and Emma inside."

"They're… h… h… hiding… s… s… something," she stammered. Elsbeth shook her head and pounded a fist into her thigh. Nancy raised an eyebrow but said nothing.

"It's okay, Elsbeth," Emma jumped in, sensing the girl's frustration that her stutter had returned. "You're just upset. We all are."

Dennis continued, "With Emma being a key shareholder, it makes sense that she'd want a tour of the facility. But it's going to be hard to convince them of that without a team of lawyers present."

"Which would make it nearly impossible for us to carry out a normal investigation," Ortega added.

"Exactly," Dennis agreed. "But, as Elsbeth pointed out to us upon her arrival, they know her. If she asks for a tour, they may be more inclined to accommodate the request and let their guard down."

"So, what's your plan?" Ortega asked.

"Well," he looked at Emma. "Why don't you tell him?"

"I found out from Mr. Lundy, Erasmus' lawyer — now *my* lawyer, as it turns out — that the three key players at the factory are Baxter Baker, the general manager who is now absent until further notice—"

"What happened to him?" Nancy asked, sitting up as if alarmed.

"He said he had to disappear for a little while. I suspect it had to do with the fact that he was trying to warn us about Erasmus' death not being an accident," Emma answered.

"Oh." Nancy leaned back into the couch. "Right," she chastised herself. That was in yesterday's brief. *Remembering all these details is harder than I thought,* Nancy mused.

"The next two are Victor Newberry, vice-president of operations, and Mordechi Sanzani, chief operating officer. Mordechi is reportedly out of town on business this week; but we'll still have to skirt around Victor Newberry."

"How do you plan to do that?" Ortega asked.

Elsbeth smirked devilishly, "I can handle Uncle Victor. Don't worry." Oddly enough, the stutter was momentarily gone.

"Where do we come in?" Sprightly was dying to know.

"First," Emma replied, "Elsbeth and I visit the factory tomorrow. We're fairly confident we can get Victor's okay between Elsbeth's family connection and the threat of me bringing lawyers, if he doesn't play nice. We don't entirely know what we're looking for yet…"

"Anything linking Vandenberg Nutraceuticals with questionable products being shipped to the Church of Infinite Love," Dennis chimed in. "Not entirely sure I'm buyin' it that everything that left that factory was on the up and up and ingredients were added later. Else, why would Erasmus be so upset?"

"Plus, Darwin Fennec phoned to give us an update on what his friend Monique found," Emma chimed in.

"What?" Ortega was almost offended. "Darwin called… you?" He'd never been sidelined before. And while he'd protested up and down to Nancy that it was Dennis' case, he really didn't expect Darwin to share with Dennis first. *But then,* he reasoned to himself, *it was pretty obvious from that call that Nancy had been purposefully kept in the dark about the details. Maybe in his strange way, he was trying to protect our marriage?*

Nancy, Sprightly, and Elsbeth all tilted their heads at once, like curious puppies, waiting for the update.

"That's right," Dennis answered uncomfortably. "It seems there were three deaths linked to the church within the past decade — all young women whose stories vanished as soon as they hit the news. It was amazing Monique found what she did."

Emma, suddenly remembering, darted from the room, returning later with manila envelopes, handing one to Nancy, one to Sprightly, and one to Elsbeth. "Inside are newspaper copies of the news stories. You can read up on the women before you visit the factory."

"So, we *are* going to get to do some sleuthing." Sprightly rubbed her hands together, excitedly.

"Don't get so excited," Dennis answered. "I'm still not keen on sending civilians in to do an officer's job. It just so happens that I can't get anyone at the precinct to believe me—"

"I think they believe you, Dennis," Ortega answered. "They just don't care."

"Money talks in this town," Dennis nodded. Then, noticing the known-to-be well off Nancy, he cleared his throat awkwardly before continuing. "We're hoping Elsbeth and Emma can do a cursory search. And, if makes sense, we'd like to send you, Nancy, and you, Sprightly, in for a few days as factory workers. We'd set you up as new hires and give you back stories."

"How exciting!" Sprightly bounced up and down in her chair.

"Unless you give yourself away," Elsbeth answered flatly. "Then, you're dead."

Sprightly stopped bouncing.

"All we're asking you to do," Emma explained, "is go through a typical day. You're not asking questions, not rifling through anything. You'll just share what you observe, if anything."

"So, how are you going to get us in?" Nancy asked logically. "Do you have access to company IDs?"

"That's what we still have to find out," Emma answered. "Let's regroup after Elsbeth and I do the rounds tomorrow."

"What do you think, Jo?" Dennis asked.

"Frankly," Ortega answered, "I think it's a terrible plan. I don't like the idea of sending this girl," Ortega motioned toward Sprightly, "and my wife into that factory. I'd much rather you send me in to go undercover first."

"No can do, Jo," Dennis answered. "One, you've been on too many high-profile cases that have gotten international attention, and two… all of their factory workers are either boys, between the ages of fourteen and seventeen, or women."

"You mean there's not a single adult male in that factory? What about Victor and Mordechi?"

"They don't count. They are executives in the company."

"I see; so why is it that there are no men actually working on the production line?"

"Good question," Dennis answered. "But look at the photos in the news stories we provided." He pulled one out and pointed. "Get a magnifying glass for a closer look… see any men there?"

"Well, I'll be—" Ortega scratched his head. "This whole case is getting weirder by the minute."

"Good thing you have us." Nancy put a hand on her husband's knee and shot an excited glance toward Sprightly. To Ortega, she added, "Don't worry, Honey. I was best in my class at improv."

"I still think this is a terrible idea," Ortega complained.

Chapter 22
Factory

Florida

Victor Newberry seemed visibly surprised when a female attendant escorted Emma and Elsbeth into his office first thing on a Monday morning.

"They're here about the tour sir," she explained sheepishly. Her gaze fell toward the floor.

"Elsbeth, how nice to see you" He plastered on a fake smile as he quickly closed the ledger he had open on his desk.

"H… h… hello, Uncle Victor," Elsbeth answered softly, shrinking behind Emma. Her behavior was so strange… confident around some people and a shrinking violet among others.

Victor eyed Emma up and down before holding her gaze intently. Whereas Baxter had a modicum of charm about him, something about Victor's gaze was somehow… letch-y. Victor was a rotund man with a double chin. He stood to greet them, his tall form towering over the women.

Elsbeth shrank a little further.

"And who is this charming young lady you have with you,

Elsbeth?" He took one of Emma's hands and cupped it between his two sweaty palms. It took everything in her power not to pull away. Instead, she smiled sweetly. "I'm Emma Post. Nice to meet you."

He dropped her hand. Victor's eyes darkened for a moment before he recovered his plastered-on smile. "Not the Emma Post who was left the entire Vandenberg fortune?"

"Not the entire fortune," Emma corrected.

"But enough," he grumbled.

"Uncle Victor," Elsbeth spoke softly. "I w… w… wanted to sh… show E… m.. ma the f… factory where Uncle Erasmus worked."

Victor paused for an unbearably long time, as if deciding to be in a sour mood or a sweet one. He tried settling on sweet. "You know that I'm not really Elsbeth's uncle," he explained, smiling coyly, as if Elsbeth weren't standing right in front of him. "But Erasmus began bringing her here on business trips. I have fond memories of little El running around with her pigtails and t-shirts with horses on them."

"Unicorns," Elsbeth corrected flatly.

"Yes, that's right," he smiled. "Unicorns. While not a Vandenberg myself, I like to think I'm an honorary member of the family." Emma smiled politely but said nothing. To Elsbeth, Victor said, "My dear girl. Don't you remember? We give tours on Tuesdays, not Mondays."

Elsbeth scratched her head absentmindedly. "Oh, that's right. Well, could you m… make an exception for Em… mm.. a s… since she's c… come all this way?"

There was something inconsistent about Elsbeth's speech patterns, but Emma couldn't quite figure out what it was. Instead, she turned her attention to Victor.

"Or," Emma suggested, "we could look around ourselves. We promise not to be in the way."

"No, that won't be necessary," Victor answered quickly. "Given that you're a shareholder and have traveled all this way to be here, let me see what I can do." He picked up the phone on his desk and hit the intercom button.

"Celia? Could you come in here, please?" The same attendant who escorted them into Victor's office returned.

"Yes, Mr. Newberry?"

"I'd like you to give my adopted niece, Elsbeth, and her friend Emma a private tour. Could you do that, please?"

It did not escape Emma's attention that he was both distancing himself *from*, and ingratiating himself *with*, the Vandenberg family, at the same time, while also diminishing Emma's position within the company, by referring to her as simply 'Elsbeth's friend.'

He's a special kind of chauvinist. Emma thought to herself but said nothing.

"Of course, Mr. Newberry," Celia answered, bowing her head slightly. After a long pause, she asked, "Now?"

"Yes, now would be perfect," he smiled, lips pursed like a cat that just ate the canary. "Now, if you don't mind, I'm very busy. But Celia will take care of you. You girls have fun." He used his fingertips to physically push Emma and Elsbeth on their backs, just between their shoulder blades, as if guiding them to evacuate his office as quickly as possible.

Once the three women were on the other side of the door, he closed it. Emma heard a loud 'click' as Victor locked them out. Next to the door was a thin glass window. Before he could turn his back on them, Elsbeth waved cautiously at him. He bent over, waving his fingers back at her. "Bye!" he could be heard saying, as he backed away.

Celia cleared her throat. She stood there, knees and ankles pressed together tightly. She was wearing a gray polyester skirt and a cream-colored blouse. Pantyhose covered her legs. Her shoes were a simple black with uncomfortable looking points on them. It was only then that Emma realized something. Celia, while polished in every other way, wasn't wearing any makeup.

That's odd, Emma thought. *I know I'm not terribly keen on the stuff, but most professional women seem pretty hung up on having their appearance 'just so.'*

"Right this way," Celia invited pleasantly. "Let me give you a brief history of the Vandenberg legacy," she began. Celia launched into Erasmus Vandenberg's early days of being a self-made man who 'pulled himself up by his bootstraps' to make a name for himself, even though he came from a family of potato farmers. At varying points during Celia's tour, Elsbeth could be seen mouthing Celia's words, metered almost exactly to Celia's speech patterns. It was uncanny… and made it clear that Elsbeth had heard this tour… a lot.

They took the stairs, not the elevator, to the lower factory floor. Celia said it was because they valued physical activity for better health. Emma wondered why, if they were so concerned about physical health, Celia was forced to go up and down the steps wearing close-toed, heeled shoes certain to cause lower back pain and hip and knee issues. But, Emma decided, maybe that was a choice, given that all the factory workers seemed to be wearing the same ugly gray pant and v-neck shirt combination. On their feet were thick black orthopedic sneakers.

Unlike the upstairs carpeted area, the floor here felt springier, like something someone would find on a running track. Emma bounced lightly.

"Synthetic rubber," Celia offered. "That's the spring you're feeling. Better than concrete when having to be on one's feet or walking back and forth for long periods of time."

The room appeared to be a giant warehouse, with assembly lines carved out, some for using machinery to assemble the packaging for products, others to systematically churn the ingredients for snack bars before sending them on the conveyor belt to the baking area. While parts of the work were manual, a large percentage of the factory consisted of specialized areas where a worker would repeat the same task, over and over.

It was as if Celia could read Emma's mind. "The difference between the use of specialized machinery and manual labor is that the product efficiency and output is one hundred times faster than if someone were to do everything by hand."

They paused by a woman who was busy loading macaroon wracks into a heating unit.

"Sounds… mind-numbing," Emma admitted.

"It's honest work," Celia smiled sweetly. "And purposeful work."

"How do you figure?" Emma asked blandly.

"We make the world a healthier place by feeding its people nutrient-rich foods they might not otherwise, normally, get in their diet. Our factory workers understand that, while their job might not *feel* glamorous, their work is very meaningful and important."

Emma searched Celia's face for sincerity. Somehow, Celia appeared to believe her own hype.

"Don't touch that!" Celia suddenly called out, just as Elsbeth was fingering the lever on one of the conveyors. Elsbeth quickly drew her hand back as several factory workers looked up from their tasks. "I'm sorry for yelling," Celia apologized. "But we have a well-oiled system in place. Any disruptions could put production back for weeks."

"Sorry," Elsbeth said absently. Emma was fairly certain that she didn't mean it.

They passed a sign that read 'Research and Development.'

"What's that about?" Emma asked.

"Oh," Celia answered, brushing past the sign and the hallway leading toward a different wing within the factory. "That's our R&D department, where they test out new recipes, do market research, and bring new product to market."

"Fascinating," Emma lied. "Can we see it?"

"Oh, I'm afraid that's not part of the tour." Celia shook her head.

"Even for a primary shareholder in the company?" Elsbeth suddenly chimed in. Celia was taken aback.

Finally, she answered, pursing her lips, "I'd have to run this by Mr. Sanzani. But, unfortunately, he's not here today."

"Then, he'll never know," Elsbeth tried again.

"Sorry, no," Celia was adamant.

At the end of the hall was a supply closet. The door was open, revealing stacks of folded uniforms and what appeared to be name tag holders on lanyards.

"Can I t-t-take t-t-two uniforms for Halloween?" Elsbeth asked suddenly.

"Hallow—" Celia was confused. "Sorry, no. And Halloween is a long way off."

Elsbeth pouted, shrinking behind Emma for the second time today. Emma took the cue.

"Celia," she leaned in, as if sharing a secret, "Elsbeth has been having a rough time adjusting to her grandfather's death. Any chance you can check with Victor and see if he might allow her a uniform… as a way of remembering Erasmus?"

"Two uniforms," Elsbeth corrected. "We need a s… slightly bigger one, too, s… so Ruth can take me trick-or-treating."

"You seem a little… old… to be trick-or-treating." Celia eyed her curiously. "And, Halloween is the Devil's work, if you ask me." She held her chin up, haughtily.

"We didn't a… ask you," Elsbeth pouted. "I'll a-a-ask Uncle Victor m-m-myself."

Suddenly, Celia's face dropped. She couldn't very well have Mr. Mayberry's adopted niece upset, now, could she? "Wait here a moment. I'll just check."

As Celia made her way to a nearby intercom, Elsbeth snagged two lanyards from the closet with red stripes across the place where name badges are slipped inside. She hid one in each of the pockets of her dress and returned to the hallway. She held up a finger to her lips as a caution to Emma as Celia returned.

"It seems that Victor has approved you to take two uniforms in whatever size you like, as long as you don't bother him again while he's trying to work."

Elsbeth grinned proudly, rushing into the closet to retrieve one small and one medium-sized women's uniform. "Which ones are w-w-women's sizes versus m—m-men's," she called loudly.

"Oh, they're all women's sizing," Celia confirmed.

"That's odd," Emma observed. "Don't men work in the factory?"

Apparently, Celia had an answer for this, too. She motioned for them to keep walking… conveniently toward one of the doors marked, 'exit.'

"Oh, they do, but they typically hold higher positions."

"Why is that?" Emma asked innocently.

Celia let out a knowing sigh. "I know, you're probably one of those feminists who feel like men and women are equal in every way."

Emma bit back her initial response. "And you don't feel that way?"

Elsbeth had a look of death across her face and hovered behind Emma like a vulture. She even slunk her shoulders forward and tilted her head downward like the carnivorous bird.

"Of *course* men and women… are equally important in the eyes of God." *Oh shit,* Emma thought. She hadn't realized she'd stepped into Jesus land. Emma bit her lip. "But most of the women here are either single gals just working until they find a good husband to care for them, single mothers whose husbands have died or abandoned them, or empty-nesters looking for purpose in their lives now that their children are grown."

"And which one are you?" Emma asked.

Celia was obviously *not* prepared for this question. She lowered her head, unnerved. "If you must know, it just so happens that I had a child out of wedlock. But Mr. Mayberry saw something special in me, took me under his wing. Through hard work, I rose to the ranks of executive assistant."

"That's… wonderful," Emma smiled politely. She tried, but Emma lacked the acting chops to pull it off. Celia became distracted a moment by something along the assembly line. Behind her back, Elsbeth pretended to stick her finger in her mouth as if about ready to vomit. Emma reached around her back and attempted to slap Elsbeth's hand from her mouth. The young woman glared at her but stopped gesturing. Celia's attention returned to them with the slightest hint of impatience crossing her face.

"Where will you go from here?" Emma mused. "From executive assistant to—"

"Wife, if I'm luck," Celia smiled dreamily.

"I was going to say, chief executive officer," Emma finished.

"Oh, no." Celia shook her head as if Emma were daft as a dodo bird. "Women are the nurturers and mothers. We don't have the same minds as men to handle the stress of all that—" she fought for the right words.

"Information? Power? Responsibility?" Emma threw out a few guesses.

"Information," Celia finished, nodding. "Our wisdom is different from a man's." She waited for Emma and Elsbeth to agree with her. Both women began eyeing the exit door with extreme interest.

"Celia," Emma finally said. "You've been so kind. We couldn't possibly take any more of your time. Perhaps Elsbeth and I can show ourselves out?"

"Thank you for your understanding." Celia nodded. "I *am* quite busy." She walked to the door and pressed hard on the bar lever that opened up to the parking lot.

Suddenly, Elsbeth turned to Celia. "Thank you… C… Cousin… C… Celia," Elsbeth stammered, wrapping her arms around the woman in an uncharacteristic show of affection. Celia was taken aback, patting the young woman cautiously on the back. "You must be a wonderful mother," she sniffed.

Elsbeth could feel Celia's body soften as the woman embraced the girl.

"Bless you, Child," Celia whispered.

Elsbeth wiped her downwardly cast eyes as they made their way to their car. Both Elsbeth and Emma felt the heat of the Florida humidity as it smacked them in the face. Emma was growing accustomed to the temperature, but Elsbeth swatted at the air as if she felt her muggy surroundings were trying to attack her.

Celia let the one-way door slam, effectively locking the women out of the factory.

Elsbeth smiled. There it was again, that Cheshire cat-like grin.

"What is it?" Emma asked.

It was only when they'd reached their car, where Sprightly was waiting behind the wheel, with feet up on the dashboard and eyes closed as she leaned into the seat, that Elsbeth flashed it… Celia's badge. "Might help us recreate what we need to get Sprightly and Nancy in this week."

At the sound of her name, Sprightly sat upright, lowering her legs. "Musta dozed off, but I'm ready!" she assured them, as Emma and Elsbeth clamored into the sports car. Elsbeth and Emma had many skills, but having lived in Manhattan for so long, driving wasn't one of them. Emma realized that the moment she almost took out Sprightly's car in the drive just two days prior. For this longer journey, she enlisted the help of Sprightly, who was only too happy to chauffeur them in Emma's Porsche.

"You little devil." Emma shook her head at Elsbeth, grabbing the badge and eyeing it.

Elsbeth put her hands behind her head and leaned back in the passenger seat, still grinning.

And suddenly, it all made sense: Elsbeth's stutter, her appearing as if autistic or in some way challenged, the way she went from meek to fierce depending on the circumstances. It was all an act… and she had the entire Vandenberg family eating out of her pretty little hands.

Chapter 23
Elsbeth

Florida

"Why the lie, Elsbeth?" Emma asked the young woman when they were safely back at Emma's residence on Treasure Island. "Your entire family thinks there is something wrong with you."

"There was," Elsbeth answered simply, taking an apple from Emma's refrigerator and biting into it without asking if she minded. Emma waited while the girl munched a large piece of it and swallowed. "By the time I was seven, it was assumed I had a neurological disorder and debilitating speech and memory issues."

"But you don't now?" Emma questioned.

Elsbeth took another bite of her apple. "Nope," she answered simply.

"Why do you let everyone believe that you do?"

Elsbeth sighed, tossing the apple core in a trash can. "Unless you compost?" Elsbeth offered, after-the-fact.

"I've been here less than a week. What do you think?" Emma asked. "And quit changing the subject."

"Well, for the longest time, I really did think something was wrong with me. But one week in private school, I traded those stupid nutritional bars. Mother always made me eat for Airheads and M&M's. For some reason, Sally, one of my classmates, was mad for them. I thought they tasted like tree bark."

"And what happened?" Emma was beginning to put two and two together.

"Sally had an inexplicable seizure — only one time; no one knew why."

"But… you did?" Emma asked cautiously.

"I was only eight at the time, and not a hundred percent sure, but I suspected."

"And what did you do, Elsbeth?"

"I started ditching the bars any chance I could, just to see what happened. And within a month, my mind sort of… cleared up."

"Why didn't you tell anyone, Elsbeth?" Elsbeth was silent. Emma tried again. "Why didn't you tell anyone?"

"At first, it was for selfish reasons," she admitted. "I was worried I'd get in trouble if I told. And… because I talked funny, Mother stopped making me go to church ceremonies with her. She thought I was an embarrassment. Then, she pulled me out of school and began homeschooling me, which I preferred. Don't know if you've noticed, but I'm not the most social of creatures."

"Oh, I noticed," Emma nodded.

"And then—"

"And then, what?" Emma coaxed.

"I heard a buzzing around the house that a woman from the Church of Infinite Love died of an overdose, and they thought it was linked to grandfather's nutrition bars. I wanted to tell grandfather but—"

"But—"

"I heard him fighting with Edwina one day about it. I wasn't a hundred percent sure he wasn't in on it."

"Did you go to the police?"

"No, I didn't go to the police!" Elsbeth yelled. "I was only eight, for Christ's sake, and just got my wits about me! I didn't even leave the house again until I was eleven, and that's only because I had an appendicitis. Mother actually asked her superiors' permission for them to operate to save my life."

"Geez, Elsbeth," Emma rubbed her forehead. "Alright, so, we need to tell Officer Dennis and —"

"No!" Elsbeth was adamant.

"Well, we have to share this information. Maybe then he can get the authorities to—"

"No!" she reiterated. "Not unless you're trying to get me killed, too." Elsbeth eyed her with a seriousness she'd never before seen in the young woman.

"So, your plan is just to pretend to have a learning disability for the rest of your life?"

"No," she corrected. "My plan was to wait until my 18th birthday and legally leave home. Only when I was out of that place could I think about reporting what I suspected. But then, a story surfaced about two more girls dying under suspicious circumstances, and I... chickened out."

"There was no one you could talk to about this... not Ferdinand, Ivy, or Ruth? Or maybe make your grandfather realize the side effects of his creation?"

"You really don't get it, do you?" Elsbeth was incredulous. "They are all members of the Church of Infinite Love. More than members... the Evangelicals." Her eyes grew wide.

"What do you mean the Evangelicals?" Emma had never heard the Vandenberg family referred to in this manner before.

Elsbeth thought a moment. "Oh," she said quietly. "I forget that outsiders wouldn't know that. The Evangelicals are the church founders. They meet in secret, and most members don't even know who they are. If they showed up at a random campus, it's unlikely anyone but the elders and deacons would know who they were."

"But Ferdinand, Ivy and Ruth… they are not family members. Are they Evangelicals, too?"

"Not exactly," she answered. "They're considered private ambassadors for the Evangelicals. It's a glorified way to refer to the servants of our house."

"So, being a member is a prerequisite for working at any of the Vandenberg residences? What about the factory?"

"Yes, to the first question. And, I'm gonna guess the factory is more of a recruitment center," Elsbeth cringed.

"So strange, though," Emma mused. "How is it that your mother is an Evangelical? I thought only men rose in rank."

"I guess the rules don't apply to those in the bloodline," Elsbeth suggested. "And even she answers to people I don't know about." She paused for an unbearably long time.

"What is it?" Emma coaxed. "You suspected Erasmus of being her superior… despite the illusion she seemed to give that she was head of the household."

Elsbeth nodded. "When I got wind that grandfather was going to close the factories and come clean, I thought maybe I could finally talk to him, but then—" Elsbeth broke down, sobbing.

"You really did love him, didn't you?" Emma put an arm around the girl. *I wish Dennis were here,* she thought. *He's so much better at this than I am.*

Elsbeth nodded. "I tried making excuses for him, but deep down I didn't trust him."

"Elsbeth," Emma considered her next question. "Was that the real reason you wanted to go with Erasmus to Florida… to come clean, yourself?"

Elsbeth nodded.

"And the others on the plane… the pilot, the flight attendant, the security guard?"

"I can't say for certain, but it stands to reason they were

somehow linked to the church. They liked to surround themselves with their own, you know?" she sniffled, smiling to herself. "I think the only innocent in all this is Uncle Edgar. But he's locked away in his castle in Ireland. What could he do, even if I had a chance to tell him? Besides, we get it drilled into our heads early on not to trust outsiders."

"So, who can you trust?" Emma asked absentmindedly.

"You," Elsbeth suddenly answered. "I'm trusting *you*."

Elsbeth was on the next available flight out of Tampa heading home before her mother returned from her latest church-related business trip. Edwina had taken Ruth with her, leaving only Ivy and Ferdinand behind. Fortunately, Ivy was preoccupied with her kids visiting from out of town and had taken a few days off to give them a tour of the Big Apple. As a single mother with grown children, it was rare for Ivy to get a chance to escape the confines of the Vandenberg high-rise for something other than grocery shopping and visits to the dry cleaners. Meanwhile, while Ferdinand insisted on driving Elsbeth to and from JFK Airport, he promised not to inform Edwina of her daughter's departure unless she expressly asked where Elsbeth was. And since Edwina forgot that Ivy was away, she assumed Elsbeth had two remaining chaperones.

"Did you have a fruitful trip, Elsbeth?" Ferdinand asked, while dragging the young woman's suitcase from the baggage claim area.

"Y… y… yes… F… Ferdinand," Elsbeth stuttered. "E… m… ma was v… very k… k… kind to m… me."

"Well, I'm glad. And you'll be happy to know that your mother hasn't phoned yet, so your secret appears to be safe with me." Ferdinand opened the door of his black sedan and Elsbeth climbed in. "Seatbelt on," he commanded. Elsbeth obeyed. It was only after he'd settled into the driver's seat that he dared to ask. "I know it's not my place, Elsbeth. But may I ask why you needed to go to Florida in such a hurry?"

"I w… wanted to m… make sure E… m… ma was okay in her new home," she answered simply.

"Well, that was very thoughtful of you," he mused. "But wouldn't a telephone call have been easier?"

Elsbeth hugged herself and shook her head adamantly. "Y… you know I h… hate phones."

Ferdinand nodded. "Ah, the whole idea of a disembodied voice on the other end."

"It's creepy," Elsbeth added. She fought back a smile as she sank into the passenger seat. Her goal was to make sure Emma got into the factory, and she knew if she were there, Victor wouldn't put up a fuss. Everything was going according to plan.

Chapter 24
Four Women, All Dead

Manhattan

"I'm telling you, Honey Bear," Monte winked into the web cam set up in Darwin and Rue's condo, where a visibly uncomfortable Ortega and his wife, sitting beside him resting one hand on his knee, were once again displayed on a large television screen. "You should let me come down there and visit the factory as Monique. I've been undercover before, and—"

"No," Ortega interrupted him. Monte placed one hand on his hips in protest, shaking his head and neck from side to side as if to say, *"Oh no, you just didn't."*

"What do you mean, 'no'?" Monte challenged.

"These people are church-loving devotees wearing no makeup and nothing that would be perceived as vain."

"So?" Monte crossed his arms indignantly. Today, he was back to his typical "Monte" wear — black jeans and a matching t-shirt. While Monique had a flair for the dramatic, Monte kept it simple.

Ortega tried again. "While I'm certain you could pass for a sufficient woman in New York—"

"Sufficient?!" Monte looked to Darwin and Rue for support. Rue stifled back a laugh. It was nice to be on the sidelines for once, where Monte was giving attitude to someone else for a change. "Let me tell you something, Honey Bear—"

"My name is former Detective José Ortega!" Ortega snapped. "Not Honey Bear, not Sweetheart, or any other term of affection!"

Nancy rubbed her husband's knee supportively. She didn't like to see him so upset, concerned that his anger would cause a spike in his blood pressure… or worse.

Monte was smart enough to know when he'd pushed too far. "Never mind." He waved a hand. "I'm not interested in flying into Tampa, anyway. Florida is absolutely grizzly this time of year."

No one was quite sure why Monte seemed to be suddenly fond of bear references, but they decided to let it go.

"Listen," Ortega tried again, eyeing Darwin and Rue for support. "I mean it as a compliment. The women in that factory aren't… shall we say… as glam as you. No makeup, no frills, and frumpy uniforms. Could you pull it off without all the… accoutrements?"

Monte surveyed his cuticles, his go-to reaction when he wasn't sure how to respond.

"Not sure, to be honest," he finally admitted.

"Then, I think it's best we send Nancy, my wife—" he motioned toward Nancy. "And Emma's helper-gal, Sprightly. No one will even notice them."

"Well, gee Honey Bear," Nancy chided, annoyed. "Glad to be so plain that I can just blend right in."

Monte stifled back a laugh.

"You know that's not what I meant," Ortega fumbled.

"Isn't it, though?" Nancy crossed her arms defiantly.

"Look." Monte held up his arms. "I get it. But let me at least share more on the case files I dug up on the three women who mysteriously died while being devoted members of the Church of Infinite Love. The church must have some pretty kick ass lawyers and publicists because it was a bitch uncovering this."

"What did you find out?" Nancy leaned in, intrigued, before Ortega had even gotten the words out. He looked at his wife, surprised at her continued interest. He'd never seen her this interested in anything… other than maybe tennis. "I mean," she continued, "beyond what you've already sent us. I read your case files several times."

Ortega, Monte, and Darwin looked over at the unassuming Nancy quizzically.

Dennis got pulled into a separate case and was stuck working late, while Emma had not yet returned from the airport with Sprightly after Elsbeth's departure. That left Ortega to collect details to share with the Florida team later.

"Help me out here?" Monte looked to Darwin who nodded. Darwin had a separate small screen set up to share images of the photos and documents Monte had secured copies of after spending hours sifting through outdated microfiche and taking rudimentary shots from the cell phone Darwin provided him.

Within minutes, Darwin had the images on display. They were grainy, having been blown up ten times their size, but good enough for their needs.

"The first is Marnie Watson," Monte began.

"The woman in her early twenties who tried to run away just days after being married off to a church deacon nearly two decades her senior." Nancy filled in.

"Very good." Monte put his hand on his hip and nodded, impressed. "She was the first reported death, of course… back in 1988. But on my first pass, it seemed the reported cause of death was 'inconclusive'." Monte put the word 'inconclusive' in air quotes. "But with the help of your friend Penelope—"

Ortega became flushed at the reference, glancing nervously at his wife. She bristled slightly but said nothing. After all, they had been married for more than a decade. That was water under the bridge, and… she trusted her husband… for the most part.

"We're hoping that she'll be able to confirm what conspiracy newspapers have been alluding to—"

"And what might that be?" Ortega asked.

"That there were antidepressants and stimulants in her system at the time of her death," Monte continued.

"Self-medicating or—" Ortega asked.

"From what we're told, she was secretly seeing a psychotherapist who was prescribing her meds for depression."

"Secretly?" Nancy asked. "Why would a 23-year-old see a shrink in secret?"

Monte cleared his throat. "Because the church frowned on outside medical interventions — physical or mental."

"I see." Nancy shook her head, disturbed. Ortega eyed his wife admirably. He'd never seen her display this kind of empathy before (not that he was an expert on the subject). To him, it was… refreshing.

"Well, there's more than reasonable evidence to suggest that the church was supplying their devotees with Vandenberg Nutraceutical bars with similar ingredients as her prescription."

"So, she accidentally overdosed?" Ortega offered.

"That's what we're trying to confirm," Monte nodded. "Unfortunately, it's been a challenge trying to recover records from a decade ago. Penelope has been trying to tap into her connections in the Pennsylvania area, as well as internal records. But so far, she's coming up empty."

"Yes, and we can't have her digging too much," Ortega squirmed in his seat. "I don't want her losing her job, or worse, getting in harm's way." He eyed Nancy, who had her eyes cast toward the floor, as if she were lost in her own thoughts.

As they continued to talk, Rue slunk away into the condo's kitchen. While out of sight from the video camera, and Ortega,

Nancy and Monte's view, Darwin had a clear line of Rue hovering by the stove, hugging herself uncomfortably.

"You okay?" he whispered.

"Yeah, just bringing back a flood of memories I worked very hard to forget."

"Why don't you wait in the bedroom while we finish up here?" Darwin suggested.

"No," Rue rubbed a tired eye. "I'm okay. I just need a moment."

"Right." Darwin rubbed her shoulders, supportively, before returning to the living room.

Monte had since moved on to the next two victims, Jessica Jones, age 17 and Linda Parker age 16. "Both of these women drowned in a lake near the church grounds in Pennsylvania… about two hours north of the church you and Rue recently visited."

"I remember those girls… vaguely," Rue piped up from the other room. "They had just transferred into our church campus and dorms right before I bolted. I know the area you're talking about. How on Earth could they have drowned in a shallow lake that couldn't have been more than four feet deep at its very center?"

Monte thought a moment, eyeing Rue quizzically with a modicum of sympathy. "So many questions."

"Story for another time," Darwin interjected, stepping in front of Rue as if to shield her from everyone's gaze.

Monte nodded before continuing. "But to at least answer your question… they were inebriated."

"What? They were drunk?" Rue asked. She had read the same file they did, but it merely listed the cause of death 'accidental drowning.'

"Another case where we only have a few conspiracy channels to go by. The toxicology reports are sealed tight at their parents' requests and because they were underage."

"How drunk do you have to be to drown in a shallow, calm

lake?" Rue pondered out loud. "And given the fact that there were cameras and security all around the compound, how the heck did no one see them out there?"

"Good question," Dennis said. "And unless we can get those cases re-opened, I'm pretty sure the church isn't going to hand over camera footage from that evening. They probably destroyed it a long time ago, anyway."

"But most of this information was in the files you sent us several days ago," Ortega reminded him. "So, other than a few new conspiracy theories about the real cause of their death, we have nothing new to go on? Is that it?"

"My, we are negative, Honey Bear," Monte teased. Before Ortega could respond, Monte waved his fingertips at the camera. "Hang on, I have one more photo to show you."

With that, he clicked over to an outdated portrait of a woman who'd obviously had her photo taken at one of those cheap mall studios.

Rue gasped. Darwin's face lit up in alarm.

"What about this woman?" Rue choked out.

"So, you know her?" Monte confirmed.

There was an old photo of Deaconess Frances… Rue's mother.

"She's my mother," Rue finally answered. "Darwin and I just spoke with her several days ago. What happened?!"

"Oh, shit, Rue." Monte looked from side to side as if seeking a place to hide. Monte rarely lost composure, but this was one of those times. "I'm… I'm sorry. I didn't know." His eyes grew red. He covered his mouth, as if shocked beyond words.

"What happened?!" she demanded. Darwin tried to put his arm around her, but she shrugged it off.

"She was found dead last night in the church's library," he answered softly.

Rue gasped. An emotional numbness overtook her, and her voice continued talking as if on autopilot. "How — how," was all that came out of her mouth.

"They found an overturned ladder with her at the bottom. The news report was vague, but forensics believe she somehow fell from the ladder while reaching for a book, hit her head, and broke her neck in the fall."

"But the ladder was overturned," was all Rue could say, as if her voice were disconnected from the rest of her body. She struggled to put a logical thought together.

"Yes," Monte confirmed. "Rue, I'm so sorry—"

"It's okay," Rue answered, her voice emotionless and seemingly very far away.

From the other end of the call, Ortega chimed in. "I'll call Penelope right away and see if she knows anyone on the forensics team out that way. I'll see what I can find out."

It was almost as if they forgot he and Nancy were still there remotely. Nancy looked at Ortega incredulously. She knew he was trying to help, but one look at Rue's face told her that this seemed as if it should be a secondary reaction, not a first.

"Rue," Nancy offered gently. "You're in shock. And you may not know what you need right now, but we are here for you."

"Thank you," Rue nodded, staring at her mother's image on the small screen, as if mesmerized by it.

"Oh, for God's sake, man," Darwin grumbled to Monte. "Shut that off, would you?" Except he didn't wait for Monte to respond. He walked over to the camera and quickly disabled it.

"Until we know what happened for sure," Darwin looked up at Ortega and Nancy grimly, "I would be very careful about your factory investigation in the morning. It seems awfully coincidental that this comes after our recent visit to the Church of Infinite Love."

Offline, Ortega turned to Nancy. "I feel like we're missing an opportunity here."

"What do you mean?" Nancy answered.

"Well," Ortega thought a moment. "If Emma's new friend, Elsbeth, is related to the Vandenberg family, and her mother has strong ties to the church, is it possible she knows more than she's letting on?"

"I doubt it," Nancy answered. "You saw how flaky she was."

"But if they have a history of drugging their members…" Ortega thought on this. "What do you think?"

"Are you actually asking my opinion about your case?" Nancy was touched.

"Yes," he answered. "I'd really like to know what you think."

"Do I think it's possible that the girl is being fed a diet of drugs to keep her in that state? I suppose it's possible, but unrealistic. Why would they want to?"

"Control?" Ortega offered.

"No." Nancy was adamant. "I can see them accidentally damaging her — and an adverse reaction and such. But no, I can't see them purposefully keeping her drugged. Who would do that to their child?" Even the thought of it made Nancy cringe.

"And Rue Brennan," Ortega continued.

"What about her?" Nancy answered.

"She and Elsbeth both grew up in the same cult. Both have high-ranking mothers. It would be interesting to get them talking—maybe interview them to see what they both know?"

"Not a bad idea, Honey Bear—" Nancy teased.

"Don't start," Ortega wagged a finger at her.

"But, given Rue's state tonight, I'd say we need to give her a few days. Not to mention the fact that Elsbeth just lost her grandfather."

"Perhaps you're right," Ortega sighed. "But I'm afraid we may not have that kind of time."

"We should get to bed," Nancy suggested, slipping into a nightgown and draping her clothes over a chair in their bedroom. "I've got a big day sleuthing tomorrow."

Ortega nodded, pulling down the covers from the bed. After

stripping down to his boxer shorts and undershirt, he climbed under the covers and pulled them up over his head. He was trying hard not to compare the two. He really was. But all he could think of was how these brainstorming sessions were far more productive with Penelope as a thought partner. Ortega knew he wasn't being fair. After all, his wife was not trained for police work, and was doing a pretty bang-up job despite her lack of experience. Still, he secretly wished he could have this conversation with Penelope instead.

Chapter 25
Blindfolds

Florida

With Elsbeth now back in New York, Emma expected to enjoy a little alone time with Dennis. Unfortunately, she quickly learned that she'd be settling in for round three of her ongoing spats with him instead.

"Damn it, Emma!" Dennis bolted into the kitchen. He had just returned from work and made the mistake of rifling through the mail before walking through the door. "What the hell's it gonna take for you to finally trust me?"

Emma looked up from the blackened tilapia she was about to throw on a small electric grill.

"What brought this on?" she asked, surprised. "Elsbeth is on a plane heading back to New York, by the way, for anyone who cares."

"This!" Dennis answered, all but shoving the document into her face, ignoring her comment. Emma peered down at it. Her cheeks became warm as her heart flooded with a mix of anger and guilt. "… Is what brought this on!" he finished angrily.

"Where did you get that?" she demanded.

"Does it matter?" Dennis' face turned pink around his cheeks and nose.

"It does when you're asking me why I don't trust you?" she defended.

"So, I'm right?" Dennis answered triumphantly.

"About what?" Emma was confused.

"That you don't trust me," Dennis continued.

Emma turned off the grill and tossed the tilapia on a plate to avoid burning the filets.

"I'm afraid I'm going to need you to be more specific." Emma's clipped tone let Dennis know that she was about to become annoyed… very annoyed, unless he did some explaining.

Dennis rubbed his forehead, searching for the right words. "It was an accident," he began, phrasing his words carefully.

"What was?" Emma was suspicious.

"If you give me a minute, I'll explain!" Dennis was frustrated.

"Stop yelling at me!" Emma whined.

"I'm not…" Dennis paused before letting out a long sigh. "Just, please give me a minute to explain."

Emma, for once, said nothing. Instead, she covered the tilapia with the lid from the frying pan and tossed it into the refrigerator for safe keeping. It seemed they weren't likely to be having dinner anytime soon, and she hated to waste food, particularly if it was fish that sacrificed their lives for their evening meal… Emma always thought about stuff like that.

After a long pause, Emma's eyes grew wide, and she motioned her hand into the air as if to say, *"Well, get on with it, then."*

"I stopped to pick up the mail just now," Dennis began.

"Oh, thanks. I forgot—"

"Found this blank envelope mixed in and opened it without thinking. Wanna explain what this is?" His cheeks and nose grew redder. She glanced at it, a sinking feeling in her chest.

"It's a prenuptial agreement," Emma answered softly.

"Emma, why?" Dennis demanded. "We're not even sleeping in the same bedroom yet because I assumed you wanted to take things slow… which is—" he ran his hand through his hair, "frustrating, but I was okay with it because I wanted to see where this was going. And, I figured you were worth… waiting for," he answered sheepishly.

"Well, obviously I'm planning for the long-term, else I wouldn't have contacted Mr. Lundy to draft that up."

"But we've never talked about marriage. Hell, there are some days when I can't even tell if you even like me all that much!"

"I like you," Emma protested. "What makes you think I don't like you?"

"Maybe because I followed your heels from New York to Florida like a lost puppy and am still sleeping in the guest bedroom, as if I were your roommate."

"Well," Emma defended. "Maybe I just wanted to be sure that this—" she motioned a finger between the two of them, "was going somewhere, and that you weren't the love 'em and leave 'em sort."

Dennis let out a sigh. He took her by the soldiers. "Emma, you've got me eating tofu and jogging… me, jogging! I had to eat meat in the garage twice already, so I didn't have to bear your look of disdain—"

"You eat meat in the garage?" Emma was surprised.

"That's not the point." Dennis changed the subject. "I think that I've more than proven myself over the past nine months. I'm not going anywhere."

"Then why are you so upset about a prenuptial agreement… assuming you're in this for the long haul?"

He dropped her shoulders and began pacing the tiny kitchen. "For one thing, we've never talked about marriage or even… well, us. 'Why do we need to put labels on it?'" he reminded her, putting his words in air quotes. "Sound familiar?"

"Well, that was before…" Emma reasoned.

"Before what?"

"Before you actually got on the plane and came down here with me."

"You thought I'd bail? I got a temporary transfer and everything."

"Yeah," she reminded him. "Temporary!"

"But, I've been helping you with the case. Obviously, I'm putting a lot on the line for our relationship."

"Well," Emma back pedaled. "I appreciate that."

But Dennis hadn't gotten everything off his chest yet.

"Up until now, I had no idea if you were interested in a long-term commitment or not, and I certainly don't love the idea that you trust me so little as to think we need to guard our money, particularly since you bring in far less than I do."

"You're forgetting about the inheritance," Emma pointed out. "If Erasmus' will holds up, I stand to be a good deal better off than I have been in the past."

"And you really think that that's what I'm about?" Dennis was hurt.

"No," Emma admitted. "But then, I've made really bad decisions about men before. What if I'm wrong about you and in two years you run off with some young redhead at work named Amber who teaches yoga on the weekends?"

"That was… oddly specific," Dennis pointed out.

Emma shook her head. "Look, I'm sorry. It was a stupid idea."

"No," Dennis' voice softened. "What was stupid was you not talking to me… about any of this? That's kinda what couples do, right? Talk about hopes, fears, and that sort of thing?"

"So, we're definitely a couple then?" Emma asked.

"I don't know," Dennis admitted. "You tell me."

"Well," Emma answered after what seemed like an eternity. "I'd like to be."

"Well then," Dennis replied. "So would I."

"Kinda convenient since we're already technically living together," Emma reasoned, her gaze falling to the floor, a little embarrassed.

"And I'm nothing if not practical," Dennis laughed, circling his arm around her waist and pulling her in for a kiss. Emma lifted her eyes to meet his. She took his face in her hands and kissed him back fervently. With the case looming over them, it was their first moment of real connection since they had arrived in Florida.

"Come with me," she smiled seductively, taking him by the hand and leading him toward her bedroom.

"Where are we going?" Dennis was afraid to get his hopes up.

"Thought maybe you might wanna finally see the inside of my bedroom… Unless you want me to go back to making dinner?"

"No!" Dennis answered and then let out a cough. He hadn't meant to yell.

Emma pushed the door to her room open. From the hallway, Dennis could see a plush brown carpet with a queen-sized bed covered in a pink blanket and pillows. Frankly, Dennis didn't see Emma as the sort of woman to like pink anything. She seemed more like a gray sweatshirt and baggy pants kinda gal, with linens to match.

"Just one more question, Dennis," Emma looked up at him innocently.

"Yes, what is it?"

"What are your thoughts on… blindfolds?" She winked at him.

Dennis' face felt flushed again, but this time, for a

completely different reason. "Should I be worried?" he asked, his voice cracking.

"Probably," she grinned, closing the bedroom door behind them.

199

Chapter 26
New Recruits

Florida

Nancy and Sprightly were filled with nervous excitement as Dennis and Ortega dropped them three blocks from the factory on a Friday morning in two separate vehicles where they were instructed to enter the Vandenberg factory at least five minutes apart. Friday was "new hire" day, as it turned out. They were wearing the uniforms Elsbeth had procured for them and name badges recreated by some guy named 'Moolah' that Darwin had recommended to Ortega. The badges matched Executive Assistant Celia's… without her title, of course. Moolah dropped them at Ortega's door at the ungodly hour of 5 a.m., along with a white delivery van with a large photo of baked bread on the side of it. Moolah made sure Ortega knew it was 'only a loan.' Ortega had no idea why the man thought he'd want to keep a battered old bakery van that had seen better days. He arrived with Nancy while Dennis dropped off Sprightly in her old Chevy Citation, which, not unlike the bakery van, had also seen better days.

"Remember," Dennis reminded them. "They'll make you pass through a metal detector and won't allow you in with any cell phones or recording devices. Nancy, you remember the plan?"

"Of course, I remember," she answered haughtily. "It was my idea!"

"Right," Dennis nodded. "But Sprightly, we're not going to have any way of tracking you. So, try to stay close to Nancy, if possible; but don't make it obvious."

Ortega sat in the borrowed van that, to him, actually felt sad from neglect. He feared the couch on wheels that Nancy bought him might be too obvious. Now, he wasn't so sure. He stationed himself in an open parking area of a neighboring print shop factory, just north of the Vandenberg factory at its back entrance. He had a recording device set up so he could listen in on what Nancy's microphone picked up.

Emma was nowhere near the factory, not with the surveillance cameras they appeared to have surrounding the place. Instead, she waited impatiently at an outdoor coffee shop a good half-mile away, sipping a latte as slowly as possible, while pretending to read a book. She had finally unwrapped the cell phone Dennis had bought her and had practiced using it last night. While it was fairly straight forward, she preferred land-lines where you could very clearly tell when you'd picked up and hung up the phone. This little contraption, she didn't entirely trust.

But Emma was there merely if she needed to suddenly show up at the factory and cause a distraction. She had no idea what that might be and silently rehearsed possible scenarios.

She recalled her earlier phone call to the security desk at Vandenberg Nutraceuticals. "Hi," she said in what she thought was a Florida accent. (Really, she had no idea.) "This is Marla from HR. I've got two new employees heading your way for the R&D department—"

Emma paused while the woman on the other end expressed

annoyance that HR never seemed to comply with Vandenberg procedures.

"Cut me some slack," Emma added in a bit of her own attitude. "I'm only two days on the job on account of some deadbeat getting arrested on a DUI. I'm the replacement. At least I showed up sober!" She waited while the woman on the phone expressed her apologies. "No matter," she continued. "You've got a Nessa O'Conner due in at 9 a.m. today… a fresh transfer from our Emerald Isle office… never worked in the Florida office before. And, there's also a Susan Brown. She's a Florida resident who's a new hire—" Emma listened at the employee's concern. "Yeah, I get that new hires don't usually get placed in Research & Development!" she all but yelled into the phone. "Maybe she's sleeping with your boss Mordachi. What do I know?!" A long silence made Emma realize she'd gone a bit too far with her act, particularly when dealing with, what appeared to be, a 'faith-based' company. Emma dialed it back with, "I apologize for my bad attitude. The truth is, I don't know why she was assigned to R&D out of the gate. Not my place to decide, is it? I mean, if that's what Mr. Mayberry requested?"

And now the Research and Development department of Vandenberg Nutraceuticals, the area where Emma, the major shareholder, and Elsbeth, the granddaughter of the founder, Erasmus Vandenberg, couldn't seem to get access to, was open to their two moles… Nancy and Sprightly. Emma continued sipping her latte and waited…

Meanwhile, Nancy arrived at the front desk first. Dressed in an ungainly gray uniform with a lanyard hanging around her neck, she stepped through the security station.

"Beep! Beep! Beep!" The metal detector chimed.

"Just one moment," an overgrown male security guard motioned toward Nancy.

"Probably my pacemaker, Hugo," Nancy explained, reading the guard's name tag. "Heart attack last year."

The guard read her name badge, "Nessa O'Conner. Just let

me check." The guard typed her last name into the small computer at his desk. "That checks out… funny, you don't sound Irish. Where are you from originally?" he asked, curiously.

Nancy remembered the pacemaker part, but forgot she was supposed to be a new transfer from Ireland. She did her best to add in what she thought might be a passable accent, "Originally from New York," she explained in a poorly blended accent. "But me dad got a job in Dublin when I was a wee thing, and I guess it's been back and forth for me between the States and Ireland ever since." She shrugged her shoulders and smiled innocently.

"Down the hall and to the left," he directed. "They should be able to get you situated from there," he finished gruffly.

"Thank you." Nancy curtsied awkwardly before heading down the very long hall that Emma and Elsbeth traveled not days earlier. Only, unlike those two, she would actually get to see what happens in the R&D department. Additionally, her 'pacemaker' was, in reality, a very tiny bug that enabled her husband and Officer Dennis to hear what was happening behind-the-scenes. This was the most fun Nancy could remember having—ever. Now, she sort of understood why Ortega loved it so much.

Moments later the guard called after her absentmindedly. "Oh… Sorry 'bout your heart attack!"

Nancy turned and nodded but kept moving.

About five minutes later, Sprightly arrived on the scene. "Susan Brown reporting for duty!" she proclaimed enthusiastically.

"Well, we'll just see about that," the guard answered. He lifted her badge from her chest and eyed it, and her, suspiciously. Sprightly shifted from side-to-side uncomfortably. He motioned her to proceed through the metal detector. Unlike Nancy, Sprightly didn't set off any alarms, and yet he still felt the need to phone the R&D department. "Yeah," he said to the person on the other end of the phone. "I've got a Susan Brown here, brand new and yet assigned to your department. I dunno—" He paused and held his hand over the phone's receiver. "They wanna know why you were recommended for a department meant for employees with tenure?"

"Don't know," Sprightly answered innocently before adding on a whim, "someone I met at church recommended I apply, and so… here I am?!"

"The Church of Infinite Love, you mean?" the guard asked. "The one in Tampa?"

"That's the one." Sprightly's eyes grew wide. "Don't tell me you're a member, too?" She feigned surprise. "I only just started going. So, I don't know too many people yet."

"Just one moment." The guard held a hand up to silence Sprightly. "I think she's okay. Got a referral from the church. Right." He hung up the phone. "Down the hall and to the right," he instructed.

Sprightly sprinted away before he could change his mind or ask her anymore questions about who referred her.

As soon as she'd arrived at the glass door leading to the Research & Development lab, she found it locked. Confused, Sprightly eyed Nancy through the glass, who was already in a factory line up, adjusting some type of syringe that appeared to be automatically infusing products in the chain as they went by. Sprightly waved emphatically. Nancy's eyes widened to suggest, *"Cut that out! You're being too obvious."* Sprightly dropped her hand. After a cursory glance to make sure no one saw her, she tipped her badge and glanced toward it. A lightbulb went off in Sprightly's head, and she held up her badge to unlock the door.

Once inside, another woman, dressed in the same drab gray onesie uniform, approached her. The only difference was that this woman's badge had some sort of star on it… possibly to indicate rank. "You must be Susan," she asked politely. "I'm Rita."

"Pleasure to make your acquaintance!" Sprightly held out a hand. The woman looked at it but made no move to return the gesture. Sprightly lowered her hand.

"This way please," she told the young woman. "We just had someone phone in sick, so your arrival today happens to be a good one."

Sprightly passed Nancy's station with disappointment. *So much for she and Nancy getting to stick together.* Instead, she passed through another set of doors with a sign marked, 'Private Shipping and Receiving.'

"Your job is pretty simple," Rita explained. "Shipments come in through there." She pointed to the receiving area where two young boys were loading boxes onto a conveyor, while two others pulled them and lined them up on a long aluminum table. She pulled an oversized brown log book and opened it to today's date. "You read each box and note what's in the box and where it's from. You've got plenty of pens in the tin." Rita motioned to a tin box filled with pens at the workstation. "Open each box to confirm you received the right product and quantity, then put the open box on this conveyer." She gestured. "So they can be added to our stock. Box cutters are next to the tins. Be careful not to cut yourself." She eyed the thin Sprightly and asked, "Some of these boxes are heavy. Think you can handle it?"

"No problem, Rita," Sprightly answered excitedly. "I'm strong as an ox. I won't let you down!"

Rita wasn't used to this much enthusiasm. She answered flatly, "The bathroom is just through that door." She motioned to a corner of the room. "Make sure you notify the manager before you leave the shipping floor. Is that clear?"

Sprightly was about to ask exactly who the manager was before her attention was drawn to a man sitting on a high-backed chair on what looked like a stage above the workers. At the word "manager" he lowered the newspaper he was reading and nodded in their direction before returning to his paper.

"Lunch is at noon. You have 45 minutes. Any questions?"

"Just one," Sprightly confessed. "Everything gets logged into that big book over there. I get that. But it seems strange that I wouldn't be logging inventory directly into a computer. Wouldn't that be more efficient?"

Rita sighed. She hated when newbies questioned the system. "Your job is not as an efficiency expert, Ms. Brown. Just fill out the logs as I've instructed. Follow the sample at the top of the page, and you should be fine."

Sprightly nodded. But the question remained bouncing around in her brain. Just beneath the counter where she stood lived stacks of old log books that must have gone back at least two decades. Another worker eyed her curiously, so Sprightly set to work at her designated station and began the mind-numbing task of opening boxes, counting bottles, and notating where they were from. Most were from medical facilities she'd never heard of in South America. They all had long names that seemed as if they were variations of popular Western medications. Sprightly's best guess was that they seemed to be a combination of sedatives, anxiety meds, and caffeine-infused energy tinctures. She carefully eyed the manager on high. He seemed to know instantly when someone's eyes were on him, as he looked up from his paper and stared back at her. Sprightly merely smiled and drew her attention back to her work.

After what seemed like an eternity, Nancy made a surprise visit to Sprightly's station, which meant that the woman had to pass from her production line, through the double doors to the Private Shipping & Receiving area that was an extension of the Research & Development area.

"Are you Susan?" Nancy asked innocently. Sprightly paused for a moment before remembering her undercover name.

"That's me!" she answered. "What can I do you for?"

Nancy showed her an invoice from a factory in Guatemala. "I was asked to see if you could check your logs for when this might have arrived. It was supposed to have come in two months ago, but we can't find it in storage. They were holding it for some new tea they're introducing."

"I'll look," Sprightly lowered her voice. "Any idea what it is?" she asked under her breath.

Nancy kept her voice at a normal level. Unlike Sprightly, she was doing a far better job at keeping a low profile. "Just check the invoice number and location." She pointed to the paper. Sprightly eyed it. Unlike the ingredients she had been checking in, this one seemed to be a cocktail of just about everything. Sprightly dug into her record book from two months back, and that's when she noticed it… a random page was missing. There were the tiniest of remnants of where someone had taken a blade and sliced it from the book. Whomever it was used enough pressure that the page beneath it was also slightly cut. It was the page between September 16 and 18.

"Sorry," Sprightly answered apologetically. "I don't see a record of it."

"Nessa!" Rita popped her head through the door, just as the lunch bell was signaled, and everything and everyone came to a grinding halt. "Never mind; we found it. Someone accidentally put them in storage cubby five instead of four. Would have been quite a mess if it got added where it shouldn't," she grimaced. "We can pick up again after lunch." Rita let the door slam behind her.

The manager promptly folded his paper and climbed down a set of wooden steps, making his way outside, presumably for lunch. He didn't wait until the floor was clear, because it seemed that no one there wanted to stay in the building a moment longer than was strictly necessary.

"Heading out for lunch, Susan?" Nancy asked. "I'll walk out with you." Sprightly caught on.

"Sure thing, let me just close out this last log." Sprightly eyed the room. When she was convinced no one was looking, she scanned the stack of log books shelved under the counter where she had been working. On the spine was the year. Sprightly sifted through her mind like a Rolodex. Finally, she grabbed two of them, 1988 and 1996, and began quickly flipping through them.

"What are you doing?" Nancy eyed over her shoulder.

"First day on the job," Sprightly answered calmly, shaking her head from side to side in case there were unseen onlookers. "I just wanna make sure my entries are consistent with the way they do things around here."

She grabbed a pen and flipped through the first book. Sure enough, there was a missing page between March 13 and 15. She took a pen and marked M14 on her hand. Then, she turned to the second book, flipping until she found another inconsistency. There was a page missing between April 8 and 10. So, she marked A9 on her hand.

"Someone's coming." Nancy heard the shuffling of feet. She helped Sprightly stash the books as Sprightly added one final mark on her hand, S17.

The two exited through the Research & Development lab as the manager returned early to his station on high, surveying the floor below as he was certain he heard voices.

Back on the R&D's main factory floor, Nancy slowed to a crawl at one of the cubbies near her workstation. There were dozens of them from floor to ceiling. The one she was looking for was labeled with a simple #5 above it, and it was at her feet on the lowest shelf. She bent to snag one of the tiny vials while Sprightly stood behind her.

"Finished tying your shoe yet?" Sprightly asked as Nancy bent over.

It was then that Nancy was hit with a sad truth… their uniforms had no pockets. *How was she supposed to get past security on their way out? They check your purses and everything?* It was the first time since grade school that she regretted having small breasts. Larger ones would have come in handy. Therefore, in a moment of desperation, she dropped the vial down her shirt, wiggling a little and catching the lump as it made its way down her leg.

Then, with some difficulty, she tucked it between her legs and squeezed as if doing a Kegel exercise… and held it.

"Let's go," Nancy said, straining. Sprightly followed at her heels. "Walk with me out front?"

Ortega heard the signal and messaged Dennis with one simple word, 'Now.' From the car he'd borrowed from Sprightly, Dennis sat three blocks away. He started up the engine once he received the text. Ortega did the same in his vehicle, waiting anxiously for his wife to return safely.

Nancy was the first through security. Once again, she beeped. "Pacemaker," she responded hurriedly. She was worried she might drop the vial and have it slide down her leg and shatter on the floor… blowing her entire cover.

"You seem to be in a hurry," the guard commented.

"Just have to use the bathroom *really* bad," she lied. "Thought I could hold out until lunch, but—"

"Go on, then." The guard motioned.

Once outside, she waved frantically for Ortega to pull in closer. Surprised, he drove right in front of the building as Nancy awkwardly climbed into the passenger seat, her upper thighs locked together. "Drive," she ordered. He didn't question her. He just drove.

Next, Sprightly went through security, politely opened her purse, and waited while they searched it.

"What's on your hand?" the guard asked, pointing to the notes she made for herself marked M14, A9, and S17. "Don't remember seeing that this morning."

"Ah," Sprightly thought quickly. "Bible verses," she answered.

"Which ones?" He wanted to know.

"You know, the popular ones from… Malachi, Acts and… Solomon," she quickly answered, trying to recall verses she had been forced to learn as a child that she had long since forgotten. Moreover, she doubted they would line up exactly with the numbers on her palm. She hoped the guard wasn't in the habit of memorizing scripture.

"Song of Solomon?" The guard raised an eyebrow. "Interesting."

"Uh, yup. That one." She squirmed nervously.

The guard bit back a laugh. "Go ahead." He motioned, noticing the growing line of antsy workers still eager to get out of the building in the hopes of having at least 30 minutes left to eat their lunches.

Sprightly darted through the door and made her way toward the main road, where Dennis pulled up alongside her. She hopped in quickly.

"Crap," Dennis said. "I think we've been spotted." He eyed a black van pulling out of the Vandenberg lot and following slowly behind them. Its windshield was splattered in one corner with bird droppings. Otherwise, it was immaculate.

"Does it matter?" Sprightly asked, eyeing the rearview mirror. "Not like I'm going back after lunch."

"Yes, it matters," Dennis growled, angry at his carelessness. "It not only puts us all in danger but could mess up any chances of getting the police to conduct a proper investigation."

"Will this help?" Sprightly reached around the back seat of her car and pulled out a magnetic police light.

"Where the heck did you get that?" Dennis asked.

"There's a reason I've never gotten a speeding ticket," she answered proudly.

"That's illegal!" he chastised. The car was getting closer.

"Wanna talk about it or use it?" Sprightly smiled sweetly.

Dennis reached a long arm out of the window and slid the light in place on the car's rooftop. From inside the car, Sprightly activated both the light and a siren just as Dennis hit the gas. The driver of the Vandenberg security vehicle kept pace for a moment, but then thought better of it, and dropped the tail.

Once at a safe distance, she turned off the siren and Dennis retrieved the light from the roof of the car. He phoned Emma, who'd left the coffee shop and relocated to a bench across the street.

"Need you to do a little recon, Honey," he told Emma.

She wasn't used to him calling her 'honey.' Emma wasn't sure how she felt about it. But, she bit her lip. "What is it?"

"Need you to phone Vandenberg HR and tell them there's been an incident."

"Is everything alright?" Emma was concerned.

"Yeah, we're good. Listen, you have to tell them that we were picking up Susan Brown for skipping her parole when she had a health incident."

"Like a miscarriage or something?" Emma offered helpfully.

"Yeah, go with that… a miscarriage. Thanks!" He hung up the phone.

Sprightly's mouth dropped open. "Really? That's the best you could come up with? Skipped parole and then had to be rushed to the hospital because of a miscarriage?"

"You got a better story?" he asked.

"Yeah," she answered. "Like, maybe you just learned my mom was injured in an accident and you were sent to bring me to the hospital! Or, maybe you're my boyfriend and you suddenly had to respond to someone going into labor on the highway, or—"

"Okay, sorry," Dennis apologized. They drove in silence for several minutes. "Now, about that bogus police equipment…"

Chapter 27
Discoveries

Florida

"Might wanna keep driving," Sprightly cautioned from the passenger seat as they neared the St. Petersburg house. Emma was in the back seat, after having been retrieved from outside the coffee shop. "Keep your head down, Em," Sprightly warned, crouching low in her seat so that her head fell below the window.

"What are you talking about?" Dennis questioned. It was then that he saw what Sprightly had spotted. Just across the street, a black van was parked. There was nothing remarkable about it, except for one thing… its windshield was decorated with bird poop… just like the van that began following them outside of the factory.

By then, he was already halfway down the block. He considered another blaring getaway, and fumbled with the police siren, now sandwiched in the center console between him and Sprightly.

Just then, a team of Girl Scouts crossed the street. Dennis

stopped to let them pass. One of the girls looked at him expectantly as another of the taller, bolder young women went up to the van and rapped on the window. The man in the van angrily rolled down his window as the girl began her cookie speech, motioning for another girl with a clipboard to take his order.

Dennis didn't wait to watch as the man shooed the scouts away, nor did he wait until they could surround his vehicle. He carefully backed slowly down the street and made a three-point turn, rounding the corner with the van unable to follow in time. He took one of the side roads before handing the phone to Sprightly. "Call Detective Ortega," he ordered.

"But I thought he wasn't a detective anymore?" Sprightly answered, missing the point.

"Just call him. Tell him we're heading to his home and we need to either ditch the car or hide it in his garage."

Sprightly nodded, scrolling through the contacts until she found his number.

"Ortega," the voice on the other end answered.

"Hi Detective Ortega," Sprightly answered enthusiastically. "Deputy Nyla Sprightly reporting for duty!"

"Er," Ortega paused. "Where's Dennis?"

"He's busy driving right now. But he said to tell you we're heading your way. I hope you've got space in your garage to hide my beater car."

"Oh," Ortega answered. "I'll put Nancy's car in the drive. How far out are you?"

Sprightly turned to Dennis, "He wants to know how far out we are?"

"Depending on if this crappy ride gets us there in one piece, I'd say about 45 minutes." Dennis answered loudly.

Sprightly held up the cell phone. To Ortega she asked, "You catch that?"

"Got it," Ortega answered. "I don't think I need to remind you to try and avoid being followed? I've already ditched my ride."

"Roger that, Detective," Sprightly answered. She was having a little too much fun playing deputy. "That's why we had to avoid the house." The phone started to crackle as they crossed the Skyway Bridge. "Better hang up now," Sprightly all but yelled into the phone. "Over and out!"

Nancy's hair was still wet from taking a shower when they'd arrived at the Ortega residence. She may have enjoyed playing undercover police officer, but somehow she felt the need to rid herself of the 'energy' of that awful jumpsuit they made her wear at the factory. Not to mention the fact that since she had the vial she'd stolen tucked securely between her unmentionables, she may have… leaked a little… trying to smuggle it out. While impressed with her quick thinking, Ortega accepted the bottle from her with a distasteful look on his face.

"What?" Nancy protested. "I rinsed it off."

Ortega let out a sigh and placed it in a sealed plastic bag.

Upon arrival, they quickly hid Sprightly's car in the garage and ushered Dennis, Sprightly, and Emma into their home. Nancy thought to draw the blinds. Meanwhile, Ortega had already scoured their house on the off chance that someone had thought to bug the place. So far, it seemed no one from Vandenberg Nutraceuticals was aware of their involvement. Darwin had promised to send Ortega something new for detecting bugs and all recording devices, telling the older man that it would be a 'game changer.' Only, it hadn't arrived yet. Therefore, he had to do his search the old-fashioned way.

Once he received the 'all-clear' from Ortega, he filled them in on what they encountered at the factory up through their arrival home.

"Yeah, well," Ortega reasoned. "You should consider staying here tonight, just to be on the safe side. This case is getting creepier by the minute."

"Here?" Nancy protested. She caught everyone's confused reaction and countered, "I just mean… is that wise? Perhaps a hotel in Tampa or someplace they wouldn't expect? Wouldn't that be safer for everyone since they don't suspect us yet?"

Emma didn't completely understand Nancy's reservations about having them there, but she wasn't particularly keen on remaining, either. All she knew for damn sure was that Nancy, for whatever reason, didn't want them to stay.

"We'll certainly do that," Emma reassured her.

"Nonsense. You and Dennis can stay in the guest room tonight," Ortega insisted, eyeing Nancy, who merely nodded reluctantly.

To Sprightly, he said, "The couch folds out into a sleeper sofa. You okay with that for the night?"

Emma took Dennis' arm and, once she'd caught his gaze, wiggled her eyebrows suggestively at him. He blushed and averted his gaze.

"Sofa is fine," Sprightly answered. "And I can take turns standing watch if you need me to."

"I don't think that will be necessary," Nancy laughed. "My husband has so many alarms and security cameras on the property, even the raccoons avoid our trash cans at night."

Sprightly nodded. Emma hadn't been in Florida long enough to know what raccoons had to do with anything, so she merely nodded. They had rats raiding the trash bins in Manhattan. *Maybe it was something like that?* She reasoned.

"Well, we've got a few frozen pizzas we can toss in the oven if you're hungry. Why don't I take care of that while you all settle in so we can recap the day?"

With only a counter dividing the space between the kitchen and the dining area, they gathered around the table. Sprightly fought back a grin as Ortega shared that Nancy had managed to smuggle a vial of, what they believed to be, a medical concoction that was about to be infused into nutrition bars. He left out exactly *how* she managed to smuggle it out.

"Any idea where the final product was going to be shipped?" Emma asked.

"No," Nancy called from the freezer. "But Sprightly discovered something interesting. Why don't you share?"

Sprightly saluted Nancy and stood, as if about to deliver a speech. She held out her hand, triumphantly. "They don't seem to like to record anything electronically at the factory, which is super weird, given that they are all about workplace efficiencies."

"What does that have to do with the numbers and letters on your palm?" Ortega asked logically.

Sprightly paused for dramatic effect before continuing. "They had me log inventory of meds coming in from other countries by hand. Only, the log books were missing pages, so I noted which days: March 14, April 8, and September 17."

"Wonder what makes those days so special?" Dennis observed.

"Don't know," Nancy chimed in, having set the oven to preheat and was now bringing a pitcher of sweet tea to set in front of the group. "But it was really odd that when I asked Sprightly to check on missing product, there was no record of it. And, someone had accidentally put the vial in the wrong bin. I'd be willing to bet someone didn't want anyone linking their inventory with traces of anything getting shipped out in those health bars."

"Brilliant thinking, Nan!" Ortega praised.

"Why, thank you, Honey." Nancy smiled gratefully at her husband. He didn't praise her often, so it meant that much more to her when he did.

"Ahem," Sprightly spoke up. "I *do* have an idea about those dates, actually."

"Go on?" Ortega encouraged.

"The first one in March was a log from 1988. The second from 1996, and the third—" She paused for dramatic effect. "This year." She waited while Ortega made the connection.

"Coincidentally, around the two times in history where the church made the news for women dying under suspicious circumstances, followed weeks later by Erasmus Vandenberg."

"Exactly!" Sprightly rocked back and forth on her heels, proud of herself.

"Good work," Ortega praised. "Any chance you got a look at any records of outbound shipments, to go along with Nancy's hypothesis?"

Sprightly's excited eyes dropped. "Sorry, no."

"That's alright," Ortega concluded. "I think we've got enough to approach someone from the sheriff's office and convince them to look into Erasmus Vandenberg's death, not to mention possibly see if we can gain access to the records surrounding the untimely death of the Deaconess and those three girls."

"But you said yourself that you're beginning to think the police are in on it," Nancy reminded him. "Or, at least they were reluctant to get involved because the Vandenberg family and the Church of Infinite Love are so powerful."

"I'm beginning to think that the family and the church aren't two different entities at all," Ortega grumbled. "The Vandenbergs seem to have their fingers in both of the most lucrative rackets in the US... nutritional supplements and religion."

"So, what? How are we going to convince anyone to help us?" Dennis was curious. He really didn't know and was all but banging his head against the wall at this point.

"I've got an idea," Ortega answered. "Are you on the beat tomorrow? Or can you go in late?"

"I am, but it shouldn't be a problem," Dennis replied. "They've got me scheduled part-time while I get settled from the move."

"Good," Ortega said. "Get some rest tonight. I'll let you in on my plan tomorrow."

Chapter 28
Contacting the Authorities

Florida

"Can I ask you a question, Jo?" Officer Dennis asked as he and Ortega made their way to the Crime Prevention Unit at the Tampa International Airport on Saturday morning, the day after their undercover work at Vandenberg Nutraceuticals.

"You just did, and—" Ortega stopped abruptly and turned toward Dennis, who all but ran into his former boss. "I know I said you could call me anything other than Detective, but maybe something different from Jo?"

"Sure thing… J…" Dennis caught himself. "But isn't your first name José?"

"It is," Ortega confirmed.

"And the English equivalent is Joe, right?"

"Yes; your point?"

"I just thought it was a fun play on words. J.O. being your initials and Joe being the same name in a different language… So… Jo." Ortega stared at Dennis expressionless. "But clearly you don't like that very much." Dennis put his thumb and fore-finger on his chin, thinking. "Do you have a middle name?"

"Yes."

"What is it?" Dennis asked as they resumed walking.

"None of your damn business." Dennis dropped his gaze. He was used to Ortega's gruff manner, but here he was starting to think that they might actually come to see each other as colleagues... friends even. Ortega saw his expression and his heart dropped for the second time in only a few days. First Nancy, now Dennis. He sure seemed to have a knack for disappointing people. "Sorry," Ortega finally answered. "Could we keep it simple and bypass the nicknames? Just call me 'José' or 'Ortega,' either one. Are you okay with that, Officer Dennis?"

"Okay," Dennis agreed. "But only if you agree to call me Dennis when we're not on official police business... like talking to the sheriff, for instance... José." Somehow, even his first name sounded weird coming from Dennis. Ortega couldn't understand it. *Am I still so tied to my old work identity that anything other than Detective Ortega sounds weird to me?* He brushed the thought aside. "Unless," Dennis took the silence as annoyance, "you hate that idea; then we can just skip it."

Ortega came out of his mind wandering. "No, that's fine Off—Dennis," he corrected. "Let's try that for a while."

"Okay, José," Dennis smiled. "Hey, could I ask you a question, man-to-man, José?"

Ortega's deadpan expression returned. "Sure," he answered hesitantly.

"Well, you're a little older than me," Dennis began. "And have more life experience and all—"

"Yes?" Ortega grew impatient. "What is it?"

"It's a personal question."

"You can ask, but I can't guarantee I'll answer."

"Fair enough," Dennis agreed. "But it's more a question on perspective."

"Would you spit it out, man!" Ortega said.

"So, for the longest time, Emma was all distant… sleeping in separate rooms and no funny business and all." The two paused to dart around a woman with a two-seater baby carriage. She also had a third child wearing a protective harness that was wrapped around his chest with a tether that wound around his mother's waist. Dennis almost tripped over the tether as her toddler ran over to a store window and began pressing his sticky fingers on the glass. "Anyway," Dennis continued. "That sort of changed recently."

"Oh, really?" Ortega's eyebrows shot up as he fought back a grin.

"Yeah, so we're sort of… serious now."

"Well, that's a good thing, right?" Ortega encouraged.

"Yeah," Dennis smiled like a cat who ate the canary. "Yeah, it's a really good thing. It's just that—" Dennis paused. "Well, it went from the well being dry to the floodgates opening, if you know what I mean?"

"I'm afraid you've lost me," Ortega confessed.

"I mean," Dennis lowered his voice in a whisper. "It's like now she wants it all the time, at night, in the morning, before dinner. Is that… normal?"

Ortega stopped abruptly once more, leaning toward Dennis in a loud whisper. "Dennis, please tell me you're not asking my advice about your girlfriend wanting to have lots of sex with you?"

"But I mean," Dennis tried again. "Should I do something about that? Honestly, it hasn't even been a week yet, but I'm kinda tired—"

"What am I supposed to do with that?!" Ortega barked. "Stay hydrated and take more vitamins. What the hell do you want from me?!"

Dennis lowered his gaze. "Okay, sorry I asked."

Ortega shuddered to think what was happening in their guest room last night. He put it out of his mind.

By then they had reached the main airport entrance. "After

you." Ortega motioned for Dennis to go first. Normally, he would have assumed that privilege, but he wasn't on the beat anymore, was he? Dennis was the one in uniform while he was just a private citizen. The gesture didn't go unnoticed by Dennis, who beamed proudly as he put his hat on and went through the revolving door to the front security desk.

Ortega followed closely behind, thinking about his failing marriage with Nancy. *Hmph,* he thought to himself. *Maybe I should be asking Dennis for relationship advice instead.*

The only other time Officer Dennis had set foot in the Tampa International Airport was when he first arrived with Emma less than two weeks ago. Once inside the main terminal, he stopped so abruptly that Ortega almost walked right into him.

"What, exactly, are we doing here?" Dennis asked, confused.

"We're looking for someone with the Crime Prevention Unit that we can trust." Ortega took the lead, and Dennis picked up the pace to keep up.

"But why not just go directly to the county Sheriff's Office?" Dennis enquired.

"You tried your precinct in New York and in Florida. And Penelope found suspiciously missing evidence in her search in the case of the three dead women at the Church of Infinite Love in upstate Pennsylvania. Nobody is willing to talk about the church nor the Vandenberg family." Ortega surveyed travelers as they struggled with heavy luggage and wove in and out of the crowds. "Makes me wonder just how big this thing really is. Where do we have to go for answers? The factory in Ireland?"

"So, why does that bring us here?" Dennis asked, as they located a sign pointing toward the police station within the airport grounds. "Because Erasmus died in flight?"

"That's part of it." Ortega seemed busy analyzing a large section of the airport with shops and restaurants. His eyes settled on a deli counter. Dennis was wondering how Ortega could possibly be thinking about food at a time like this. "I'm looking for someone… adjacent to this situation, who we can trust to help us."

"What does ordering a corned beef on rye from the man at the deli counter have to do with anything?" Dennis asked sourly as Ortega approached the small restaurant.

"Not him." Ortega pointed to the man behind the counter. "*Him*." Dennis followed Ortega's line of vision and spotted a man wearing a hunter green sheriff's uniform. He was hunched over a small red table, munching on a bagel.

"Why him?" Dennis was confused.

"Look at his head," Ortega answered. Dennis, dumbfounded, looked. The man was wearing a yarmulke on the crown of his head. His hair was a curly brown with long sideburns on the side of his round face and narrow chin. A lightbulb went off in Dennis's head.

"Not likely to be a member of the Church of Infinite Love is he?"

"Probably not," Ortega agreed. "Not that it means he's not taking a payoff or part of a coverup. But he's also not directly tied to your precinct, so—"

"There's a chance," Dennis finished.

"Exactly."

The two men approached the sheriff, who looked up in surprise. "Can I help you, Officer?" he asked Dennis, before eyeing Ortega, who was wearing a white linen shirt and jeans.

Dennis stammered a little, not sure where to begin. Ortega chimed in.

"Sorry to interrupt your lunch," Ortega apologized. "I'm former Police Detective José Ortega from Manhattan. I have an unusual request. May I?" He motioned toward the seat.

"Of course," the man answered, standing, removing the napkin he had tucked under his chin, and offering his hand. "I'm Deputy Sheriff Shep Stern. What can I do for you?"

The two men joined the deputy sheriff and sat.

"We've got a case that spans two countries, three states, several counties, and three major cities," Ortega began.

"This sounds serious," Shep acknowledged. "Why come to me?" Surprisingly, there was something trusting in Shep's eyes. Unlike Ortega, who assumed that everyone was up to no good, Deputy Sheriff Shep Stern had a gentle way about him, and he was willing to give a man the benefit of the doubt.

"Because it involves the Church of Infinite Love and Vandenberg Nutraceuticals. I'm going to go out on a limb and guess that you're not a member of a Christian organization and don't ingest non-kosher snack bars."

"I see," Shep grinned, pointing to his yarmulke. "Wonder what gave me away... But, why does that matter?"

"Go ahead, son," Ortega motioned to Officer Dennis.

Shep Stern looked curiously at Dennis.

Dennis provided, as quickly and succinctly as he could, what they'd encountered so far, beginning with Erasmus' death and working backward until their convoluted story was told. Then, he waited with bated breath as Shep took it all in.

"So, let me see if I've got this straight?" Shep asked, gathering the remains of his half-eaten bagel and brushing the crumbs from his hands onto a small serving tray. He pushed it to one side, and a deli attendant scooped it up almost immediately. He pointed a finger first at Dennis. "You're a police officer from New York on a temporary exchange program in Florida with a girlfriend who was a suspect in a past murder investigation and is now a millionaire." He turned his meaty finger to Ortega, "And, you're a retired police detective whose wife made you move here. You both enlisted the help of a questionable undercover investigator and a New York forensic scientist who "called in a favor" on your behalf, not to mention several civilians who have no business doing undercover work because you suspect that tycoon Erasmus Vandenberg was murdered. And everyone, including law enforcement in three states, is helping to cover it up?"

Both Dennis and Ortega paused. It sounded ludicrous when put so succinctly like that.

"Pretty much," Ortega clasped his fingers together and rested his elbows on the table. "You're not going to help us, are you?"

After another dramatic pause, Shep began laughing so hard his belly jiggled up and down. "Of course, I'm going to help you... if I can. This is the most insane thing I've heard all day. I love it. I'm in."

And with that, the team of misfits had one more player — Deputy Sheriff Shep Stern.

Chapter 29
Moolah

Florida

Ortega had just dropped off Dennis and Emma at their St. Pete residence, but only after Dennis agreed to let Ortega come by later to set up a few cameras. He trusted Dennis' skills as an officer. Although, while he would never admit it to himself, he was beginning to treat Dennis like the son he'd never had. And he was worried about him. Sprightly promised to return home and stash her car out of sight for a few days.

"Not a problem," she agreed. "I use my bike most times anyway."

Now, Ortega's current challenge, after he'd picked up the dry-cleaning, was trying to figure out the best way to lay it in the backseat of his Lincoln Town Car without getting it ruffled. He didn't understand the need for his new overgrown car, but somehow Nancy thought it was a nice show of gratitude for him agreeing to retire early and move to Florida. *A nice gesture would have been bringing me coffee and the Sunday paper in bed,* he thought. This was overkill.

The phone rang as he was settling into the driver's seat. *The car is so fancy, it's even got its own phone.*

"Hello, Honey," he answered. He was expecting Nancy.

"Hi, Doll," a man's voice answered, not without a hint of sarcasm.

"Oh, Moolah," Ortega remembered. "Forgot I gave you this number. You got the van back okay, right?" In the mess of everything that was happening, he forgot to check back in.

"Yeah, I got it. But never mind that. Are you sitting down?" Moolah asked.

"I'm in my car, Moolah," Ortega barked. "What do you think?"

"But you're not driving?" Moolah confirmed.

"Was just about to, why?"

"Got some info about your Lady Love," Moolah sighed. "You're not gonna like it."

"Oh." Ortega's chest sank.

Nancy had assumed that when Moolah dropped off the assets for their factory coup, that it was the first time Ortega had spoken to the man. It wasn't. On an earlier call with Darwin, he had asked him for a favor.

Darwin agreed, and suggested he phone a man named 'Moolah.' "Just tell him 'Finn' sent you, and he'll help you out."

"Where are you now? I can drop some photos your way," Moolah offered hastily.

Ortega looked around. "You know the dry cleaner on 301 near Ellenton? Connected to the laundromat?"

"Yeah," Moolah confirmed. "I know it. I can be there in less than ten minutes."

"Okay, I'll wait. I'm in the metered parking out front. Look for an obnoxious tan Lincoln Town Car."

"Gotcha. Be there in two shakes of a lamb's tail."

"Uh, okay. Bye." Ortega hung up the phone. He didn't get

the expression. Nor did he try. He was more concerned about what he'd dug up on Nancy.

As if her ears were buzzing, the car phone rang again.

"Hello," Ortega answered, this time, not certain who was on the other end.

"Is that any way to greet your wife?" Nancy teased.

"Uh, sorry," Ortega fumbled, trying to sound natural. "Still not used to all this new technology."

"Welcome to the 20th Century," she joked. "Hey, listen. Dominic can squeeze me in for a late lesson today. Thought I'd meet some of the girls at the club for cocktails after. Can you manage dinner on your own tonight?"

Ortega thought a moment, just as a beaten up dark green compact car pulled up alongside him. It was a little too worn, even for the likes of this town, so Ortega assumed it must have been Moolah. He was right.

"Yeah, sure," he answered, hitting a few buttons in an attempt to roll down the window. Instead, the car locked and unlocked and his seat shifted. "Damn it!" he cursed, as Moolah, who was now standing just outside the car, waited impatiently, taking furtive glances around him.

"What's wrong?" Nancy asked, concerned.

"Nothing," he sucked in a breath, powering down the window and accepting the manila envelope from Moolah. "Technology and all," he let out a forced laugh. "No, that's fine," he answered, reaching into his pocket to pull out a smaller envelop filled with cash. He handed it to Moolah, who accepted it quickly, gave him a two-finger salute as if tipping a hat to him, and darted off in his green monstrosity. "I can manage."

"Thanks, hon," Nancy cooed. "I'll make it up to you by cooking a nice roast beef dinner tomorrow night. M'wah!" She made a kissing noise into the phone before hanging up.

Ortega hung up the phone. Just then, he spotted a parking meter attendant making the rounds. He looked up and saw that his time had expired. *Ah well,* he thought. *Probably best to look at these when I get home, anyway.*

Ten minutes later, Ortega was pulling into his subdivision. He waved to his neighbor, Bob, as he pulled into his driveway, but Bob merely wrinkled his upper lip, turned his back toward him, and continued to water his lawn. *Guess he's still sore about the newspaper,* Ortega thought.

Once inside, Ortega set the envelope on the kitchen counter, as if trying to mentally prepare himself. He looked up to see that Nancy had left out a bottle of his favorite bourbon and a small, crystal bourbon tumbler with the letter "J" carved into it. Next to it was a handwritten note: *"Thanks for being so understanding about dinner. There's some leftover chicken in the fridge and green beans. Love you oodles, Nancy."*

Ortega poured himself a hearty serving of bourbon and took a long sip before procuring a butter knife from the drawer and slicing open the envelope. Had Nancy been home, she would have protested his using a food knife to open an envelope. But then, she wasn't here, was she? No, she was having a tennis lesson with Dominic.

After an eternity, he finally pulled the black and white photos from the envelope and fought back a reaction, as if there were other people in the room and he wanted to remain calm. His lower lip quivered. It appeared Nancy was doing more than playing tennis with her instructor. The photos started out innocently enough, pictures of her and Dominic standing next to the court, tennis rackets in hand, sipping water and laughing about some shared joke. But they got progressively worse, showing the couple kissing in the pool… the pool at the Ortega residence. And another featured some indelicate shots of them naked in the water, wrapped together tighter than two river otters on a cold day. There was no mistaking what they were doing, as there were other photos of her leaving what Ortega presumed was Dominic's apartment, hand in hand, and even one outdoors on the grounds of the tennis club… literally, in full display on the grass. Perhaps if Dominic and Nancy hadn't found the potential for getting caught such a turn on, had they been more discreet, maybe Moolah wouldn't have found anything.

Ortega took another long sip of his bourbon. The thing that plagued him the most was not even the infidelity, nor that he had given up everything, his career and his life, to uproot and move to Florida in an effort to save their marriage. It wasn't even the fact that she had lied to him. It was the fact that she thought so little of him as to bring her lover into their home. He forced himself to look at the photos by the pool again, in case he somehow got it wrong. But no, there were the red fire plants and small Areca palms and a money tree that she'd had the land-scapers add on one side of the pool. He could even spot the edge of one of their outdoor lounge chairs and the corner of one of their beach towels.

Ortega was not one to cry, but his eyes teared up just a little, his heart aching in a way that it hadn't since —

The phone rang. This time, it was his cell phone. He recognized the number.

"Hi Penelope," Ortega greeted weakly.

"What's wrong?" Penelope immediately asked. "You don't sound right."

Ortega let out a sigh. "Just a long day?" he lied. "Got something for me?"

"Uh, yeah," Penelope finally answered. "I don't know what's happening down there in Florida, but it seems the forensics guy on the case has got his head up his ass."

"Oh?" Ortega's eyebrows shot up.

"Samples of the 'healthy tea' that Erasmus was supposedly drinking the night he died were conveniently absent from the report, along with anything other than the dinner his on-board chef made. And, the coroner attributed the death to natural causes, except—"

"Except what?" Ortega asked.

"Except that he had a mild rash on his forearms, and his lips were swollen, suggesting—"

"An allergic reaction to antibiotics?"

"Possibly, or some other drug," Penelope concluded. "But Erasmus was as healthy as a horse. He didn't take prescription meds for anything."

"So why would the local coroner and forensic expert cover this up?" Ortega asked.

"Must be a lot of money in Vandenberg Nutraceuticals," Penelope suggested.

"I'll say," Ortega finished. "And since Erasmus was conveniently cremated, we'll never know for sure if something was slipped into his food… Come to think of it—" Ortega replayed the news story that Monte shared with him, letting it tumble in his head for a moment. Penelope waited patiently for him to continue. She knew the sign of Ortega about to have an "aha" moment. Finally, he continued.

"Didn't the newspaper say they found valerian root packed in his overnight bag? Could something have conflicted with that… something he ate or drank?"

"There might be something to that," Penelope continued. "And at that high altitude, even being in a pressurized cabin, whatever it was still would have affected him more so than when on land. If he took that on top of what I found… Woo Wee," Penelope huffed into the phone.

"Really? What else have you found?"

"The food samples that your guy Darwin got me each had traces of prescription meds in them. The bar in the red wrapping had traces of ephedrine. The purple one, zolpidem. The green macaroon snacks, opium, and the yellow wafers, sertraline."

"Wow, these guys weren't messing around, a drug for every occasion, energy, sleep, pain relief, depression—"

"And I saved the best for last." Penelope paused dramatically. "The stain on Darwin's shirt had traces of fruit pectin on it."

"Why is that important?" Ortega was confused.

"Think about it, José," Penelope added. "What do drug users do when they want to try fooling a drug test by cleaning out their system?"

"Oh." Ortega's eyes lit up. "So perhaps the church wanted to make sure that no one discovered their 'miracles' by creating a system by which the meds went through someone's bloodstream quickly."

"Or someone serving a healthy tea on a plane heading to Florida," Penelope offered.

"You're a genius. Thank you, Penelope. I can always count on you."

"Sure thing, José." Her voice softened. "José?" she said again.

"Yes, Penelope."

"You know you can always talk to me, right?" She paused for a moment on the other end of the line. Ortega could hear her breathing softly. "About anything… not just work stuff."

"I know, Penelope. I appreciate that," he answered quietly.

"Goodnight, José."

"Goodnight, Penelope."

Chapter 30
Mother

Back in Manhattan

Rue paced the floor of the condo nervously, occasionally peering out the window at the near-desolate street below, as if looking for someone or something. Snow mixed with sleet pelted hard on the building, and she watched as it quickly piled up on the sidewalk and the cars below. With the high winds and blizzard outside that struck with little warning, there was nothing to do but pace inside, in a condo that was large by Manhattan standards, but was no match for a woman in distress.

"Shall we talk about it?" Darwin finally asked, offering her a glass of her favorite Willamette Valley wine.

Rue paused, accepted the glass, took a giant swig of it, and handed it back to Darwin. She returned to her pacing.

Oh, this is bad, Darwin thought to himself. In the short time they had been together, Rue had developed quite the refined palate for wine. She didn't guzzle wine, and she rarely drank it unless it was paired with what she deemed were the proper cheese, nuts, and dried fruits or main course. He set the small dish of dried apricots, gruyere cheese cubes, and hazelnuts aside. Apparently, he had read the room wrong.

"No," Rue finally answered, exasperated. "If there weren't a God-damned blizzard outside, I could at least go for a power walk in Central Park."

That didn't exactly answer Darwin's question. He tried again, this time pacing beside her. "Would it help if I walked beside you and you shared what's on your mind?"

Rue stopped abruptly, agitated. "No, and that's really annoying. I just need a little — space."

Darwin's face dropped. This was the first time since they'd met over a year ago that she'd needed 'space.' He felt helpless.

"Look," Rue huffed, seeing Darwin's crestfallen expression. "This has nothing to do with you—-"

Oh, crap, he thought. He was about to get the '*It's not you; It's me*' speech.

"This is just something I need to work through," she finished.

"Okay." Darwin put his hands in the air and backed away a few paces. "I'm just going to say one more thing, and then I promise I'll leave you alone. I'll disappear into the bedroom for a while until you tell me it's okay to come out… deal?"

"Fine." Rue dropped her arms. "What is it?"

"I realize that everyone grieves in their own way, but you seem to be bottling up an awful lot of emotion lately since you learned of your mother's death."

"It was only a few days ago!" Rue's voice went up an octave.

"I recognize that," he answered. "All I'm saying is that it's okay for you to be however you need to be. You're in mourning, so if you need to cry—"

"That's just it," Rue slammed a hand down on the computer desk. Darwin was startled. This was a side of her he'd never seen before. "I'm not grieving." Darwin winced, unsure how to respond. "If anything, I feel… relieved."

"I see," Darwin answered calmly.

"No, Darwin, you don't see!" She knew she was taking her anger out on him, but she didn't know how else to channel what she was feeling at that moment. "How terrible of a daughter am I that I actually feel *relieved* that my mother is dead?"

"Well, one, I don't think you're a terrible daughter, and—" Rue turned her back on him, wrapping her arms around herself as she started sobbing uncontrollably. Darwin dared not touch her given the icy reception the last time he tried to reach out to her. "Shall I go away for a bit?" Darwin offered helplessly.

Finally, Rue relented, reaching for a tissue on the desk. After blowing her nose and tossing the tissue into a wastepaper basket, she motioned to their couch. He obliged by settling in next to her, noticing that she had backed away to the opposite end. "Sorry," she whimpered. "It just feels as if my skin is all pins and needles, as if every nerve in my body is frayed."

Darwin understood that feeling. That's exactly how he'd felt when he learned his ex-wife had died. And even though he wasn't in love with her, he had still cared deeply about her. He sat back on his side of the couch, stretching his long legs out in front of him, nearly knocking his feet against the base of the coffee table. Rue, by contrast, had managed to fold herself into the tiniest of balls and sat nestled into the couch like a curled-up greyhound.

"It's just that—" Rue tried again. This wasn't easy for her, since she'd never really opened up to anyone before. She simply never trusted anyone enough. The closest she'd found before Darwin was her friend Midge, but that was before — She brought her wandering thoughts back into the room. "It's as if, with her death, I'm closing the door on a part of my life that should have been shut a long time ago."

Darwin bit his tongue. Everything he'd said so far was a miss, so he thought his best option was to nod and just wait for what seemed like an agonizingly long time for her to continue.

"And with the church," she continued hesitantly. "My mom

was never actually my mom, really. It was as if we all belonged to the cause. And when I finally escaped that life, she kept tabs on me. I don't know that anyone else would bother, honestly. Hence the —"

"Relief," Darwin finished. Rue nodded. "The door is closed and after years of looking over your shoulder, no one is following you."

"Yes, except—"

"What is it?" He instinctively reached out a hand to her before remembering himself and pulling it back.

"That's not exactly true, is it?"

"What do you mean?"

"We stirred up a hornet's nest by visiting the Church of Infinite Love, Darwin. Don't you realize that? And, in addition to the guilt over not grieving my mother's death, is the added guilt of feeling responsible for her death."

"Responsible, how?"

"You think it was a coincidence that she 'accidentally' fell to her death after she'd helped us by slipping us a few clues that day? Because I don't."

"Nor do I, but that doesn't mean—"

"It kinda does!" Rue insisted. "We're not cops. And while you are an investigator for hire, the guy who hired you isn't even a police detective anymore. So, what the hell were we doing there, Darwin?"

Darwin's face grew flushed. Up until that moment, he was sympathetic toward Rue, assuming that she was grieving the loss of her mother. Now, however, it seemed she was blaming them — both of them — for her mother's death. It was unfair, he reasoned, and hurtful to an ego that was more fragile than he realized. *How dare she suggest that I, as a trained investigator, had no business being there? And that somehow this was our fault!*

Darwin clenched his jaw but said nothing.

Chapter 31
The Commitments

A Special Gathering in Pennsylvania

The parents of the late Marnie Watson, Jessica Jones, and Linda Parker all sat quietly at the decadent religious ceremony of the Evangelicals. With one exception… Linda Parker's father died of a grief-stricken heart attack not six months after his daughter's death, leaving Linda's mother to mourn both the loss of her husband and her daughter with nothing but the support of the church to guide her.

As long-term members, they had signed non-disclosure agreements following the suspicious deaths of their children… standard procedure, of course.

The church's brainwashing and gaslighting techniques did a fair job of convincing them that their children died because they disobeyed their parents and the laws of God. That's why Marnie Watson had mental health problems. "A demon got in," they reasoned. Meanwhile, Jessica Jones and Linda Parker had been drinking underage and out on the grounds after dark — which was strictly forbidden. Yes, other children had made mistakes in the past without such dire consequences, but more was expected from those young women who grew up in the church from birth, and whose parents were considered among the most well-respected elders.

Still, with Erasmus Vandenberg's recent death, the Evangelicals were concerned the parents of the deceased might be questioning their beliefs. And they wanted to ensure that they were briefed about the right 'message' to tell reporters, detectives, and anyone who might ask. After all, non-believers couldn't possibly understand their larger mission — that of saving humanity from the gates of hell. Sadness and discomfort in this life were minor when compared to the bliss to be enjoyed in the heavenly afterworld.

The ceremony was attended by a dozen Evangelicals, including Edwina Vandenberg, and their Ambassadors. Among the Ambassadors were, as Elsbeth had indicated, servants of the Vandenberg's, Ruth, Ivy, Hugo the security agent, and Vivian the flight attendant. Also in attendance was Reverend Simon from the Pennsylvania church and several of the elders who supported him from nearby church campuses. Had Deaconess Frances not met with an untimely death, she would have been in attendance as well. Ferdinand was *not* in attendance, as he was told to stay behind and look after Elsbeth.

With Erasmus gone, Edwina Vandenberg was next in line to take control of the Church of Infinite Love but was meeting opposition.

"Thank you all for being here on this somber and yet glorious occasion." A short man stood. He was wearing a well-tailored black suit and red tie … It was Bernie, the pilot on Erasmus' final voyage. "Every pilot needs a co-pilot," he joked. "Thank you, Edwina Vandenberg, for being my co-pilot in light of the very troubling and sad loss of your father, Erasmus."

He stood on a large theater stage, looking freakishly small by comparison. The small crowd seated in the first few rows bowed their head in prayer. Edwina bit the corners of her lip, agitated, so hard that she drew blood that mixed with her deep red lipstick. While the lesser members of the church were told that makeup was vanity, Edwina had no such restriction, nor did she feel the need to explain why she was exempt.

How does Bernie Forger think he can just jump the ranks and take my father's place? Edwina never bought into the idea that women were less capable than men in matters of leadership and business. She just went along with it when it suited her. And, at this moment, it did not suit her.

"Since dear Erasmus had no male children, and women are not called to be in such positions of authority, naturally, the next in line to lead as Governing Evangelist is myself, Bernard Forger. I was anointed by Erasmus to be second in command ten years ago." Bernie paused to take in the somber looks of the family members… Uncle Morris, Aunt Stella… but no Baxter, no Edgar, no Elsbeth… *No matter,* he thought to himself. *Who needs them, anyway?* "Let us pause to recite the seven commitments!"

Like the Ten Commandments, only more streamlined, mercenary, and self-serving, the group droned on in unison, as follows…

We commit to serving God and His supreme will at the expense of our own safety and happiness.

We understand that the Evangelicals must be pure of mind, body, and spirit and act as guardians of their flock, even though it may require sacrifices for the good of all.

We acknowledge the unquestionable authority of the male elders of the church and value the service of the female nurturers.

We vow never to lie, steal, or kill for personal gain, and will engage in warfare only as directed by God for the greater enlightenment and overall salvation of his people.

We promise to set aside personal and professional desires that do not align with the mission of the Church of Infinite Love.

We commit ourselves to spreading love throughout the world, under-standing that sometimes love requires punishment for the greater alignment to one's highest purpose.

We vow to serve as beacons of light unto all that we encounter, believers and non-believers, so that they may one day understand the true awesomeness of faith in the Highest.

Amen.

After the 'Amen,' the Ambassadors jumped to attention at the flick of Bernie's wrist and escorted the Evangelicals and the elders into a side room that opened to reveal a long dining table. Mr. and Mrs. Watson, Mr. and Mrs. Jones, and Mrs. Parker were seated along one of the long ends of the table, with the Evangelicals and other elders surrounding them. The Ambassadors began serving food and beverage from an adjacent kitchen.

"How are you getting on, my Dear?" Mrs. Watson asked Mrs. Parker softly. Mrs. Watson had ten years to grieve, and while one never gets over the loss of a child, she empathized with the fact that Mrs. Parker was two years in, after losing both a spouse and a child.

Mrs. Parker sat there, gaunt and pale, trembling slightly. An Ambassador set a bowl of soup in front of the woman. "Thank you," Mrs. Parker answered weakly, before slowly turning her head toward Mrs. Watson, as if it pained her to do so. "I've been better," she confessed. "But I'm trying." Her lip trembled.

"Just remember, my Dear," Edwina—who was sitting at the head of the table — piped up. "Your loss is an opportunity to demonstrate to the world that living an ungodly life leads to misery." Mrs. Parker's face crumbled, as the other parents eyed Edwina with horror. She tried to backpedal. "What I mean is," she softened her voice. "You will be reunited with your husband and daughter again in the afterworld, where God will bless you beyond anything you can imagine. You must remain faithful to the Church, and it will all be okay."

Mrs. Parker nodded, skeptically. But since she had no one to turn to, aside from other members of the Church of Infinite Light, she received no grief support. Therefore, there was no voice of reason to suggest that maybe this life was worth living, instead of what she was currently doing — which was essentially, waiting to die.

A call came in at 8 p.m., just as Dennis and Emma were going to, for the first time since their arrival, settle in and take the night off. It took a while, but they finally agreed on a rental movie, and Dennis had the cassette in the VCR and was about to hit 'play.'

Just then, a commercial popped up selling a collection of the "Greatest Oldies of All Time," available in CD, cassette, and — for a limited time — in 8-track format. That's when she heard it, Bing Crosby singing, *"Every time it rains, it rains pennies from heaven—"*

"That's it!" Emma squealed.

"What is?" Dennis sat up, alarmed.

"I don't have it all worked out yet," Emma admitted, "But I'll bet any amount of money that there's a connection between that song and this case. He kept singing *Pennies from Heaven* over and over again."

"Who did?"

"Erasmus!" Emma explained.

Dennis opened his mouth to speak, but Emma was already on her cell phone calling the Vandenberg residence in New York. Ferdinand answered the phone.

"You want to talk to Elsbeth?" Ferdinand was surprised. "Now? Seems a little late."

Elsbeth's ears must have been burning, but suddenly there was a click from another line, as Elsbeth picked up the call from a separate phone in the library. "I'll t.. take it, F… Ferdinand."

"Very well," he acknowledged, hanging up the phone.

"What is it?" Elsbeth asked knowingly, whispering into the phone. "I can't talk long. Ivy's asleep, but Mother and Ruth are arriving home from their church travels any minute now."

"I need to know if you still have your grandfather's record collection, the one he wanted to take on the plane with him?"

Elsbeth let out a groan, "No," she lamented. "I would have, but Mother's taken over the entire estate and wanted to get rid of most of grandfather's things, records, art collection, even half the furniture—"

"Get rid of them?" Emma's voice went up in pitch.

"Keep it down," Elsbeth whispered. "Yes, but I phoned Uncle Edgar and let him know of her plans. He put a call in and asked her to ship him everything. She didn't understand why, but he claimed to be sentimental—even offered to pay for it."

"So, all the possessions that Erasmus loved most are—"

"Heading to Ireland," Elsbeth nodded. "If they aren't there already."

"Elsbeth?" Emma asked suddenly. "I need you to do me a favor."

"What is it?" Elsbeth heard the jingle from the front door. "And hurry! They're home."

"I need you to call Edgar, tell him I'm heading to Dublin on the next available flight, and will meet him at the Leitrim estate. Can you do that?"

"Yes," Elsbeth answered, hanging up the phone abruptly.

"Elsbeth?" Edwina eyed her daughter standing in the hallway wearing a nightgown and fuzzy pink slippers. "What are you doing up at this hour?"

Elsbeth thought quickly. Ferdinand knew who was on the other end of the phone line, so she couldn't lie. "It w-w-was Emma," she stuttered. "W-w-wanted to s-s-see how we w-w-ere g-g-getting on after grandfather's death."

"Really?" Edwina was surprised. "Why so late?"

Elsbeth merely shrugged her shoulders and yawned. To herself, she thought, *I need to figure out how to get a message to Edgar without Mother knowing. But how?*

Chapter 32
Leitrim

Ireland

Despite Dennis' concern, Emma arrived at the Ireland estate early morning after flying from Tampa to New York and catching the red eye from LaGuardia airport just two days after her call with Elsbeth. Stressed and sleep deprived, Emma dropped her single carry-on bag on the ground and dragged herself up the stone steps leading to Edgar's front door. After several attempts at ringing the bell and even peering through a few of the windows, she realized that Edgar was most likely not at home. *Maybe Elsbeth hadn't gotten the message to him?* Severely jet-lagged, Emma sat on one of the steps, leaning slightly against the thick, cold railing.

With two suspected murders on their hands... one being Rue Brennan's mother and the other being Erasmus Vandenberg, Emma had no intention of staying in the home for longer than what was absolutely necessary. She closed her eyes momentarily to see if she could get rid of the brain fog that had settled in and let out a long yawn. For the briefest of moments, the sun came out, warming her face.

Sprightly had offered to accompany her, but Emma was concerned it would be too dangerous. Unlike the stubborn Emma, Sprightly understood, and promised to stay behind to water the grounds on Emma's new property and make sure that Emma's 'main squeeze,' didn't forget to eat. Emma knew this was a kind gesture. But, one, she never understood that expression, since she only had 'one squeeze' (Dennis), and two, Dennis never forgot to eat… not once. On the plus side, Sprightly was a health nut, so no doubt she'd have a thing or two to say about Dennis' BBQ takeout habits while Emma wasn't home to cook sensibly.

"Ahem," a female voice called out, clearing her throat, just loud enough to jar Emma. It was only then that Emma realized that she was now leaning her cheek against the cool stone railing where she sat, her face pressed so hard against it that it left a mark.

"Oh." She sat upright, rubbing her cheek. She hadn't realized she had dozed off.

Ruth, the housekeeper, stood with a solitary small black suitcase in her hand, wearing an equally black, starched polyester dress, and white Mary Jane shoes with white matching gloves. Elsbeth was next to her, with her severely chopped bangs and bob haircut, button down black blazer and skirt, and a look on her face that suggested she would rather be anywhere but there.

"Are you alright, my Dear?" Ruth asked sympathetically.

"Yes." Emma bolted to her feet. "Just a little jet-lagged is all." She paused to eye them both. "But, what are you doing here?"

"I suppose we could ask you the same thing, my Dear," Ruth answered softly.

Elsbeth shot Emma what could only be described as an unspoken apology. In other words, Elsbeth hadn't intended on being there, and if she had, she hadn't planned on being accompanied.

"Oh." Emma sifted through her mind, trying to sort out her thoughts quickly. "Edgar let me know that Edwina had sent much of Erasmus' things here to be put in storage," she lied, saving involving Elsbeth in all this. "I was hoping to collect a few sentimental pieces to add to my newly acquired Florida home."

"Sentimental," Ruth repeated quietly.

"Yes, that's right," Emma nodded.

"With you being Erasmus' portrait model and all," Ruth pursed her lips. (To be clear, her lips actually did come together like an old coin purse.)

"He was my friend, and I miss him," Emma stammered a little as she tried to defend her position. She wasn't a timid woman, but it was the first time she found herself actually talking about her feelings for Erasmus.

"Enough to fly all this way?" Ruth was unconvinced.

Elsbeth intervened. "I m… miss him too!" She suddenly wailed, running to pull Emma into a tight embrace. Under her breath, she whispered so that only Emma could hear, "I'm sorry. They weren't supposed to come with me."

Ruth was visibly shocked. "Elsbeth," she chastised, her tone ever gentle. "Compose yourself. What would your mother say?" Elsbeth released her hug and backed away slightly, rubbing her eyes until they appeared red.

"What's going on?" Ferdinand's tall frame appeared next to the smaller and wider Ruth.

"The girls are crying over Erasmus' death," Ruth answered softly.

Unlike Ruth, who kept a neutral, serene look on her face at all times, Ferdinand's was very expressive. He dropped into a frown. "I know how you feel, young ladies," Ferdinand acknowledged. "I miss him, too." He shook his head solemnly.

"But the good Lord knows what he's doing," Ruth reminded Ferdinand, who smiled and nodded in a way that suggested he was not so sure anymore. "Well," she turned to Emma. "Get about your business, then." Under her breath she muttered to Elsbeth, "Don't understand how she and Edgar got to be such good friends all of a sudden."

Elsbeth merely shrugged then bolted ahead with the key to the front door, grabbing Emma's arm along the way and pulling her after her. Emma nearly tripped, which would have led to her falling face-first on the stone but managed to catch her footing in time.

Before Ruth and Ferdinand could catch up, Elsbeth whispered to Emma, "I told 'em Uncle was going to meet me at the airport, but they refused to let me travel alone," she explained. "I'll try to distract them as best as I can, though, while you look around."

Emma would have preferred that Elsbeth hadn't interfered and just passed the message on to Edgar as promised, but she'd come to learn that Elsbeth had a stubborn streak, and now that she had Emma as an ally, her courage to stand up to her family was building.

"Where is Edgar?" Emma whispered back.

Elsbeth shrugged. "I couldn't get a hold of him," she confessed. "That's why I'm here." She clammed up when Ruth reached the door.

Ruth crossed the threshold of the household and eyed the room distastefully. She even tsked a little under her breath. At that moment, she wished Ivy were there to help her, but Edwina insisted she needed 'Housekeeper' to stay behind to manage the New York household... even though the household currently contained one very capable woman.

Isaac, the only caretaker of this estate, was currently accompanying Edgar in Dublin for a naturalist convention, but they had no way of knowing that. Ruth made a mental note to give Edwina a full report of her findings when she returned. Although Erasmus' will had made it very clear that the Ireland home now belonged to Edgar, surely Edwina could do… something?

"Ruth," Elsbeth pulled the older woman from her thoughts. "I'm very t-t-tired," she yawned, adopting a childlike voice. "Could y-y-you help me get s-s-settled in one of the rooms upstairs?"

Ruth eyed the girl curiously before shooting Emma a suspicious look. Emma, who was now surveying the room for signs of Erasmus' belongings, pretended not to notice.

"Of course, but—" Ruth answered hesitantly.

"Maybe Ferdinand could g-g-go into t-t-town and get us some groceries… y… you could provide the list." Elsbeth's mood brightened.

"But what about—" She nodded toward Emma, pursing her lips, yet again.

"Emma will have no t-t-trouble finding the s-s-storage unit on the property… It's just by the empty s-s-stables." She paused to fill Emma in. "Let her l-l-look around." Elsbeth was keenly aware of Ruth's apprehension and added, "Grandfather Erasmus s-s-saw fit to t-t-trust her," she reminded Ruth.

"Yes." Ruth eyed Emma head to toe judgmentally. "You certainly have your charms over the men in this household… But how were you planning to get inside, anyway? Edgar isn't home."

"I was… waiting for him," Emma answered. "That's why you found me sitting on the front steps."

"Fine," Ruth eventually relented. Frankly, Ruth liked it better when Elsbeth was younger and needier and didn't have someone like Emma feeding the girl bad ideas. Elsbeth used to be much easier to control. "Let's go." Ruth pointed Elsbeth toward the steps. "Incompetent that man is," Ruth grumbled. "I thought he was supposed to meet us at the airport?"

As Elsbeth and Ruth made their way to one of the spare bedrooms, with Elsbeth doing her best to distract Ruth from the facts, Ferdinand offered, "I can show you where the storage unit is, Emma. I'm heading out, anyway."

The air was crisp when they walked back outside. It seemed as if the sun had immediately vanished and the wind suddenly picked up speed, the icy coolness shocking her face. She hugged herself. Somehow her wool jacket keeping her warm, contrasted by the sudden biting air, refreshed her. She spotted the storage house in the distance.

"I see it, thanks!" she called to Ferdinand. With her newfound second wind, she headed past the stables until she found an old stone building with a rotting wooden door. She tugged at it, and the old door finally gave way and opened, kicking up a mountain of dust that landed in her hair. She coughed a moment, doing her best to brush off the particles with gloved hands. "It's unlocked!" she called again.

No one ventured out to their remote estate, so Edgar was lax about locking the shed. And, even if someone did come by, if they wanted Erasmus' old furniture that badly, they could have it. Edgar had already selected a few pieces from his uncle's collection as keepsakes and had relocated them to the main house. He was more concerned about keeping his collection of reptiles, amphibians, and arachnids behind glass, under lock and key.

Emma watched as Ferdinand climbed into an all-black Citroen he'd rented at the airport, once they realized that Edgar was unreachable. He waved in acknowledgement seeing that she was successful in getting inside.

Whomever was responsible for transporting Erasmus' belongings did a very poor job of it, as old couches, lamps, end tables, several mattresses, framed pictures, and all manner of household appliances appeared to be haphazardly piled on top of one another. Emma sighed as she saw what had become of the very couch she sat on the last time she modeled for Erasmus. Several costumes, including the dress she wore, were strewn on top of it. She made a mental note to tag some of these pieces and ask Edgar to hold them for her so she could have them shipped to her new home in Florida. It didn't exactly go with the decor, but she didn't care.

Suddenly, she saw something scurrying in the corner. Emma let out a scream as a large rat ran across her foot. "Geez!" She grabbed her heart, jumping backward and almost sailing into a very large hallway mirror. "And I thought the subway rats were bad."

Think, Emma, she said to herself. *Where would Erasmus have stored detailed, hard copy records of the underhanded transactions happening at Vandenberg Nutraceuticals?*

It was then that she remembered his vinyl records. And that was what clued her in that he might have been the one who removed the pages from the log books that Sprightly discovered. *But was the song a clue, somehow?* She replayed the lyrics in her mind, over and over again.

She found herself shimmying between pieces of furniture, often getting the hem of her coat stuck on the edge of something as she carefully climbed among the household items. But there was nothing obvious… no old file cabinets, boxes filled with paper, no music… nothing. Perhaps this was a wasted trip.

Hmm, she thought to herself. *Edgar did say he recovered a few sentimental pieces from Erasmus' collection. Maybe there's something in the house?* She did one final, cursory search of the storage unit before climbing, twisting, turning, and all but biting her way out of the room, shutting the old door behind her.

As she made her way to the main house, she saw that Ferdinand's car wasn't back yet. She crept through the front door quietly, tiptoeing past the staircase. Upstairs, she could hear Ruth fussing with Elsbeth about something.

They didn't hear her. She had a little more time.

Emma left the main foyer and headed to the adjacent living room, sparsely filled with two leather couches and a pub chair, surrounding a green Turkish throw rug. Behind one of the couches was a curio cabinet filled with souvenirs from someone's travels… she assumed Erasmus', Edgar's, or one of several of the family members that stayed there from time to time.

That's when she noticed something. All around the room were remnants of Erasmus' old art studio, several of the paintings that hung on the walls in his New York condo were now hanging here, somewhat out of place with the decor. His tea set sat neatly arranged on one of the end tables, and his easel stood by the window, just the way Erasmus would have placed it to catch the right natural light from outside.

Her heart sank a little, knowing that she'd never get to talk with him again, work together, or share the odd afternoon tea. She brought herself out of her thoughts as she heard a thump from one of the rooms upstairs… she needed to work quickly and made her way through the archway to the small dining area, next to the kitchen. While there, she noticed several more paintings, the odd sculpture, and even Erasmus' old world globe that opened to reveal a secret mini-bar. Just to be sure, she inched up to the globe and carefully lifted the lid… no documents of any kind, just a few aged whiskeys. She closed the lid.

While the estate was sprawling, with several smaller guest houses and servants' quarters, the main house, itself, was rather small. Aside from the kitchen on the ground level, and a small study that was connected to the main bedroom on the second floor, that left only one other possible place to search… the main study. The only thing Emma knew about it was that Erasmus joked that Edgar was converting his research room into a taxidermy shop full of spiders… this made no sense to her, except for this one reference to Edgar's 'collection of death.'

After one more cursory glance to make sure neither Ruth nor Ferdinand were there looking over her shoulder, she scurried down the hallway leading to the study…

Chapter 33
Revelations

Manhattan

"Come take a look at these, won't you, Rue?" Darwin asked, popping a 3.5" floppy disc into the computer drive and clicking to open the contents on his desktop.

"Sure." Rue emerged from the kitchen, gnawing on a breadstick that was left over from last night's takeout dinner. She had on red, striped flannel pajamas and matching socks.

Two days had passed since her earlier emotional breakdown. Both found the entire situation unsettling. Beyond the accident surrounding the death of Rue's mother, and the fact that someone tried to injure them by tampering with their rental car, there was something else… What was consuming both of their minds now was that since they had been together, they never really fought. Now they wondered if that was simply because they rarely talked about their respective pasts. And now that they had, and the discussion didn't go well, were there further arguments on the horizon?

Darwin smiled to himself and shook his head. *It'll be okay,* he told himself. They had been living together for months now, but he still wasn't used to Rue being a permanent resident in his condo. Even with the pantyhose hanging over the shower rod to dry, the assortment of cosmetics strewn on the bathroom counter, and the fact that she had so easily claimed one side of the bed and end table as her own, Darwin still felt as if this was all a dream, and he was worried he might wake up at any moment. The truth of the matter was, he liked her being there… a lot.

"What's that goofy expression on your face for?" she smiled back at him, crunching loudly into her breadstick and chewing.

"Nothing," he smiled. "Here, take a look."

Rue looked at the files Darwin had opened. "What am I looking for?" she asked.

"Not sure, really," Darwin admitted. "This is a compilation of everyone even marginally related to this case, along with screenshots of newspaper clippings, and copies of files previously on microfiche. I've gone through it a thousand times. I'm missing something, but I don't know what."

"Don't know if I can help, but I'll try." Rue plopped into the computer chair and set her remaining piece of breadstick on the table, crumbs scattering all around it in a very unhygienic mess. Darwin opened his mouth to say something but decided better of it. He was learning to pick his battles. For example, squabbles over the correct way to load the dishwasher, why you should hang wet towels up instead of leaving them on the floor, and what happens when you run the vacuum cleaner over the carpet without cutting any stray strands with a pair of scissors first, were not that important in the grand scheme of things. He was beginning to learn that 90% of the time none of it was particularly important and, certainly, not worth fighting over.

"Have I lost you?" Rue asked, bringing Darwin back from his daydream.

"Sorry, no," Darwin answered. "These are also a few digital

copies of old newspaper stories, three of which link the Church of Infinite Love, and Vandenberg Nutraceuticals to the death of three people. And the last—" Darwin's voice trailed off.

"The last what?"

"The last is a story about… um… the suspicious nature of your mother's death…Look, we can skip that one if—"

"No," Rue was adamant. "It's okay. I can handle it." She motioned toward the file, and Darwin clicked to enlarge it.

The article was published just days after the deaconess' death. Rue's head was spinning. It was surreal. Her mother died just after she and Darwin had visited the church, where her death was deemed a tragic accident. In some strange way, Rue actually thought that maybe some God or the universe had given her the gift of seeing her mother one more time; but now she feared that she may have been partially responsible.

So, now Rue had two things to feel guilty about… being responsible for her mother's death and not grieving properly after it happened. She blinked back a few tears.

"You sure you're okay?" Darwin was concerned.

"Yes," Rue reassured him. "I have to work through this. I have to know what happened." Rue turned and read the headline, "Church Deaconess Dies Following Faith Healing Ritual." The article was deliberate in pointing out how, despite the church's claiming to conduct "thousands of successful healings" each year, one of its highest-ranking members could not be saved, and, in point of fact, may have been the target of God's wrath. This was all said tongue-in-cheek, of course, and had it been someone other than Rue's mother, she might have shared the sentiment.

Her eyes gave a cursory glance over the black and white images that accompanied the article… Reverend Simon holding his hands over a sick woman's head while her mother stood dutifully in the background, a practitioner falling backward in a swoon with a tall man reaching out to catch her, and an outside shot of the Church of Infinite Love building—obviously taken from the parking lot. Nothing stood out as—

"Hang on a minute." Rue sat up, a look of shock on her face.

"What is it?" Darwin asked.

"That woman." Rue pointed to the swooning woman.

"What about her?"

"See the mole on her face?" Rue circled a finger above the image.

"Yes?"

"That was the woman attending to my mother the day we were in her private quarters. Do you remember?"

"Not really," Darwin admitted. "I mean, I remember a woman being there, but she sort of… blended in with the background." Darwin felt bad admitting this. One, because he prided himself on paying attention to the people around him and two, he was an investigator, after all. Of course, unbeknownst to him at the time, they had also given him a special cocktail laced with painkillers, according to Penelope's findings. That had no doubt clouded his judgment and memory of the evening.

"I've seen her before. But where—" Rue grabbed the mouse from Darwin and began clicking through the photos, stopping at the article announcing Erasmus' death. "There!" Rue pointed. She spotted the small woman getting on the plane, following closely behind Erasmus Vandenberg, Elsbeth, and Ferdinand. The caption of the photo identified everyone who was boarding the plane, including Erasmus' in-house chef, and Edwina and Elsbeth's personal attendant, a woman named Ruth Fenstermeier.

"Let's zoom in on her," she muttered, clicking to enlarge the screen. "Look," Rue confirmed. "Same mole, same facial features… it's the same woman."

"So, what was the Vandenberg's personal attendant doing at

the Church of Infinite Love, serving your high-ranking mother, not long after Erasmus' death?"

"Was she in attendance at the reading of Erasmus' will?" Rue wanted to know.

"Easy enough to find out," he answered. He pointed to another log. "Click on that one," he instructed. "Should have everyone's name who was at the reading.

"There she is again." Rue pointed. "How can she be both in service to the church *and* a full-time servant in the Vandenberg household?

"Good question," Darwin agreed. "And, where is this woman now?"

He made a quick phone call to Officer Dennis, who relayed Emma's call with Elsbeth.

"So," Darwin confirmed, "Ruth was accompanying Edwina to a church event. Does this happen a lot?" Darwin listened. "I see."

"What is it?" Rue asked after he'd hung up the phone.

"It seems that Ruth travels with Edwina quite often on church business."

"So why wasn't Edwina there when we visited?"

"Maybe she was, and we didn't see her?" Darwin suggested.

"Maybe," Rue thought on this. "But Ruth was also on the plane when Erasmus died. Edwina wasn't."

"Hmmm," Darwin thought a moment.

"What, 'hmmm'?" Rue asked.

"Dennis said that Emma got on a plane to Ireland after Edwina shipped a number of Erasmus' belongings to Edgar Vandenberg."

"Emma thinks there's something in Erasmus' belongings that could provide evidence tying Vandenberg Nutraceuticals directly to the deaths at the church?" Rue was surprised.

"That's what it sounds like," Darwin agreed.

"And no one is there with her?" Rue's voice was shaky.

"She insisted on going alone," Darwin explained. He could see the heat rising in Rue's face as she became flushed.

"Officer Dennis is a dumb ass," Rue spat flatly. "If she suspects something is there, then so will any number of people in the Vandenberg family. You have any leftover connections in the Emerald Isle?" Rue asked pointedly. "Because if you do, you better use them to check in on Emma."

Chapter 34
Myrna

Leitrim, Ireland

The study door creaked loudly, as if announcing her arrival. Emma found herself inching it open slowly, cringing the entire time. Finally, she entered the room and looked around with awe.

The three main walls were filled with books, beakers, microscopes, and all manner of scientific equipment—most of which were unrecognizable to Emma. On the center table was the small cage where Myrna the mole lived. Edgar had set up an automatic feeding machine and water dispenser for her while he was away. Unfortunately for Myrna, who had gotten used to a daily diet of earthworms and insects, it was filled with kitten kibble and dried fruits and vegetables—just to tied her over until Edgar returned home.

Finally, the fourth wall, alongside the doorway through which she'd just entered, contained a large, office storage cabinet. She twisted the handle and tugged, in an attempt to open it, eagerly hoping for it to reveal paper files that would prove that

Vandenberg Nutraceuticals was not only aware of the Church of Infinite drugging its members in the name of control and 'faith healing,' but that a small sub-division of the factory in Florida was actually dedicated to creating the branded products meant exclusively for the church. Unfortunately, since the church had been growing worldwide for the past decade, there was plenty of time and opportunity to convert lots of new followers, with the church and Vandenberg Nutraceuticals making a killing in profit. And if that amounted to a few hundred deaths over the years? Well, that might be considered 'collateral damage.'

Except that Erasmus didn't see it that way. And when he discovered what was happening, he aimed to put a stop to it. Only someone stopped *him* first.

The cabinet was resistant as Emma tugged at it a second time. The door refused to budge.

"Might want to try these," a male voice called over her shoulder.

The hairs on the back of her neck stood up. She knew that voice. Emma shuddered for a moment.

"I hope I make you nervous for the right reasons, Emma Post."

Emma spun around to see none other than Baxter Baker standing there with a tiny key dangling from his finger, presumably to open the cabinet with which she was currently struggling.

She sucked in her breath. "You just caught me off guard, is all," she barked back, snatching the key from his finger and inserting it in the lock. But the nervousness returned.

"Why *are* you here, Mr. Baker?"

"If you'll remember, Emma, I did tell you that the information I shared with you put me in danger and that I needed to disappear for a while."

"Yeah, but I thought you were going on a trip to the Maldives... or wherever it is that rich people go." Emma opened the cabinet to reveal old stacks of magazines, newspapers, a few VHS tapes, and even several old film reels. She began rifling haphazardly through the stack.

"Uh, no," he answered, pausing with amusement as he watched her trying to focus, even though, it was clear his presence undoubtedly unnerved her. "Media files," he finally said.

"What?" Emma paused, looking up at him.

"Media files," he said again. "This was Erasmus' way of collecting all the press coverage of Vandenberg Nutraceuticals over the years. Not sure how they ended up here but—"

"So, you've already been through all these?"

Baxter leaned a shoulder against the side of the cabinet. "Yes," he answered simply. "Been staying in one of the guest-houses for the past month. Funny, Edgar was so wrapped up in his own work that neither he nor Isaac seemed aware that I was here."

"And you managed to go through the contents of this cabinet? What, exactly, were you looking for, Baxter?"

"The same thing as you, Emma."

"Why?" Emma demanded. "You said yourself that you knowingly allowed the Church of Infinite Love to tamper with the vitamin bars your company was selling, even going as far as to eventually set up a lab in Florida to streamline the process. Wouldn't this incriminate you, among others?"

Baxter took a step toward her. Emma instinctively backed away. "Stop," she demanded, holding out her arm, palm facing him like a stop sign. He held his hands up and backed away.

"Relax, Emma. I'm not here to hurt you."

"Aren't you?" Her thoughts returned to Rue's mother and then to Erasmus. But if Baxter wasn't responsible for their deaths… then who was?

Just then, she saw it. Hanging on the wall, behind glass, were a series of Erasmus' old vinyl records, still in their original cases. Perhaps this was Edgar's last attempt at immortalizing his uncle. Right in the center was Bing Crosby's Greatest Hits.

"Pennies from Heaven," Emma murmured under her breath.

Baxter followed her gaze curiously.

Unlike the cabinet, this case wasn't locked. Of course it wasn't—Edgar put them in there, and he was a trusting soul, except when it came to his 'collection of death' that he kept under glass. Once Emma reached the case, she slid it open with ease. She paused to glance at Baxter once more.

As if reading her thoughts, he answered, "I want to know who killed Uncle Erasmus, too."

Emma furrowed her brows in distrust.

"Fine." He tilted his head from side to side. "And possibly remove any documents or evidence that might tie my name to any connection with the church or the deaths caused by Vandenberg Nutraceuticals."

Emma shook her head, disappointed.

"As I've said before, Emma," he lowered his voice, as if suddenly remembering there were other people in the house. "I'm exactly as you'd expect me to be. I've never tried to hide from you, or anyone, who I really am."

"Except where criminal activity is concerned," she corrected.

He held up his hands again. "I am nothing, if not a practical man," he smiled. "So, what is it you've found?"

"Yes," a woman's voice called from the doorway. There stood Ruth, still in her unpleasant black garb, but this time, wearing crisp white lace gloves. She was also distinctly pointing a Sig Sauer 9mm at Emma's chest. "Show us, Emma, what you've found."

For a moment, both Baxter and Emma froze. Since she already had the case open, there was no getting around it. She began to reach for one of the lesser-known records.

"Not that one," Ruth corrected. "The one in the center. *Pennies from Heaven* — one of Erasmus' favorites, wasn't it? Used to hear you both singing it while you were supposedly modeling for him."

Emma let the 'supposedly' go, but only because she currently had a gun pointed at her. She reached for the album and carefully removed it from the stand Edgar had it hooked to behind the case. Turning to set it on the counter, she carefully reached inside to slide the record out, except that wrapped around the vinyl wasn't a sleeve to hold it, but a handwritten sales log.

"Well, what have we here?" Ruth moved into the room. "Unfold that paper," she commanded. Emma did so. On it were a series of transactions between the Church of Infinite Love and Vandenberg Nutraceuticals. "Pull another record down," Ruth ordered. Emma pulled a second from the display, sliding out more documents that revealed information about payments being made to the Watson, Jones and Parker families as quiet settlements for the loss of their children due to negligence.

"I don't know whether Erasmus was crafty or stupid," Ruth chuckled. "Hiding the records inside actual record sleeves was clever, but paper documents are so easy to destroy."

"You killed him," Emma stated.

"Let's just say, I played my part," Ruth agreed. "And, my dear Miss Post, I'm afraid this is the end of the line for you." Ruth's finger twitched against the trigger as she took aim. Just as she fired, Baxter lunged at Emma, tackling her to the ground. A shot rang out as Baxter landed on top of the woman, who narrowly escaped hitting her head on the concrete floor by instinctively tucking her chin. In the commotion, Myrna's cage was disrupted, sending it toppling over.

Emma scrambled to sit upright, Baxter still laying in a heap across her lap. His shirt was covered in blood.

"Baxter," Ruth was aghast. "What have you done?!"

"What have *I* done?" he choked out, grabbing his belly and wincing at the pain.

Emma was frantic, unsure of which emergency to deal with

first, Ruth trying to kill her, or an injured Baxter who, from what she could tell, had been shot near the center of his chest.

Ruth was close enough now that there was no missing her target. She pointed the Sig at Emma's head.

"No!" Elsbeth screamed from the doorway.

Suddenly, Ruth's vengeful face contorted. The older woman hollered in pain as her leg began to buckle. At her feet, Myrna the mole scurried behind the woman, giving her a nasty bite on her Achilles heel. The distraction provided just enough time for Elsbeth to knock her guardian to the ground and grab the gun. She pointed it at Ruth.

"Elsbeth?" Ruth asked. "How are you awake, I gave you a sedative?"

"I didn't eat that stupid nutrition bar!"

"Don't do anything rash, my Dear Child," Ruth implored. "You don't know what you're doing."

"Oh, I'm pretty sure I do!" Elsbeth answered before finally realizing the state Baxter was in, who looked as if he'd coughed up a little blood. Meanwhile, Emma tried in vain to remove her coat and use it to apply pressure to the wound. Baxter let out a groan as he started to lose consciousness.

"What's going on?" Ferdinand burst in the room. "I heard a gunshot—" Then he saw Elsbeth. "Elsbeth, no!" He went to wrap his arms around her.

"That's right," Ruth's eyes widened. "She tried to kill Emma!"

Ferdinand paused in his struggle to contain Elsbeth, who had already wiggled herself free. Unfortunately, she dropped the gun, which Ruth lunged for. "Tried to kill—Emma?" Ferdinand was confused. Something didn't add up.

Just then, a booming voice could be heard from outside. "This is the Garda Síochána; we're coming in!" Several constables burst through the door of the study, immediately grabbing Ruth's arms and roughly dragging her to her feet.

"What are you grabbing me for?" Ruth wailed. "She's the one with the gun! She tried to kill Baxter!"

Moments later, two paramedics arrived, rushing to Baxter's aid. It seemed that Darwin still had a few connections left in Ireland after all.

Before being lifted from Emma's lap, Baxter whispered softly, "I always said that you'd be the death of me, Emma Post."

Chapter 35
Hospital

Ireland

"Well, I must say, you're the last person I'd expect to be visiting me in the hospital," Baxter croaked out.

"Yeah, well, Emma is flying back to Florida today under police protection to ensure she, and the missing logs she found, are safe and land in the right hands for a change," Dennis offered.

"But," Baxter's head was throbbing as he thought it through. "Aren't *you* the police?"

"Yes, but I'm here with you," Dennis answered sarcastically. "I just flew in this morning to babysit."

"Lucky me," Baxter answered. Dennis closed the hospital door and pulled a chair bedside and took a seat next to the patient. "Oh, goody. You're staying."

"Cut the crap, Baxter," Dennis whispered as he leaned in. "I'm here to help you, and only because you risked your life to save Emma."

"Did more than risk," Baxter coughed. "I was technically dead for fifteen whole seconds. Saw the light at the end of the tunnel with someone who suspiciously resembled Erasmus at the end." Dennis seemed unconvinced. "Check the medical records," Baxter insisted. "Your woman was nearly the death of me."

"That's right, my woman," Dennis answered possessively. "We'll get back to Emma in a moment, but first—"

"Mind handing me a cup of water," Baxter interrupted. He was still hooked up to an IV and his chest was bandaged. He tried to sit up and let out a groan.

"Here," Dennis relented, hitting the bed's automatic adjustment, and bringing Baxter's torso to a semi-reclined position.

"Oh!" Baxter complained. "Easy man!"

"Sorry," Dennis answered in a way that suggested that he wasn't particularly sorry at all. Though, he did feel a small pang of guilt, so he went behind Baxter and gently helped him prop himself up on pillows. Then, he poured him a small paper cup full of water that was on the nightstand by the bed.

"Thanks." Baxter accepted the water and struggled to get a few sips in. He handed the cup back to Dennis, who set it aside. "How is it that you plan to help me, exactly?"

"Because you know way more than you're letting on about what was happening behind-the-scenes at Vandenberg Nutraceuticals."

"Do I?" Baxter feigned innocence. "As everyone at the company can attest, I wasn't around much these past few years. I was more of a… figurehead."

"Mr. Baker, we now have evidence to connect four out of five deaths…*actual* deaths," Dennis emphasized, "to complications directly resulting from people ingesting health bars laced with varied prescription medications."

"But I had nothing to do with that," Baxter protested.

"But you know people who did. And you kept your mouth shut until it started hitting close to home." For once, Baxter remained quiet. Finally, he asked, "You mentioned *five* deaths? Aside from the three young women in the newspapers years ago, and now Erasmus, who else?"

Dennis surveyed Baxter's face. He was telling the truth. "A deaconess at the Church of Infinite Love was allegedly murdered by the same woman who tried to shoot Emma and got you by mistake."

"Ruth." Baxter shook his head. "Always the quiet ones… But why?"

"The same reason she came after Emma. The deaconess was trying to help a few of our colleagues with the case. Ruth, a devoted member of the church, took it upon herself to take care of things."

"And Elsbeth? Please tell me she wasn't involved in any of this." There was something half-hearted about the question, but Dennis couldn't quite figure out why. "No," Dennis answered, finally. "Most likely not. We're still questioning Edwina, however. While it seems that Ruth acted alone in her attack against Emma, Edwina must have had keen insight into the happenings of the church, being on the high counsel."

"What's going to happen to Elsbeth?" Baxter asked softly.

Dennis was surprised. It seemed that Cousin Baxter really did care about the young woman.

"She'll be just fine," Dennis grinned. "She's not nearly as helpless as you think, you know?"

An odd looked crossed Baxter's face. "I really don't know what to think anymore," Baxter touched a hand to his head. "Any chance we can hold off on questioning until I'm marginally better?"

"Of course," Dennis agreed. "You have to be healthy enough to fly."

"To fly?" Baxter asked. "Where exactly are we flying to, may I ask?"

"We need you back in Florida." It was then that Baxter saw the travel backpack strapped to Officer Dennis, and only then because he slung it forward to retrieve some documents. "Sorry to have to do this to you when you're in such a state, but it's a subpoena to appear in court."

"Ah, I see," Baxter sunk back onto his pillow and slid down the bed slightly, adjusting his torso uncomfortably. "And in the meantime, will I have police protection while I'm stuck in the hospital… and in Florida?"

"What … here?" Dennis was surprised. "Why would you need a Garda Síochána here?"

"Do you know how damn big the Church of Infinite Love is?" Baxter asked. "I came to the Leitrim estate because I thought no one would think to look for me in this forgotten place. And if Edwina hadn't decided to ship Erasmus' things off to Edgar, and Edgar hadn't been so damn sentimental, I might not be lying in a hospital bed right now."

"But this was one woman with an agenda," Dennis protested.

"Officer Dennis, please tell me you're smarter than that." Dennis curled his lip, insulted. He was about to protest, but Baxter wasn't finished yet. "*Think* how devoted Ruth was despite having no rank in the church but was brainwashed enough to act violently on its behalf, as if she were a mama bear defending her cub. Now, work in Victor Newberry, Mordechi Sanzani, and the other executives at Vandenberg Nutraceuticals, likely to be tied to five deaths, who are not as nice as I am—"

Officer Dennis snorted.

"Trust me, Dennis. I know I'm no prize, but I'm a good deal better than they are."

"Okay," Officer Dennis agreed. "I'll see that you have protection. Let me make a few calls. In the meantime," Dennis pulled a cord next to the bed and, within minutes, a nurse arrived.

"Is something the matter?" she asked, concerned, eyeing Baxter. The nurse seemed flustered, as if in a hurry… given the ratio of patients to nurses, she probably was.

"Yes," Officer Dennis answered. "No rush, but I'm going to need at least one bed, or a stretcher if you don't have a bed, that we can keep in this room."

"May I ask why?" The nurse seemed annoyed.

"Of course," Dennis smiled sweetly. "Because we're going to have a guard on rotation, outside this room, at all times. They'll need somewhere to sleep in between their shifts."

"Oh." The nurse eyed Dennis and Baxter in surprise. "Well, this is unexpected." She thought quickly. "I'll let the doctor on site know and see what I can do." She made a hasty exit.

Dennis began dragging a chair around Baxter's bed and through the front door.

"What are you doing?" Baxter asked, curious.

"Until I can assemble a team, I've got first watch."

"You mean *you're* going to protect me?"

"You got any other options?" Dennis asked, yawning. The effects of the time change were just now beginning to catch up with him.

"No, but how do I know you won't smother me in my sleep for making the moves on your girlfriend?"

"Yeah," Dennis nodded. "About that. I'd appreciate it if you would respect the fact that Emma is with me and not you. Just… keep your distance."

"I'll keep my distance as long as it suits me." Baxter's face grew red. Dennis whipped his head around angrily. "What I'm getting at is," Baxter finished, "you've got a good woman there, Dennis. Don't screw it up. Because if you do, good 'ol Baxter Baker will be there to pick up the pieces."

"Hmph." Dennis accidentally banged the back of the chair against the hospital wall as he set it down with a clatter outside of Baxter's room, raising attention from nurses, other patients, and visitors in the hallway. "I have no intention of screwing it up," he grumbled under his breath. "Quite the opposite. I'm a good boyfriend. Scratch that… a *great* boyfriend. Why else would she take the time to draw up that ridiculous prenup if she didn't I—" Suddenly, it hit Dennis like a ton of bricks. He sat down in front of Baxter's hospital room, crossed his arms, and began grinning from ear to ear. *Emma is nothing if not practical. She wouldn't have drawn up that prenuptial agreement if she didn't love me.* He replayed that notion in his brain several more times. *She loves me!* Thinking about it further, he nodded satisfactorily to himself as a few passersby eyed him curiously. *She may have trust issues, but we can work on that. I'm a very patient man.*

That last part wasn't entirely true. Dennis lacked patience, and he knew it. But Emma was worth the investment. And so, for the next five hours, he sat outside of Baxter Baker's hospital room with a stupid grin on his face until someone from the Guard was able to relieve him.

Chapter 36
Good Thing

Back in Florida

Ortega was waiting by the front door with two suitcases, three cardboard boxes, and a half-empty bottle of bourbon… the fancy kind that Nancy had given him when he agreed to retire.

He sat on the edge of one of his suitcases and sipped a tumbler of bourbon. He had no idea when Nancy was getting home, as she'd forgotten to call, yet again. But he was in no hurry.

Finally, at half past six, he could hear the jingling of her keys in the lock. She bounded through the door, giggling something into her cell phone. Nancy used it a lot ever since he bought her one at Christmas. They were becoming more popular, but they were still considered a novelty. When she saw her husband's face, and then the suitcases, she spoke quickly into her phone, "Listen… uh… Liz… I'll have to call you back. Okay, bye." She folded her phone and set it on the counter.

Ortega had no idea if she was really talking to a *Liz*. He assumed not. But he didn't care anymore.

Nancy eyed the suitcases and boxes. "What's going on, José?" she asked quietly.

Ortega didn't answer. Instead, he handed her a manila envelope. She slowly unclipped it and glanced, cautiously, inside. She sucked in her breath and held it for a moment before roughly sighing it out.

"You had me followed," she stated quietly.

"I had no choice," Ortega answered softly.

"Of course you had a choice," she whispered back, lacking the energy to even get angry. "You could have talked to me."

"And would talking to you have made a difference?" Ortega was incredulous. "That's all we've been doing is talking…And, I did everything you asked. I quit my job. I retired early. I moved to Florida with you. I've tried everything I could to make you happy."

After an unbearably long time, Nancy answered calmly, "Yes, you did."

"Then, why?" Tears filled his eyes.

"I don't know," Nancy whined. "I thought it was the job. I thought it was because you and my son never got along. Then, I thought it was New York. I never thought it was just —"

"Us," Ortega finished.

"I'm sorry," Nancy sniffed back a few tears as her eyes grew redder. "We just don't work, and I tried—"

"No." Ortega held up a hand. "That," he pointed to the envelope, "is not trying."

"Oh, c'mon now," she challenged.

"What is that supposed to mean?"

"It means that you think I don't know there's a forensic scientist in your life that you just never truly got over?" She gently smiled at him, as if letting him in on the secret she'd known all along.

"You mean, Penelope?" Ortega was surprised. "There's

nothing going on with me and Penelope. That was over long ago!"

"I know, José." She held up her hands. "I know. All I'm saying is… maybe there should be."

"Are you honestly trying to justify your affair by suggesting I have one with my ex?"

"José, your bags are packed. You think I don't know what that means?" Ortega hung his head. "Look," Nancy tried again. "We had a good thing once. But maybe we're just too different." She put a hand on his shoulder and watched as he began sobbing uncontrollably. Not a good look for a man who prided himself on keeping his emotions in check at all times. "I'm sorry about—"

"Dominic—" José finished.

"Yes," she whispered. "I know he's only using me for my money. I know I'm a good bit older than him. And I sure as hell know it won't last."

"So, it was worth ruining our marriage over?"

"Our marriage was over a long time ago, José. We just didn't realize it."

"But we were just starting to have fun," he whined. He thought about how keen Nancy was on working on the case with him, giving him renewed hope in their relationship.

"It was fun, wasn't it?" Nancy confirmed. "And for a few moments there, I thought we might have had something salvageable."

"Were you ever planning on telling me?" He lifted his sunken eyes to meet hers.

After a moment, she confessed, "I'm not sure." After a moment more, she added, "Every time, I swore it would be the last. He was just a bandage for my broken ego."

Ortega sighed. He planned on confronting Nancy. He'd even planned on packing. But he hadn't actually thought about the… leaving. And despite everything, he never intended on hurting Nancy any more than she set out to hurt him. He loved her, but it was abundantly clear that he'd done a terrible job at showing it. Ortega blamed himself for Nancy's affair as much, if not more, than he did her.

"Stay here tonight," Nancy offered gently. "I can go visit my sister. In the morning, after you've slept off the bourbon, we can figure out together the best way to end this… as amicably as possible."

Ortega nodded.

Nancy picked up her car keys once again. Before leaving, she turned and said, "I do love you, you know? But I stand behind what I said. I think your heart still belongs to someone else."

Chapter 37
Best Friends

Manhattan

Elsbeth Ions knocked on the door of Rue and Darwin's condo at 4:30 p.m. two days after she and Ferdinand returned from Ireland sans Ruth. She waited until Ivy and Edwina were running errands. Ferdinand had the day off.

"Are we expecting anyone? Rue asked cautiously.

"Not that I'm aware of."

The two eyed the door. No one got in without first stopping at the front security desk and being admitted and announced.

"A neighbor?" Rue eyed the keyhole where she spotted a young woman dressed all in black. Having never met Elsbeth, she had no idea who the woman was.

Darwin, while not fond of weapons, pulled a small retractable metal baton from his desk drawer and stood on the opposite side of the door while Rue opened it a tiny crack, peering an eye out.

"Can I help you?" Rue was not typically this paranoid, but when they learned of Emma's nearly getting shot and that she

274

had uncovered evidence that would connect Vandenberg Nutraceuticals with the Church of Infinite Love, just after learning about the death of her mother, both she and Darwin were on edge.

"That's an odd way for a detective agency to answer the door," Elsbeth answered, emotionless.

The lightbulb clicked as Rue realized who the woman was. She had seen a picture of the young girl in one of their briefs, but it must have been taken several years ago. Other than that, she had nothing else to go by.

"Elsbeth Ions?" Rue asked.

"Pretty good super sleuthing, Rue Brennan." Elsbeth's voice remained deadpan. "May I come in or would you prefer to conduct this meeting in the hallway?"

Rue bit back a rebuttal, but only because she was concerned about the woman's safety, knowing that she was an ally of Emma's.

"Come on in." Rue opened the door wider.

Elsbeth stepped inside, spotting Darwin standing beside the front door, shoulder blades pinned against the wall in an effort to minimize himself. Given that Darwin was on the rather tall side, and about as intimidating as a house plant, he looked nothing short of ridiculous.

"Please tell me you're not on the security team?"

Darwin stepped away from the door, crossed the room, and put the baton back from where he had retrieved it. "Hmm," was all he said, grumbling to himself.

Elsbeth eyed the room curiously. Unlike Emma's estimation of the high-end Midtown condo, Elsbeth wasn't impressed. "Cute," she finally offered.

Darwin opened his mouth to speak. Rue, catching the look on his face, smacked the back of her hand lightly into his stomach to silence him.

"Would you care to have a seat, Ms. Ions?" Rue asked politely.

"Sure." Elsbeth sat on the edge of the couch, poised to leave at a moment's notice.

After an unusually long silence, during which each woman waited for the other to speak, Rue finally asked, "Is there something we can help you with, Ms. Ions?"

Elsbeth was surprised. "You tell me. You're the ones who asked me to meet you here."

Rue eyed Darwin. "Uh no," Rue answered. "We didn't."

"Then who the hell sent me this note?" Elsbeth reached into her pocket to retrieve a note that someone had left with the concierge at her place of residence.

"I did," a female voice answered from the hallway. "Knock, knock!" she continued in a blended New York-mixed-with-Philly accent. "Who's there?" She spoke deeply, as if imitating a different male voice.

"Midge," Rue's words got stuck in her throat as her face went pale.

Darwin regretted having put the baton away so quickly. He thought frantically, grabbing the door in an attempt to slam it before Midge could cross the threshold. She blocked it with the bottom of her foot, kicking it back open violently, almost smacking Darwin in the face in the process.

"Not so fast," she answered. The last time Rue saw Midge she wore her hair in frizzy, bright red curls, that looked like a Raggedy Ann doll, and colorful clothes about two decades out of style. Today, her hair was shaved on the sides with the top and back spiked in high, dark-green colored locks. She wore a stud leather necklace and a black and white plaid-print dress with oversized brown leather boots. If Rue wasn't mistaken, they were the same boots that she wore when—

"I come in peace." She held her hands up. To Rue she said, "I am alone and unarmed. You can search me if you like?" She wriggled her eyes first at Rue and then at Darwin.

"Am I missing something?" Elsbeth eyed the scene, confused.

"Lots of things," Midge answered, taking a seat on a lounger next to the couch, putting her boots up on their end table and settling back in the chair. "But don't worry. I'll catch you up."

"You have two seconds to leave before I call the cops," Rue threatened.

"Who? That dough boy Dennis?" she mocked. "Maybe, if he were still in the same state… or country, for that matter, but even then, I doubt that boy could jog to the end of the block without getting winded. Maybe his girlfriend will help whip him into shape."

"What do you know of it?" Rue demanded.

"Ah, curious now, are ya?" Midge grinned. "Have a seat, Rue, so we can have a chat. It's been a while."

Darwin was already dialing 9-1-1.

"Listen, my tall drink of water," Midge addressed Darwin. "Turn me in and lots of people are gonna get hurt… or worse. Hang up the phone." Darwin ended the call, just as an emergency representative picked up the phone.

"Elsbeth," Rue said carefully. "You should probably leave."

"No." Midge shook her head. "For her safety, she should probably stay."

Elsbeth didn't share Rue and Darwin's fear. After all, she spent her entire life fearing her family, fearing the cult they belonged to, and fearing what might happen if she spoke up. But this green-haired little woman didn't seem intimidating at all. If anything, Elsbeth found her adorable and fascinating — like discovering that unicorns were real.

Rue framed her words carefully, speaking in a measured tone, "Midge? Friends don't threaten other friends. Besties, remember?"

Midge eyed Rue momentarily before bursting out laughing. "Oh, you are too funny my friend, trying to use my words against me and all." She chuckled uncontrollably for several seconds. "But I'm not threatening you." Her voice turned serious. "I'm trying to protect you."

"Why would you do that?" Rue asked carefully. After all, it was she and Darwin who were instrumental in putting her behind bars.

"Look, I get that we all have a different moral compass—"

"That's one way of describing it," Rue bit the side of her lip.

"Don't get all high and mighty on me, just because your mom is a high-ranking deaconess and all... well... was... Sorry about your mom, by the way."

Rue felt something at the center of her chest. If it had been an image, it would have been a steel trap that wrapped around her heart, not letting any of the hurt in. Midge didn't have empathy, at least not the way most people did. Rue was fairly confident that her former friend had a strange loyalty toward her and cared about her in her own weird and twisted way, but she wouldn't have understood the depth of pain associated with loss, the guilt of feeling responsible, nor the nuanced feelings of trying to forgive and love someone who, for most of your life, convinced you that the world was a dark and scary place.

"Earth to Rue." Midge snapped her fingers. "As I was saying, I'm trying to protect you. *That's* what besties do."

"Okay, I'll bite," Rue answered, finally. "What are you protecting me from?"

"Not just you," Midge clarified. "*All* of you."

"What did you mean by 'for her safety, she should probably stay'?" Elsbeth asked quietly.

"Good question," Midge praised. "I suspect you are very smart. Not as smart as I am, of course, but—" she paused to assess her nails before rubbing them against her chest as if buffing them, "few are." Midge waited for an absurdly long period of time before answering. "Youse guys sure know how to poke the bear and start trouble; that's for sure," she laughed. "Between youse guys visiting the Church of Infinite Love in

Pennsylvania and Emma poking her nose around where it didn't belong, it's a wonder I got here in time to save you."

"What the hell are you talking about, Midge?" Rue remained standing a safe distance from Midge.

"You know, you can sit down if you like," Midge offered. "It's not like I bite… at least not often." She chuckled at her own joke.

"You murdered two people and a busload of women. I think I'll stand."

Instead of running for cover, Elsbeth actually leaned in, as if hanging on Midge's every word.

"Correction," Midge replied. "I had nothing to do with the women escaping from prison. That was all Jaks. Had I known he was going to kill 'em, I woulda never gone along with it."

"Really?" Rue crossed her arms. "And given your track record, why should we believe that?"

"Because the women I took out deserved it." Midge waved her hand in the air before Rue could protest. "I'll admit that my initial motivations were, perhaps, somewhat misguided—"

"Misguided?!" Rue's voice shifted a pitch.

"But they were no angels, believe me," Midge reassured her, as if somehow that would make their murders 'acceptable.' "In some ways, I did your new pal Emma Post a favor. I misjudged her, I think. Doesn't happen often, but I'll admit when I'm… er —" Her voice trailed off.

"Wrong?" Rue finished.

"Yeah," Midge confirmed. "That. Or, shall we say, less than right."

"And where is Jaks these days?" Rue was suspicious.

"Damned if I know." Midge looked around the room nervously, as if he would suddenly appear. "That guy is crazy." She eyed Rue and Darwin back and forth, as if waiting for a reaction that didn't come. "Anyhoo," she finally considered. "That's how I found out about your little situation here. Kinda a coincidink, don'tcha think?"

"Why are you here, Midge?" Rue demanded.

"I'm here because youse guys are in way over your head. If Emma had just taken the money and kept quiet, everything woulda been fine. But she had to go all high and mighty on us."

"But we caught the woman who murdered Erasmus, and—" Darwin eyed Rue sympathetically, "the others."

"Who? Ruth?" Midge laughed. "She ain't even the tip of the iceberg. You have no idea."

"So, you're here to—" Darwin egged her on.

"Help you," Midge finished. "Yes."

"Why?" Rue tried again.

"Because Jaks Liebling is batshit cuckoo. When he broke me outta prison and we headed to Florida, he hooked up with someone who worked at Vandenberg Nutraceuticals. Once he realized what they were up to, he devised a scheme to insert himself into their game plan — securing a nice future for us. Except—"

"Except what?" Rue encouraged.

"Different moral compass," Midge sighed. "I, at least have a reason for the stuff I do. Jaks just seems to get off on hurting people. Jaks reacts to killing like most men respond to a sexual conquest. It's weird… even for me."

Rue crinkled her mouth up, as if she'd just discovered moldy bread in the refrigerator or a dead roach under her loofa in the bathroom.

"If I were to read between the lines here," Darwin interjected, "you're helping us because you are afraid of what Jaks Liebling might do to *you*."

"See? I always knew you were more than just a pretty face, you sexy string bean, you." Midge eyed Darwin up and down and winked.

Now it was Elsbeth's turn to crinkle her mouth and wrinkle her nose. She eyed Darwin, then Midge, shrugged her shoulders and assumed there was just no accounting for taste.

"So, you want… protection?" Rue confirmed.

Midge huffed, as if it took too much energy to explain to those who clearly didn't have the mental grasp of reality that she possessed. "What I'm offering is… a compromise. Isn't that what people do in relationships?" She reached a hand toward Rue, cupping her hand over her former friend's.

"We're not in a relationship." Rue drew her hand away. And, as if it needed clarification, she added, "We never were."

Midge sat back and hugged herself. "Disappointing," she sighed, before eyeing Elsbeth, who, unlike Rue, hung onto her every word. Midge winked at the girl, who immediately mirrored Midge, hugging herself and flopping back against the couch, embarrassed. Elsbeth, despite being in her twenties, had no interactions of the romantic or flirtatious nature of any kind, unless you count Baxter. But since he was family and, obviously (to her), an idiot playboy, she didn't take his 'kissing cousins' jokes seriously. They were inappropriate, to be clear, but not enough to cause the level of discomfort she was now feeling as Midge seemed to eye her like one might a prime roast beef.

While Rue may have experienced an arrested development early on, unlike Elsbeth, she'd had more time to work through it. She intervened on Elsbeth's behalf.

"Midge," Rue declared. "You have exactly five minutes to explain what it is you came here to explain."

Midge opened her mouth to say something sarcastic, but her smile suddenly dropped as she eyed Rue's facial expression. She recognized that look from hundreds of times before, from many people… she had gone too far. Only, she never really seemed to 'get' where that 'too far' boundary was located. It was like a moving target.

Midge thought carefully. "Ruth Fenstermeier is now the scapegoat. But make no mistake, while the Vandenberg factory in Florida has been shut down, and the church in the U.S. is under investigation, they will simply rebrand and move elsewhere."

"Rebrand?" Darwin raised an eyebrow.

Midge nodded. "The old Dublin factory is getting a dust off. And if my suspicions are correct, the Church of Infinite Love will come back as the Church of… something else."

"What do you propose we do about it?" Darwin asked simply.

For once, Midge was serious. "My ex-cuckoo-head is likely to be at the center of it. I promise to help you bring the Vandenbergs down… present company excluded." She eyed Elsbeth, who waved a hand as if she'd dismissed her lineage a long time ago. "I can help protect you from retaliation, but—"

"But?" Rue asked.

"But I need you to protect me from Jaks," Midge finished.

"Midge, you're supposed to be in prison for murder," Rue reminded her.

"I know that, silly! And all cuz of you—"

"Don't you even go there," Rue warned. "I had nothing to do with your warped sense of loyalty."

Darwin intervened. "And how are we supposed to do that? Protect you from Jaks?"

"I want a new identity," Midge finished. "I get that I'll end up back in prison. I accept that. But I don't want my death to be because of some lunatic."

Rue blinked a few times, looking at Midge meaningfully. *Lunatic, you say,* Rue thought to herself. But self-reflection was largely lost on Midge.

"I'm just an investigator," Darwin explained. "I have no connection to the police department, the Feds, no one."

"I'm sure you could pull a few strings." She meaningfully rolled her eyes up to meet his. "And if you can't, your pal Ortega can."

There was a knock at the door.

Again, Darwin thought. Rue and Midge braced themselves, as if expecting the worst. Elsbeth was on the edge of her seat, literally, her eyes wide with fascination.

"You all okay in here?" a security guard from the building asked when Darwin finally answered,

"Of course, why wouldn't we be?" Darwin's voice wavered.

"Well, the last guard on duty got a strange call about her home being on fire and left her post. It was a false alarm, and I'm just making sure nothing out of the ordinary happened while she was gone." The guard eyed Darwin questioningly.

Darwin shot a brief glance over his shoulder at Midge before addressing the guard. "No," he finally answered. "Nothing out of the ordinary here," he confirmed. "But thank you for checking."

He closed the door and returned his attention to Midge. "So, what's your plan?"

"So glad you asked," Midge responded, rubbing her palms together. "How do you feel about a vay-cay in Ireland?"

Chapter 38
Shep

Florida

Shep sat in small corner of a local library mid-way between Tampa and Parrish. He was careful to pick a spot where they were not likely to be heard, and one where he could finish his coffee and bagel without a librarian telling him he wasn't allowed to eat there.

Moments later, Emma arrived, and then Dennis, and finally, Ortega, a few minutes after that.

They thought it was safest to have Sprightly browse books in the area surrounding their cubby, keeping an eye out for anyone who looked suspicious or could potentially overhear them. Plus, they reasoned, while she was key in turning up evidence, she was not subtle in voice or manner, which worked out perfectly in this instance. Whenever someone got close to them, she would hang over a visitor's shoulder, asking what they were reading with an overabundance of curiosity and little regard for personal space. Since the section closest to the group featured categories of books about sex education, sexual disfunction, and how to save a sexless marriage, her curiosity was not welcome. And, if that didn't deter them, she would scratch her butt and ask if anyone had seen that book about STDs and how to identify them. Sprightly managed to clear the space in record time and keep it that way.

Deputy Sheriff Shep Stern refused to meet at anyone's home, both to avoid suspicion and surveillance, and because he was convinced that their homes were bugged.

But Ortega came prepared. When he arrived, he put a forefinger to his lips and began walking the perimeters of their space, waving his arm curiously. Unlike his usual attire, today he wore a tan Member's Only racer jacket and sporty wristbands that Nancy had bought him last year for Christmas.

"All clear," he whispered.

"What was that all about, Jo?" Dennis asked, falling back to his old naming pattern for his former boss. Ortega let it go for the time being.

Ortega lifted the edge of the terry cloth wristband to reveal a small black wire. He tapped his jacket. "Bug detector," he answered simply. "Not even on the market yet." Darwin Fennec had come through for him again, sending him a TRD-800 recorder-detector that wasn't to be released until later that year. But Darwin had his connections.

"Impressive," Shep said with a mouthful of food as he chewed his bagel.

"Are you ever *not* eating?" Ortega challenged. Shep was by no means a small man, but his size didn't seem to match his appetite.

Shep merely shrugged, crumbling up his napkin and tossing it in a paper bag that he set beside his chair. "We got bigger problems than my eating habits." He licked his fingers and then wiped them on his sleeve. Ortega wrinkled his nose but said nothing.

Shep leaned in and so did the rest of the group. "I nearly got my ass handed to me for asking a few questions at work.

Apparently, both the Church of Infinite Love and Vandenberg Nutraceuticals have a history of making very large donations to certain political campaigns, and let's just say their contributions at the Policemen's Charity Ball are exceptionally generous."

"How generous?" Ortega asked.

"In the millions generous."

"Geez." Ortega rubbed his forehead.

"I did a little schmoozing, but any records I could find about Erasmus Vandenberg's death, and anything related to complaints about the church or company, were scrubbed clean. All cases were dismissed and closed."

"I hate to state the obvious," Dennis interjected. "But if Emma gets to keep her house and the money, can't we just lay low for a while? They have their scapegoat in prison. This is too dangerous."

Shep was outraged as he whispered back, little bits of spit coming out of his mouth as he spoke. "Where's your chutzpah? You come to me for help, put my ass on the line, and when we uncover the crime of the century, you just wanna pack it up and go home?"

"Hey pal," Emma spoke up, and then remembering where they were, lowered her voice. "He was just trying to protect me, so lay off."

Shep would never have accused Emma of lacking chutzpah.

Shep held his palms up in surrender and sat back in his chair. He was beginning to question his decision to get involved with this motley crew.

"So, where the hell do we go from here?" Ortega asked.

"Ireland," Shep answered simply.

"What do you mean, Ireland?"

"That dumb schmuck Baxter Baker thought he'd escape the family by hiding out in Leitrim with his Uncle Edgar. Elsbeth was supposed to join him."

"Elsbeth?" Emma sat up. "What does she have to do with any of this?"

"A lot, apparently," Shep answered. "Got an anonymous tip from a gal from New York. At least, that's what her accent sounded like to me. Seems the two were trying to cut all ties with the family. Edgar was the only one they trusted to help them. He was such a hermit that he seemed to fly under the radar of the rest of the family."

Emma was a little hurt. Elsbeth, it appeared, still had secrets.

"But how can you know the source can be trusted?" Dennis asked.

"She said that if I needed confirmation that she was telling the truth, I should reach out to a Rue Brennan directly. I did, and she confirmed that a Midge Pasternack recently visited them. The voice, and information she gave, added up."

The color drained from Emma's face, as she bounced to her feet. "No, no, no, no, no, no, no!" Emma called out. The group stood, alarmed.

"What did I say?" Shep was concerned. Somehow, in his research, he hadn't yet connected all the dots.

"Emma, let's take this outside," Dennis whispered, wrapping an arm around her shoulder and leading her toward the front of the library, just as a librarian was making her way toward them. "Sorry," he apologized quickly. "She just learned that Betty Davis died. She was a huge, huge fan."

The librarian merely nodded, gesturing her head toward the front door in a polite, unspoken request for them to leave.

Outside, Emma paced angrily back and forth. "The nerve of that… that murderer! Wandering free after what she did!"

Moments later, Shep emerged first, approaching them cautiously. "Look, I'm sorry," he apologized. "I was investigating *this* case. I didn't realize you had been connected to the woman in the past."

Emma sniffed and wiped her eyes with the back of her sleeve.

"But I gotta ask," he continued. "How is it that you seem to be at the center of both of these… eh… situations?"

"Not here." Ortega rushed out to meet them. A loud buzzing could be heard from his sleeve… the bug detector had fired up.

As quickly as they'd come together, the group disbanded. Unfortunately, no one remembered to tell Sprightly, who became immersed in a newly revised book called *The Joy of Sex* and momentarily forgot why she was there. When she finally realized they were gone, a red-faced Sprightly returned the book to the shelf and, after a cursory search of the library, drove to Emma and Dennis's residence, and waited.

"You can't go," Dennis told Emma, once back home and after he and Ortega confirmed there were no listening devices on the premises.

"Why not? I can help," Emma protested. "Besides, I'm the one who got you into this mess."

"He's right," Shep acknowledged, sucking down a bowl of vegetable soup and rye bread that Emma prepared for him. Suddenly, he became self-conscious. "Low blood sugar," he explained as he slurped.

After having been given the run down, Deputy Sheriff Shep Stern requested an immediate leave of absence, citing a family emergency. He was planning to join Ortega in Ireland to continue their investigation into the Church of Infinite Love and look for evidence that they were, in fact, rebranding their church and nutraceutical company into something unrecognizable but equally profitable.

"Em," Dennis reasoned, "you're still a civilian. So is Sprightly. I'm still on the force, so I can hang behind and assist from here if needed."

"But you gotta lay low for a bit." Shep pointed the corner of a piece of toast at him. "Should have thought it through before I chewed you out earlier… sorry 'bout that."

"I know. I know," Dennis nodded. "The point is, Emmam this is the safest and best solution. You think they're not going to notice your sudden interest in the Leitrim estate? Particularly after you uncovered what turned out to be a whole mess of sales receipts and shipping records, both to and from the Florida factory?"

"Yeah, okay," she conceded. "You've got a point. But it still feels weird to have Rue Brennan doing what I think I should be doing." It had only recently been made clear to her that, while *she* was not going to Ireland, it appeared that Rue *was*.

"She knows a lot about the inner workings of the church and can help us."

"But what about Midge? You're not seriously going to be working with *her*, are you?"

"Calm down," Shep answered. Dennis went on high alert, drawing the side of his hand across his neck as if to let Shep know it was curtains if he didn't shut his mouth. Telling Emma to calm down was likely to produce the exact opposite effect. He was right.

"Calm down?" she squealed. "I may not be a huge Rue Brennan fan, but I sure as hell don't want her, or anybody else, dead."

"Midge Pasternak has agreed to remain under surveillance the entire time she's working with us," Shep explained.

"It's a crappy plan, if you ask me," Emma retorted.

"You gotta a better one, Miss High and Mighty?" Shep challenged.

"You know what—" Emma pointed a finger.

"Stop!" Dennis intervened. "It's settled. We stay put and keep a low profile, for now."

"What about Elsbeth?" Emma asked.

"Elsbeth is not in any danger as long as she plays along for a little while longer," Dennis explained.

"You mean, continue to act as if she's mentally challenged in some way? How is *that* a solution?"

Shep sighed. "It's not a solution. But if she bolts now, or comes clean, her mother and the family will know she's involved."

"Well, that's just crap." Emma folded her arms, leaning against the kitchen counter.

"I agree," Shep nodded. "But Rome wasn't built in a day."

"What the hell does Rome have to do with anything?"

Dennis gave up. It was clear that Shep and Emma were not likely to become fast friends. But it didn't matter. Elsbeth was a grown woman capable of deciding for herself what do to, and for the time being, she decided to keep her family in the dark. Darwin made it clear he was staying in New York. So that left Shep, Ortega, and Rue to carry the torch and solve this mystery once and for all.

Chapter 39
New Beginnings

Manhattan

"I have to go," Rue insisted.

"No, Rue. You don't!" Darwin rarely raised his voice and certainly never to Rue. He ran a hand through his hair as a strange look crossed his face. It was the first time Rue had ever witnessed that expression. Then, she recognized it… fear.

"You could go with me if you want" Rue offered.

"No, Rue. I can't!" Darwin insisted.

"Well, why not? It's not as if we're swimming in cases at the moment. We could—"

"I can't go back to Ireland," he interrupted.

"Well, why the hell not?" Rue demanded. Darwin turned his back, rapping the edge of his fist on the back of their couch, frustrated. "Why not, Darwin?" Rue tried again, touching his shoulder.

"I can't set foot in Ireland," he repeated, looking over his shoulder at her, as if pleading with her not to ask him anymore questions.

"I see." Rue dropped her hand. "It seems there are still lots of things we don't know about one another," she answered softly.

"But why do you have to go, Rue? You said yourself, you tried for years to get away from your mother and that church, and now you're free."

"But that's just it," she explained. "I might be, but there are a lot of women… just like me, just like Elsbeth… who aren't. Between her and me, we can provide valuable information to take down the entire cult operation… for good."

"And you actually trust Midge to be telling you the truth?" He was incredulous.

"No, but we need her. And she wouldn't hurt me. You know that."

"No, I don't really know that," Darwin answered angrily. "She's a psychopathic killer."

"What choice do I have?"

"You have the choice not to go." Darwin was defiant.

"I have to. In some way, I was responsible for—"

"For what, Rue?" Rue's lip began to quiver. "For your mother's death?" Darwin asked. "Look at the life she brought you up in. What happened to her was a result of her choices."

"I have to go," she answered finally.

"Well, unfortunately, I can't go with you," Darwin replied quietly.

Rue felt a tightening in her chest and her face began to crumble. She began sobbing uncontrollably as she ran into Darwin's arms.

"Despite my sometimes-disagreeable nature, I do love you, you know?" Rue sniffed.

"Yes, I know." Darwin gave a half-hearted smile mixed with sadness. "I love you too."

After a moment, Rue asked, "Is this the end of.. us?"

"No, no, no." Darwin hugged her fiercely and kissed the top of her head. "I'm not going anywhere." He paused, holding her in his arms as if it might be the last time. "But, I don't know, maybe a little time apart might not be a bad thing? Hell, we hardly know each other despite living together."

Rue understood, but that didn't stop the horrible sinking feeling in her belly. Darwin had been her rock for the better part of a year. He was her friend, lover, confidante. She couldn't even explain the driving need she felt within her. She just knew she had to go.

"Knock, knock," a voice called from the other side of the door. Ortega was busy loading up several suitcases into the back of his car and had left the front door ajar.

"Penelope?" Ortega stood there with a large suitcase in one hand and an oversized duffle bag slung over the opposite shoulder. They were heavy, and the strap felt like it was cutting into his shoulder… He didn't notice. He was still in a state of shock.

"Need some help?" She eyed his luggage.

"Uh, no." He set his bags down and eyed her curiously. She stood there wearing a flowered sun dress with ruffled sleeves. It was as if he hadn't seen her in a lifetime. "You… here… Not New York?" he stammered.

"How about a hug, first," she laughed, opening her arms.

Ortega didn't hesitate. He wrapped his arms around her small frame, hugging her tightly.

"Need… to… breathe," she joked. He lessened his bear hug, but only slightly.

"Why are you here?" he finally asked, releasing her.

"Nice to see you too, José," she teased.

"Of course, I'm happy you're here. Just surprised is all." He paused awkwardly, staring at her, as if memorizing her face and trying to capture this moment in time.

"Well, to answer your question," she leaned an arm on the counter, "I'm going with you."

"With me? What are you talking about?"

"To Ireland," she answered plainly. "I've sorted it all with Shep. You, me, him, and Rue… we're heading to the Vandenberg estate and the old factory in Dublin."

"No," Ortega shook his head. "I don't want you mixed up in all of this. Besides, what about your work?"

"What work? My poking around on your behalf got me fired. So, you have no choice. I'm going with you."

"But—" he protested.

"It'll be just like old times." She smiled up at him and flashed her eyes wide gleefully.

"Well." He thought about it, remembering how he let his work interfere with their relationship. "Hopefully, not just like before. But, hey," he remembered, "what about Garth?"

"Gareth," she corrected. "We broke up." Ortega's eyes lit up like a kid on Christmas before he realized it and lowered his gaze. "You don't have to look so overjoyed," she laughed.

"Can I be a little happy about it? Seeing as, well, I am soon to be unattached as well."

"Don't push it," Penelope joked, grabbing a camera bag he had on the floor. "Let me help you load up." He retrieved his shoulder bag and suitcase, following her as she opened the door wider for him to get through. "Maybe just a little happy," she whispered flirtatiously, as he crossed the threshold.

Ortega glanced behind him at the house and let out a sigh. Sprightly would be along soon to look after things until he and Nancy could decide the best way to divide everything. They agreed to do their best to keep it as amicable as possible.

"Meet you at the airport?" he asked, after his car was loaded up.

Penelope stood with the door of her rental car open. "Yup," she answered. "I'll be right behind you."

Ortega shook his head. He couldn't believe she was there

and that they were back on a case together. If you had asked him, 'what's the last thing you think will happen at this moment?' He would have said it was *this very moment*. And yet, here she was. Ortega hoped he wasn't dreaming.

"What is it?" Penelope asked quizzically.

"I'm getting too old for this shit," he reminisced, a lopsided grin on his face.

"Who are you kidding?" Penelope played along. "You *live* for this shit."

Chapter 40
Mr. Lundy

"How are they treating you, Ruth?" Mr. Lundy was granted access to a private cell where Ruth Fenstermeier, Erasmus Vandenberg's personal chef and Edwina Vandenberg's religious Ambassador, was being held on two counts of alleged murder charges and one count of attempted murder.

"I was Edwina's assistant for years," she smirked sourly. "This is a walk in the park by comparison." Ruth sat on the edge of her prison bed, wearing a hunter green uniform and slippers.

Mr. Lundy nodded, sitting on a small metal bench that was bolted into the floor and setting his briefcase on his lap. Mr. Lundy glanced at the guard standing at the end of the hallway… most likely out of earshot. His briefcase had already been inspected upon arrival. He was let in only after they had confirmed two things: one, that there was nothing in his case but a pencil and legal documents, and two, his status as the family attorney.

"Why don't you sit beside me, Ruth, so I can accurately take your statement?"

Ruth eyed the briefcase nervously, surveying Mr. Lundy's face for any sign of anger or aggression. But no, Mr. Lundy had always been the calm sort, she decided. She stood, shuffling her feet across the prison floor before sitting beside her lawyer.

A guard eyed them from a distance but said nothing.

Mr. Lundy pulled out a pad of paper and pencil. "Now," he announced a little louder than necessary. "Let's start at the beginning—"

Ruth smiled cautiously and nodded. She sighed gratefully. Mr. Lundy would make everything all right. Mr. Lundy *always* made everything all right. After all, he was paid good money to protect the family.

"You screwed up, Ruth," he whispered calmly into the older woman's ear.

Ruth bristled, the hairs on the back of her arms standing up. This was not what she expected from the lawyer at all. Tears began forming in the corners of her eyes. She fought them back defiantly. "I had to do something," she defended quietly. "They were going to ruin everything."

"But who gave you permission to act out on your own?" Mr. Lundy challenged. "You're an Ambassador. You don't make decisions. You take direction," he explained.

She nodded again, "But—"

"But, what?"

"I *was* taking orders."

Mr. Lundy eyed the guard, who weas busy talking to another security officer, as if giving instructions.

"From whom?" he asked, surprised.

"Well," Ruth answered. "From God."

"From God?" Mr. Lundy shifted in his seat, biting back his

incredulousness. "Since when does God speak through you and not the Evangelicals?"

"I felt it in my bones, I tell you," Ruth tried in vain to explain.

"No, Ruth," Mr. Lundy disagreed. The guard was almost finished talking. He had to work fast.

Before she could react, Mr. Lundy touched the point of the lead pencil to Ruth's arm, pressing on the eraser like a plunger. A small needle poked through the tip of the pencil. The woman's eyes met his, surprised. And then, he held it there momentarily as he met Ruth's fearful gaze.

Mr. Lundy yanked the pencil away and began scribbling something on his notepad just as the guard turned his attention back to them.

"Now," Mr. Lundy whispered calmly. "I'm going to take your statement, in which you will take full responsibility for the murders of Deaconess Frances and Erasmus Vandenberg, as well as the attempted murder of Emma Post." Ruth sucked in her breath but remained silent. "You will wait 24 hours before requesting to make your confession to the police, asking for my presence, where I will confirm that you had made such a confession to me, but I requested you think about your decision fully before coming forward."

"And then what?" Ruth looked at her arm. "What did you do to me?"

"A very concentrated thallium poisoning. You'll get another from me in 24 hours when we talk to the police." He saw her forlorn expression. "It has to be this way, I'm afraid. Remember, you acted alone. No one knew what you had planned. Throw in that God told you to do it, that was a good one."

"But it's the truth," Ruth insisted.

"Of course, it is," Mr. Lundy agreed patronizingly.

"But I can still help you. I know things," Ruth whispered, eyes darting back and forth frantically.

"What sort of things?" Mr. Lundy asked.

"For one thing," Ruth tried, "I know that it was Baxter Baker who stole shipping and receiving logs, along with sales receipts that Erasmus kept hidden. He turned them over to Erasmus on the condition that Erasmus keep Baxter's name out of it when he closed the factory."

"How do you know this?" Mr. Lundy was surprised.

"I'm just the help," she explained. "People let lots of things slip when there's an invisible old woman in the room." Ruth took a moment to run her hands over her legs as if she were smoothing a skirt. "Erasmus was going to shut down our work. His actions would have bankrupted the church and the Vandenberg family. You don't think that would have gotten the attention of the media? He would have ruined everything for all of us."

"Why didn't you tell Edwina?" Mr. Lundy asked.

"Because I—" Ruth stammered.

"Yes?" Mr. Lundy persuaded.

"Because I thought she might look on me favorably if I took swift action. Besides, without the actual evidence, I didn't know if she'd believe me. I didn't know it was right in front of our flippin' eyes the whole time with those stupid records."

"And you murdered him on the plane because?"

"It was supposed to be the night of his birthday party," Ruth explained. "But then Erasmus surprised everyone with his last-minute trip. I knew I had to act fast so—"

"You drugged his food?"

Ruth nodded, smiling at her cleverness. "He had no idea that the experimental cocktail he found record of was the very thing that killed him. I added fruit pectin to the tea, just like we do in church, to make it absorb quickly and go through his system faster. I wasn't 100% sure it would work, but it did the trick."

"Hmm." Mr. Lundy tapped the pencil on the legal pad, before jotting down a few more notes.

"What, 'hmm'?" Ruth asked, trying to peer in vain over his shoulder.

"I wonder if he did know."

"How could he?"

"I don't know. But given his last adaptation to the will, I wonder if he suspected he was a target… or at least knew he would be after shutting the factory down."

"Makes no sense." Ruth hugged herself. "With him dead, the factory would go on as it always has. Why would he willingly sacrifice himself?"

"Maybe he wanted an investigation," Mr. Lundy suggested. "Perhaps *that's* why he went along with it."

"You mean you think he *let* me drug him?" Ruth was filled with a mix of surprise and annoyance. Ruth began rubbing her legs again. She felt itchy all of a sudden.

"Possibly," Mr. Lundy answered, putting his pencil and paper away. He stood.

Ruth eyed him pleadingly. "No chance you'll take pity on an old woman and save me?"

"I'm sorry, Ruth," was all that Mr. Lundy said.

Finally, Ruth asked the dreaded question, "How long have I got?"

"Hard to say," Mr. Lundy answered calmly. "After tomorrow's dosage, maybe a week, a month? Everyone is different."

"And if I *don't* confess tomorrow?"

"Oh, Ruth," Mr. Lundy smiled. "We both know that this is not an option."

Epilogue

A Hospital Room in Ireland, 1998

The phone rang in Baxter Baker's hospital room. Baxter rubbed his eyes groggily as he checked the time on the clock next to his bed… 8 a.m. Wondering who would be phoning him this early in the morning, he lifted the receiver tentatively.

"We've got a problem, Baxter." It was Elsbeth.

Baxter struggled to sit up in his bed. "Elsbeth? Are you okay? It's like, what… 3 a.m. in New York?"

"Yeah," Elsbeth whispered. "Listen, I only have a minute to explain, but in case you weren't aware of it, there's a team heading to the Dublin factory to investigate. No doubt they'll want to case the Leitrim house, too."

Baxter sighed. "I was worried that would happen." He eyed the door where a member of the Garda Síochána was stationed out front.

"So much for me and you hiding out with Edgar for a while," Elsbeth lamented. If only I had the courage to leave with Baxter the night I sent a text to warn him. Maybe if he had texted back, she thought. She didn't know that he was having dinner with Emma at the time.

"Yeah, well," Baxter whispered. "That wasn't likely to happen anyway. The police are going to fly me back to the States in connection with Vandenberg Nutraceuticals and the deaths at the Church of Infinite Love."

"Hmmm," Elsbeth thought a moment. "If only we could think of a way to hide you."

"Who's we?" Baxter asked. "And I don't want you mixed up in this, Elsbeth. I've already got a bullseye on my back because of my involvement. Just lay low for a while longer, El. Really, it's for your safety."

"Fortunately for you, that's not going to happen," Elsbeth answered.

"Why?" Baxter was concerned. "What are you gonna do?"

"Let's just say, I'm heading your way and leave it at that."

"El, no," Baxter protested. The call ended and a loud dial tone buzzed in Baxter's ear. He hung up the phone and collapsed back on the bed. He was healing quickly, but still had bouts of grogginess and pain.

"Knock, knock," a gentle male voice called from the door to Baxter's room. It was a member of the Garda Síochána dressed in a black and yellow uniform. "May I come in?"

"Uh, sure," Baxter answered. How much had he heard? He wondered to himself.

"I couldn't help but notice that you were in a bit of a pickle," the small man continued. His voice was deep and had a slithery quality to it.

"I don't know what you're talking about," Baxter lied.

"Oh, no need to be coy, Mr. Baker. I'm here to help. Allow me to introduce myself." He grinned widely as he stood over Baxter's hospital bed. "My name is Jax… Jax Liebling."

To be continued… in Ireland.

About the Author

Danielle Palli is a multi-genre author, Board Certified Positive Psychology & Mindfulness coach, and multimedia content creator & book coach. She lives in Florida with her husband and a plethora of pets. She finds joy in nature, travel, music, theater and the arts, and is known for singing and dancing around the living room at any hour of the day or night. As a free-spirited outlier enamored with life, she finds that life is more exciting when you color outside the lines. Learn more:

www.DaniellePalli.com.